STONE COLD FOXE

The Skyler Foxe Novels by Haley Walsh

Foxe Tail

Foxe Hunt

Out-Foxed

Foxe Den: A Holiday Collection (Novella)

Foxe Fire

Desert Foxe

Foxe Den 2: Summer Vacation (Novella)

Crazy Like A Foxe

A Very Merry Foxemas (Novella)

STONE COLD FOXE

A Skyler Foxe Mystery

Haley Walsh

Foxe Press

Cover design by Jeri Westerson

**Sign up for my newsletter at
SkylerFoxeMysteries.com**

Foxe Press
PO Box 799
Sun City, CA 92586

For my long-suffering husband.
To him, I'm his "stone cold fox."

"The fox condemns the trap, not himself." – **William Blake**

INTRODUCTION

STONE COLD FOXE continues directly from the last scene of CRAZY LIKE A FOXE, so it is very much advised to have read that book first. In fact, unlike some of the books in this series, this is not a standalone. I don't think you can really enjoy *this* book unless you've read the series up to this point. And MAJOR SPOILER ALERT! If you haven't read any of the previous Skyler Foxe Mysteries, there are some *huge* spoilers ahead. I mean, truly story-spoiling spoilers for every mystery. Best be advised to stop now, go back and read the series, and then get up to speed here. I don't want the mysteries ruined for you.

If you are reading the ebook, pay special attention to the hyperlinks! Check them out! It is truly interactive. Enjoy!

Part One

"I was married by a judge. I should have asked for a jury."
– **Groucho Marx**

CHAPTER ONE

IT WASN'T SO MUCH THAT SKYLER HAD SAID IT, BUT that he'd said it *twice*. The first time was in the throes of passion. And so he'd said it a second time just to make sure Keith had really heard him. And now that the seconds were ticking by and Keith wasn't saying anything back and had, frankly, a deer-in-the-headlights look in his eye, Skyler was getting that itchy feeling of buyer's remorse.

Why had he said it? Why now? Did he really want to make that kind of commitment? *Wait, wait.* He *knew* why. After all the crap they had just been through with a harassing ex-boyfriend of Keith's showing up out of the blue, of Sidney and Mike's elopement, of murder, and of the reassurance of their love for one another, Skyler had suddenly felt the bone-deep urge to keep it all that way, to *be* with Keith and only Keith. Yup, he'd said it, words he never, *ever* expected to come out of his mouth.

"Will you marry me?"

And still, Keith said nothing in reply.

"Um…" Skyler twisted the sticky sheets in his fingers. "So…what do you think?"

"About what?" Keith's expression was shut up tight, and he turned away to lay his head on the pillow and stare up at the ceiling.

"What do you mean? About what I just said. About…" His voice dropped in volume, as if not wanting the neighbors to hear. "About marrying me."

Keith's sigh spoke volumes. "Skyler...I know there was a lot going on. A huge adrenalin rush. Catching a murderer, Sidney's wedding reception...sex. So I know that you didn't really mean it. It's okay."

Skyler jerked up, pushing the sheets into his lap. "What do you mean I didn't mean it? Of *course* I meant it. I never would have said it if I didn't mean it. Keith. Come on. Talk to me. Look at me."

Keith turned his head. Yet he still wore that same placid, expressionless face. "It's okay. In the heat of the moment, lots of things are said. I won't hold you to it. No harm, no foul."

Skyler looked to the heavens for help. "But...Keith..."

The man reached over and planted a quick kiss to the side of Skyler's mouth. "Let's go to sleep, huh?"

"No! We will *not* go to sleep. We will talk about this." *What's with all the sighing*, he thought, as Keith gave him another one.

"Skyler, do you really want to be having this conversation in the middle of the night? I get you, babe. I know you. In the morning you'll be sorry you ever said it. It's *okay*."

"I won't be sorry. Keith, I love you. I want to spend the rest of my life with you. I want us to do this."

"We haven't even been together a whole year. Hell, we haven't even *known* each other a whole year."

"So? Lots of people get married quickly."

"I thought you didn't want to ever get married."

"I didn't. But now I do."

Keith slowly moved up and sat against the headboard, sheets and hands in his lap. He kept his eyes on his restless fingers. "I know this thing with my ex and the woman has freaked you out. And I know you jump at things without really thinking them through. So I'm saying that I love you, and that I understand, and that we can just forget you ever said it."

"Will you *look* at me, for Christ's sake!" Keith did. "I. Love. You. I want what we have to go on and on. And I don't think it matters one bit that we haven't known each other that long. I don't need more time. I know what I want, just as I've known that I wanted to be a teacher and to stay in Redlands and everything else in my life. *This* is my life. *You* are my life." He paused to breathe. And in that moment, a horrible thought struck him. "Don't you *want* to marry me?" he said in a small voice. Because the possibility was just beginning to cross his mind that Keith, though loving and seemingly committed, might just be a bit gun shy of Skyler's on again, off again emotional roller coaster.

Keith reached over and curled his fingers around Skyler's jaw, rubbing it with his thumb, scraping on the nearly invisible white-blond stubble just beginning to form. "You know I do," he said, voice gruff with emotion. "Nothing would make me happier, make my life more complete than to make that commitment to you. But you're not ready."

Keith's hand fell away and he slowly sat back.

"Yes, I am."

"No, you're not."

"Dammit! Where do you get off telling me whether I'm ready or not?"

"Because I know it with every fiber of my being. We've been through a lot, you and I. Lots of ups and downs. I think we can put off this discussion for at least a few years, don't you?"

"No! When the time is right, it's right. I'm really surprised at you. And a little insulted."

"I'm sorry, it's just how I see it."

"So the answer is 'no'?"

"It's not 'no', it's just…'later'."

"Really. Fine." Skyler slammed himself down on the bed, his back to Keith, and yanked up the sheets to his shoulder. "Good night!" he said sharply.

"Skyler…"

"Good *night*!"

That sigh again, until Keith gave up, switched off the light, and hunkered down into the bed.

He could not believe it. After everything. After dragging an "I love you" out of Skyler when he never intended to fall in love. And he had. He so had. And every crazy thing that happened to them since only made him feel that much stronger an emotion toward Keith. It was insulting. It really was.

He jolted upright again and switched on his light.

Keith turned onto his back, started to sigh, but then blew a breath out of his nose instead.

"We are not going to sleep until we talk this out."

"I thought we had."

"*You* had. You know, it's really insulting the way you treat me sometimes, like I'm a kid who doesn't know his own mind. Okay, so sometimes I do behave that way, but this is serious. I would never just cavalierly come out with something like this just because of emotional turmoil. I really gave it a lot of thought."

"Okay. So how long have you been thinking about it?"

"What do you mean?"

"You said you've been thinking it through. For how long? A few days? A week? Longer?"

"Uh…" He'd only actually come to the conclusion while they were making love. But it had solidified in his mind and he was sure about it. But with Keith laying it out there like that, it did seem slightly irresponsible. Maybe. And that made him mad, too.

"What difference does it make? I feel that way. That should be valid enough for anyone."

Keith scowled. "I refuse to acquiesce to a last second decision you made because of the presence of an ex-boyfriend. Is that clear enough for you?"

"Is that what you really think?"

"Yeah. It's what I really think. So have we talked it through? Can we go to sleep now?"

"Sure we can." Skyler scooped up his pillow and marched toward the door.

"Where are you going?" said Keith wearily.

"To the couch. I can't sleep with someone who thinks everything I do is based on a spur-of-the-moment whim. I guess you're right. You shouldn't marry anyone whom you don't trust." He jutted his chin in the air, threw open the door, and promptly tripped over Fishbreath, their fat tabby cat.

The cat yowled indignantly as Skyler clambered to his feet.

"You all right, Skyler?"

"I'm fine! Good night!"

"Skyler...Jesus Christ."

Skyler threw his pillow at the couch and snatched up the knitted throw. The bed squeaked in the other room as Keith climbed out of it. He slid on his sweat pants as he moved into the doorway, rubbing his hair. "Are you really suggesting you can't see my side of things?"

"All I see is that I opened my heart to you and you laugh in its face. If it had a face... You know what I mean!"

"You must be frazzled if you're mixing your metaphors," he mumbled.

Skyler sat heavily on the couch and clutched a pillow to his chest. It didn't look as if Keith had the courage to sit beside him. He stayed in the bedroom doorway, fidgeting.

"I..." Keith began, and then stopped. Shaking his head, he raised his gaze toward Skyler. "Maybe I don't know *what* to say."

"I had assumed something in the affirmative," said Skyler huffily.

"It's just that..." Keith swallowed, looked away, and then fastened his eyes on Skyler once more. "I pretty much gave up hope that you'd be interested in that. You've said it enough times in all kinds of ways."

Skyler said nothing. He hugged the pillow tighter.

"I mean...we've had a few false starts. It took you a long time to say you loved me. That...kind of hurt."

Sneaking a look at Keith, Skyler tried to keep his body directed away.

"And the most logical thing in the world — my moving in with you when I had nowhere else to go — wasn't your idea. Sidney had to ask."

"And that still pisses me off," Skyler muttered.

"And then...when I did move in...it took you ages to actually give me a key."

"It was only...three weeks." Skyler winced after saying it. Had he really waited that long? Shit. That was kind of rude.

"And then it was still sort of a trial."

"Aha!" Skyler pointed a finger at Keith's bare chest. "That's on *you*. You're the one who said it was a trial."

Keith nodded. "Yeah. That was me. Can you blame me?"

"A little, yeah."

"I was scared, Skyler. I'm scared right now. I'm scared that maybe you don't really mean it. That you asked me because you were still feeling a bit insecure about Ethan. And about Laurie Henderson. And maybe…even Sidney. And your parents. All of these things separately might give a person pause, but put all together, when you're insecure about relationships in the first place…"

"I'm not insecure about relationships. Not anymore."

"Yes, I will concede that. We seem to be a nice solid couple. And I want to keep it that way. I don't want you to say you want a commitment like this when you really don't want it. I don't want to be jilted like that."

Keith pressed his lips together. Was his chin trembling? *Oh my God. Have I done that to him?*

Skyler found himself rising, and he threw the pillow aside. He came up to Keith and lightly touched his arm. They were crossed tightly, protectively over his chest. "God, Keith. I'm so sorry. I've really put you through some stuff, haven't I?"

"It's not your fault. You've never had relationships like this before."

"That's no excuse. I've been a shit to you."

"You didn't know what you wanted."

"Why are you defending my shitty behavior?"

"Because I love you."

Skyler slowly closed him in a hug, resting his head against the man's cheek. "Keith," he said softly, "I love you, too. You know I do. I love you so much. And I do want this. I really do. I wouldn't back out at the last minute. I won't! This is…this is really important to me. This is the most serious thing I've ever decided. And it's done. It's a done decision. But it only takes you to believe me. You've gotta believe me." He rubbed his cheek against that scruffy face. "Ever since marriage equality passed I thought, 'Good for us. Now anyone in the community can get married if they want to.' And then for a teensy bit, I wondered if now maybe it was okay for me to think about it, too. Just a smidge. Because it never occurred to me before. Before *you*, that is. And then…I dared to think it. A few times. Just a little. And all I saw was you. Spending the rest of my days with you. And it seemed okay. Maybe still a little scary, all right, I admit it. But…whenever *you* were in the equation, it was right. And then, when all this shit went down, yeah, I was worried. I wondered if maybe you were bi and I was worried about losing you to some woman. But then it soon wasn't about *losing* you, but about going the next step *with* you. Do you understand?"

He drew back to look at Keith, whose eyes were shimmering, and — damn! There was a tear running down his face. Skyler's gut hurt. He reached up and wiped gently at that tear track and held back his own.

"I love you, Keith. That isn't going to change. And I want to continue on this journey with you, tied to you. Ring and all. I really, really do."

Keith loosened his arms and ran his hand down his own face, leaving a damp swath of spent tears across his cheeks and nose.

"So…Keith Fletcher…" Skyler gently took Keith's hand and slowly got down on one knee. "Knowing how much I love you, knowing who I am with my wacky friends, my strange anxieties, my willful nature, and my penchant for Hawaiian pizza which I can't understand you not liking…can you see your way to do me the honor of marrying me? Please say 'yes' this time."

Keith gasped a laugh even as the tears came again. "You're such a little idiot," he choked out.

"I know…but will you?" Skyler clutched his hand harder.

"God, you are so…annoying."

"Persistent."

"Persistently annoying." Keith wiped his face again and yanked Skyler to his feet. He slid his damp hands under Skyler's jaw. "I love you," he said fiercely. Drawing Skyler closer and with his lips almost touching Skyler's, said, "And yes…I will marry you, you little idiot. And don't you dare back out of it."

"Never." He grabbed Keith's torso, pulled him the rest of the way in, and kissed him deeply.

In his head, his thoughts sprinted: *Omigod he can kiss. I love the feel of his lips and tongue. And his body. It's so warm and hairy and…and…oh my God we're getting married… Help.*

Chapter Two

"GOOD MORNING, SLEEPY HEAD."

Skyler woke to Keith smiling over him and leaning on his pillow.

"G'morning." He tried to smile back but Keith was kissing him gently.

"I can see it all on your face, you know."

"See what?" He wiped his face as if wiping off whatever it was Keith was seeing.

"You've made up your mind but you're still worried. You see, I know you. And I love you. Nothing has to happen overnight, Skyler. We're engaged, but it can be for as long as you need, babe. I've got my man and that's all I care about."

He felt flushed, embarrassed. He tried to look away but Keith was *right there*. "You don't have to do that. I'm fine. We can plan this whenever you want to."

"I'll wait for you to decide. In the meantime, seems a shame to waste this morning wood." He waggled his brows, looking down at the tented blanket over Skyler's lap. Before Skyler could say anything, Keith slipped under the covers and enveloped his dick in a warm, wet mouth.

"Oh shit," he whimpered.

Warm fingers slid over his sac, thumbs rubbing over the pebbly skin. Skyler squirmed, feeling the sharp ache deep in his belly, seeping into his extremities with rising heat. Wet lips and tongue moved over him and he spread his legs, inviting the intimate fingers to do their evil down the sensitive skin on the inside of thighs, behind his balls, up his crack…

The blankets fell away and Keith's dark ruffled hair emerged. Hands suddenly grabbed his ass cheeks, gripping hard into the muscle, and lifted. Keith dropped Skyler's legs over his shoulders, and he dipped his head and feasted on his cock, one hand holding Skyler steady, the other stroking himself.

Skyler let himself feel. He loved a good blowjob and Keith was a master of them, but the fact that it wasn't some disembodied guy—just any old guy—giving it to him, that it was *Keith*, seemed to make all the difference. And as he drifted in the sensation, he began to realize that this was the crux of it. It was all about Keith and the two of them together.

"Keith," he whispered. True, anyone sucking on his dick could make him feel good, but no one but Keith could make him feel loved.

Skyler moaned as Keith sloppily sucked and slurped, bobbing his head, nose dug deep into white blond pubic hair. Opening his eyes to slits, Skyler watched him, watched his cheeks suck in when he drew on Skyler's cock, watched his dark brows contract over his closed eyes. Skyler wished he'd open them so he could see what was in them, see his emotions as raw as Skyler felt right now as he lay open and exposed, letting himself go, letting the heat and the sensations overwhelm him. And then Keith snapped open his eyes and looked directly at Skyler, even as his shoulders shook as he pumped on his own cock, as he grunted and moaned out his own completion, cum spattering Skyler's back. That was enough to tilt Skyler over the edge and he cried out, pumping down Keith's open throat, toes clenching, heels digging into Keith's back.

Keith sucked and licked him a moment more before letting the spent cock drop out of his mouth. His lips were wet and swollen and Skyler wanted to kiss them, taste himself there. Keith seemed to know that and let his legs fall, leaned over him, and planted his mouth to Skyler's, kissing him languidly, over and over, turning his face to catch each corner and taper of his mouth. Keith sighed and fell down beside him, scooping him into his arms in one graceful move. "Mm mmm, Mr. Foxe. My favorite breakfast."

"Uh huh," said Skyler vaguely, feeling suddenly sleepy. So warm. So comfortable in his arms. He had felt tense but he couldn't remember why anymore.

All the rest of the morning, Keith wouldn't let Skyler sulk or worry. He smiled every time Skyler looked his way and seemed particularly affectionate. He took to grabbing Skyler every time he walked by, hugging and kissing him. Once they'd dressed and closed and locked the front door, Keith cornered him on the landing, embraced him, and tilted up his chin. "See you at lunch today?"

"Yeah. Let's do that." Lips softly touched Skyler's, and though he was momentarily caught up in the sensations, he was also slightly ruffled by his scrambled emotions. No, he was not doing this! *He* had asked Keith. He was not going to screw this up!

"Let's keep this to ourselves for a bit, though," said Keith, still holding him. "No need to let the school know just yet."

"Oh, I agree. Let's keep it on the downlow for now."

"We're not hiding," he said sternly. "It's just…for us for now." He kissed Skyler's nose and gave his butt a pinch as Skyler led the way down the steps.

Midday, they met for lunch and mooned over each other, laughing stupidly at nothing. Skyler felt good about it…as long as he was in Keith's presence. But it seemed the moment he was out of his sphere of influence, he'd go back to anxious worrying again.

He almost headed to The Bean after school, but even as he slowly drove his white VW Bug toward a parking space in front of the green awning and rainbow flag out front, he quickly changed his mind. He couldn't tell Philip first. Besides, he got the feeling Keith didn't want it broadcast just yet. Philip and his boyfriend Rodolfo were probably busy anyway, what with their taking over the store next door for Rodolfo's pastry shop. At least, that's the excuse he told himself as he made an illegal U-turn and cut someone off.

"Sorry!" he yelled out the window, though they probably didn't hear him as the other driver was leaning heavily on the horn.

He even toyed with the idea of going over to his mom's house. But he didn't quite want to face his mom and dad, now that they were living together without any intention of getting re-married. He felt weird about that. And a little hypocritical. He felt that people their age needed the formality of marriage, even though his mom was the one who had refused it. His staid, proper mother, of all people. But he supposed she was wary of marriage after hers had gone so wrong. He guessed that's what he felt the most hypocritical about, the fact that he had disdained marriage for much the same reason.

But he really wanted to tell someone, and the only person he could see to tell, *should* tell first, was Sidney. Would it be okay? Keith wanted to keep it just for them. He could call and ask him…but he was keener on asking for forgiveness rather than permission.

He drove toward Mike and Sidney's place on Tamarisk, a pleasant street lined with pines and sycamores. The Rachel Court apartments were made up of duplexes and theirs was in the front, street-side.

Parking, he sat in the car, staring at their curving concrete pathway lit with Malibu lights. *What are you waiting for, Skyler?* He really didn't know why he hesitated. He finally pocketed his keys and got out.

Ringing the doorbell, he waited. He could smell someone's outdoor cooking wafting down toward him. Barbeque. It was a homey smell, made him feel comforted, even as anxious as he was to face his friend with his news. *And why are you anxious?* he wondered.

The door flung open and Sidney posed in the doorway. Her long ringlets were gathered up in a bun on the top of her head and she was wearing shorts and a halter top with no shoes. "Hey, Skyler. Whatcha doing here? Come on in, you're letting all the air-conditioning out." She gave him a quick hug and ushered him inside. "Is Keith with you?"

"No, it's just me."

"How come?" She snatched up a sweaty glass and took a drink. "You want something? I've made a pitcher of Long Island Iced Teas."

"Oooh, that sounds good. Just a little one. I'm driving."

She took a highball glass from the rolling cart she and Mike used as a bar, dumped in ice, and then poured from the pitcher. "There you go. A small one."

He took it gratefully and sipped. Wow. She always made them strong. "You're not working today?"

"I got off early. Mike is still at the station though. He's got a report to write up."

"Don't you write them together?"

"It's *his* collar. I was back at the station at the time."

"Oh. I just assumed you were always joined at the hip. Cagney and Lacy."

"Which one is he supposed to be?"

He sipped, blinking away the harsh alcohol. "I don't know. I always forget which is which."

"Sit down, Skyler. Any reason why you stopped by?" She made herself comfortable on the sofa, tucking one leg under her. The place was still pretty much as Mike had originally decorated it, with what Skyler called Filipino kitsch. The walls were covered with pictures of his large extended family, and there was a palm frond fan on the opposite wall, and a carved teak cross next to the kitchen. He was sure Sidney's very Jewish mother just loved that.

The only touches he could see that belonged to Sidney were a pair of nunchucks hanging on the wall, a picture of Sidney at her bat mitzvah, and another of her from her police academy graduation.

He held the glass in both hands. "Well, yeah there was something." He took another sip. The alcohol served to sooth his nerves this time. "So, um, how's married life?"

"Fine. Since the last time you asked me only two days ago at our reception."

"Oh yeah." Which had sort of started this whole thing rolling. He took another sip, and couldn't seem to sit still. Rising, he carried his drink with him as he walked to the far wall and looked over Mike's family gallery, including a few of Mike's parents and what he assumed were his grandparents' wedding photos. Everyone looked so happy in the pictures.

She got up to stand beside him. "They do. They're wedding pictures."

He hadn't realized he'd said that out loud.

"Skyler, what's up? You all right? You and Keith?"

"Oh yeah. Couldn't be better. In fact..." He turned to look at her, really look at her. She was beautiful. He'd known her since they were both gangly nine-year-olds. Her face was a little long in a Sarah Jessica Parker sort of way, but her curled hair softened her chiseled features, made her eyes bigger, even as they narrowed in suspicion at him. "How...how did you feel when you got married?"

"What?" She grabbed his drink out of his hand and pushed him up against the wall with her forearm. "Skyler, what the fuck is going on? You're acting weird."

"Am I? Okay. Maybe I am. It's just that...Sid. Oh my God. I asked Keith to marry me."

"You *what*?"

He wrung his hands. "I asked him to marry me."

"Oh my God." She sipped both drinks, one after the other. "Were you drunk?"

"No. I was stone cold sober. But we *were* having sex."

"You asked him while you were having sex?"

"Yeah. It just came out. And then I asked him again when we were through...just to make sure he knew I meant it."

"And did you?"

He turned away from her, rolling his shoulder along the wall. "Yes. Of course... At the time."

"Skyler!"

"And I still mean it now! It's just...I think I'm a little overwhelmed with what happened. I mean, he didn't react well. And I had to talk him into it."

"Oh for Christ's sake. Come here, sit down with me, and tell me everything."

She set both glasses down on a table, took his hand, and dragged him back to the sofa. She held his hand in both of hers while he told the whole story. Wincing when he'd finished, he looked at her. "Do you think I did the right thing?"

"You are one fucked-up dude, you know that, right?" He nodded sadly. "Okay. Let's look at what happened. You asked him because you were insecure about your folks, and about Keith's old boyfriend, and the scare about his having a kid."

"I wasn't insecure about all that."

"Oh really?"

"Yes, really. Okay, maybe about the Ethan thing…a-and the kid…that turned out to be a false alarm."

"But you said you were afraid that Keith was bi. Not that you'd have to worry. I'd say he was pretty fixated on you."

"But a girl who looked like me could —"

"Oh my God, shut up about that already. You know that's not true. And by the way, this is the very definition of insecure, I hope you know."

He folded his arms and looked at the floor.

"Oh, Skyler." She leaned over and took him in an embrace. He untucked his arms and hugged her, sighing with his chin resting on her shoulder.

"Oh, Sid. I *am* fucked up. I want this. And then I don't. But when he holds me and kisses me…" He pulled out of her embrace and sat back. "I just…go melty. But then later when I think about marriage, I shut down."

She looked him in the eye. "Can you live without him? Tell me honestly. If this were your last day together, how would you feel?"

He thought about it, thought about their quiet evenings, about their trips to Trixx and dancing together, about how Keith made him laugh, how he made him feel, the security of knowing he was there day and night—and he knew what she meant. "No. I can't live without him."

"Then there's your answer."

"I know all that in my gut, but my brain is on turbocharge, running a million miles an hour."

"Then turn your brain off. It hasn't done you much good lately anyway."

He gave her a withering look. "Keith is the right choice. It's just the marriage thing. Am I ready for it right now?"

"What else have you got going? Are you afraid you won't get to trick anymore? 'Cause you won't. But you already knew that because Keith would hate sharing you."

"I *know*. And I don't particularly want to, it's just that it's permanently off the table now."

"And so what? What do you need to do that for?"

"Oh, excuse me? Do I sense a bit of sexism here? I remember you were open for business quite a lot back in the day. Did that *thang* of yours ever snap back to pre-carousing size?"

"My vag is perfectly fine, thanks for asking. And I certainly don't miss the meat market."

"Well, it's different for you."

"Now who's being sexist?"

"Well...all right, I concede it. We're just a couple of former sluts, I guess."

"That's right. We have nothing to apologize for. And we don't have to reconcile anything. Times change. *We* change. Carousing is expensive, all those drinks in a bar. And who has time for that anymore?"

He took her hand, smiling. "We always made time."

"I know." She gave him a friendly elbow. "But you have school hours to keep these days and I have cop hours. You're twenty-six, I'm twenty-seven…we're getting older. Getting settled."

"Maybe that's what it is. Getting settled. I just never thought I'd do that. Let alone at this stage of my life."

"Why? You're a responsible person, Skyler. You've got your students and school projects like the Gay-Straight Alliance. Aren't you busy and fulfilled enough?"

"I guess."

"And then there's Keith always there to support you. Always there to love you. Isn't that a nice thing?"

"It's very nice," he sighed. "Sid, what's wrong with me?"

"You're still in Twink mode. You think the world is laid at your feet. You think that all you have to do is wiggle that cute ass of yours and men will come running. And they would. And you're having a hard time reconciling that to this new world order of responsibilities and relationships and everyday life. But when you break it all down to its elements, you do like your life, right?"

He squeezed her hand. "I do. I really do."

"As for me, what's married life like? It's like nothing I've ever experienced. It's like coming home even when you aren't home. It's knowing that there's always someone there on your side. It's a partnership that goes deep, deeper than friendship. The ultimate friendship."

"Wow. I've never heard you talk like that before."

"Like I said, I've changed. And you will, too." She kissed his shoulder. "This is a good thing, sweetie. I'm proud of you."

"You're proud of me?"

"Yeah." She took his chin. "You really want this, whether you realize it now or not. Give yourself time. Have a longish engagement."

"That's what Keith said."

"And besides, you'll need time to plan the wedding."

He sat straight up, losing her hand. "Omigosh! I have a wedding to plan."

"Calm down, Skyler. You know I'll help you. And so will the guys."

Something clicked inside. He brightened. "It will be the wedding of the century."

"Whoa, boy. Don't go nuts. You need to talk it over with Keith. I have a feeling he's a small affair kind of guy."

"Yeah, yeah," he said distractedly. He was picturing doves, he was seeing garlands of voile and gold everywhere, a string quartet, and champagne served by handsome young waiters in crisp uniforms. "A reception to die for," he muttered.

"Oh Jesus, Keith is gonna kill me. Come on. Earth calling Skyler," she said, waving her hand in front of his face. "Come back down, dude."

"What?"

"You haven't told the guys yet, have you?"

"No. I had to come to you first." He squared with her and took up her hands again. "Sidney, will you be my best man?"

"Of course! And as your newly elected best man, I will tell you right now to calm the fuck down and don't go crazy. First you have to pick a date. And before you go and put Keith in a kilt" — Skyler's eyes bulged — "you have to find out what *he* wants. Promise me."

"Wha—oh yeah, sure."

"Promise me, Skyler."

"Yes, yes, I promise." They both rose and she escorted him to the door. But before he could leave, she took him into a hug again.

"Don't do it for the party, do you hear me? If for any reason it just doesn't feel right—even to the moment you are supposed to walk down the aisle—you tell me and I'll fix it. I'll have a car out front ready to roll. Are you listening?"

"Yes, mother. Oh! I've gotta tell my mom and dad."

"You should do that next. You should go over there right now. She'll kill you if you don't."

"You're right. Okay. What would I do without you, Sidney?" He hugged her again.

"You'd fall apart into little blond Twinkie crumbles. Now go! Go talk to your mother! She'll be over the moon."

"She'll want to plan the wedding."

"I'll take care of her. Don't worry. Go, Skyler. Be the dutiful son."

He saluted. "I'm off, *mon capitaine*! Wish me luck."

"*Bon chance*," she said in a bad French accent, and closed the door on him.

He stood on her concrete step for a moment longer, inhaling that smoky barbecue, the heat of the air finally cooling as the sun sank below the mountains, and stepped off.

When he got into his car, his player spilled out the strains of Al Green telling him to *Get Yourself Together*. "That's for sure," he muttered, humming along with it. When he passed his own apartment, he didn't see Keith's truck parked out front yet. "Good." He'd have time to swing by his mom's, tell her, and get home to start dinner before Keith knew he was out and about. Not that he had anything to hide. Well. He had promised not to tell anyone. But Sidney and his parents weren't just *anyone*.

He was actually feeling better about it. Maybe it wasn't going to be so bad after all. Maybe he just needed to get it out of his system a bit. That thought took him all the way to his mother's, where he parked out front and shut off the engine. Both his parents' cars were in the driveway, and he hurried up the walk to get out of the heat and rang the bell.

"Well, Skyler!" said his mother, reaching out to grab him into a hug. "What are you doing here? Where's Keith?"

"It's just me. Is, uh, Dad here?"

"You know he is," she said, but her cheeks colored slightly. She dragged him in, and when he turned, his dad was getting up from the armchair. "Son," said Dale.

"Hi Dad. I'm glad you're both here. I have something to tell you."

His mother gasped. "Oh God, you have a disease. A gay disease!"

"Mom!"

"Cynthia!" Dale hurried to his former wife and took her shoulders. "Skyler does *not* have a disease... *Do* you, son?"

"No! Jeez! Can I at least get through the door before you push me into an early grave?"

Cynthia Foxe shook her head and walked toward the sofa in the living room. "I wish you wouldn't announce things like that. It gets me very upset."

"All I said was I wanted to talk to you. Why does that mean I'm suddenly dying?"

"I worry, that's all."

"And I don't have any 'gay diseases'. God!"

"Fine, then." She sat primly and Dale sat again in his chair. There were cocktails in front of them on the table. How cozy. No, he wasn't going to start anything. He'd already made his displeasure known that they had moved in together and everyone had called a truce. No reason to bring it all up again. Besides, this was good news. He hoped.

"It's good news," he said, sitting next to his mother. He held his breath and then blurted, "I'm getting married."

"Oh!" Cynthia seemed so shocked that she froze.

"To that Keith fella?" asked Dale.

"Well, yeah, Dad. He's the person I live with."

Dale's eyes narrowed. He didn't miss the jab.

"Oh my Lord!" Cynthia grabbed him into a hug and squeezed. "Oh Skyler! I'm so happy for you!"

Her Chanel scent lingered on his nose as he hugged her tight. "I'm pretty happy for me, too." The sentiment sunk in, and his emotions ramped up to a happy place again.

Then Dale was suddenly there and he pulled Skyler to his feet and was hugging him as well. "Congratulations, son."

"Thanks, Dad."

Dale was trying for a serious but man-to-man tone. At least that's how Skyler interpreted it. "Is this a sudden thing or have you been discussing this a while?"

"Kind of sudden, I guess."

"It's because of Sidney, isn't it?" His mother dabbed at her wet eyes with a tissue. "Weddings are contagious, especially among friends of the same age."

He shrugged. "I don't know about that. All I know is that I didn't want anything to come between me and Keith and…"

"Wait, Skyler," said his dad. "I thought you were soured on marriage."

"I was. For a long time. And now…I'm not."

Cynthia sprang to her feet. "This calls for champagne. I know we have some in the fridge. Dale, will you do the honors?"

"You've got it, hon."

Strange, the casual endearment. Though, Skyler supposed, if his mom could get used to his being gay, he should try to get used to her life choices.

Dale returned with three sparkling flutes of champagne carefully grasped between his fingers. "Take this, son," he said. Skyler extricated one while Cynthia took another. Dale held up his glass. "A toast, then, to Skyler and Keith. May their marriage be a long and happy one."

They all clinked and drank.

Cynthia sighed. "Keith should be here."

"I know, but I wanted to tell you myself, by myself. As a family. In case you had any…embarrassing questions."

"Questions like what?" She blinked, puzzled.

"Like which one will wear the wedding dress." Dale laughed. Skyler didn't. "Oh come on, son. It's a joke."

"Okay, like that, Dad. That's not funny."

He slapped Skyler on the back. "Lighten up, Skyler. It's hilarious."

"No, Dad." He set his glass down. "It isn't. Don't you think I've had that sort of thing tossed at me all my life? I am not a girl."

He quickly sobered, especially after Cynthia slapped his arm. "I'm…I'm sorry, Skyler. You're right. That was in poor taste."

He blew out a breath. "Listen, I have to go."

"Wait!" said his mom. "You didn't tell us the date yet."

"I don't have one. This all just happened. We have yet to discuss dates."

"And the wedding reception. Now I have some ideas…"

"Mom, I think I would like to take care of this myself. I mean, this is all different for me. I want a chance to think about it all. I don't know how I want to handle this yet. Maybe a small wedding."

"Oh no! It has to be a big wedding. We have so many relatives. I'll make a list."

"I don't know about a big one, Mom. Small seems more—"

"But I've helped so many others with their wedding planning."

"Cyn, I think he'd like to do it himself. He's a grown man. Let him decide."

They both fell silent. Skyler excused himself and walked to the door. With his arm around Cynthia's shoulders Dale followed. "Skyler," said Dale, "I really didn't mean to offend you. I never knew a lot of gay folks. Please forgive me, okay? It seems I'll be saying that to you till I drop."

"I know you didn't mean anything by it, Dad, but there will be a lot of my friends there. A lot of gay people. You are going to have to learn not to offend them."

"I will." He looked to Cynthia. "We both will."

"Good. I love you both." He kissed his mother's cheek and endured another hug from his father before trotted out the door to his car.

That was…weird. But he supposed they were trying.

When he got to his apartment, he parked out front behind Keith's truck, and took the steps up to his door two at a time. When he opened the door the entire compliment of the Skyler Fuck Club rose, turned to him, and screamed at the top of their lungs.

He nearly fell out of the door, but he caught himself on the door jamb.

Sidney! he growled.

The Skyler Fuck Club — or SFC — was his loyal posse who had begun as hook-ups and ended up friends. Keith had learned to tolerate their history because of that loyalty, but he hated that name that one of them had coined long ago.

"And here comes the other groom at last!" said Philip, Skyler's coffee-house-owner friend. Philip's glasses and nerdy good looks were what had attracted Skyler to him all those years ago, long before Keith had ever entered the picture.

Everyone was holding flutes of champagne. Skyler knew that he hadn't had any on hand. One of *them* must have brought it.

After his heart's hammering began to settle down, he closed the door and accepted a glass Jamie handed him, until he enclosed Skyler in his arms. Jamie was slim but well-toned, with brilliant scarlet-dyed hair draping over his forehead. "Congratulations, Skyboy! I can't believe it."

Then it was Rodolfo's turn. Tears streamed down his face, and between sobs, he blurted out, "Oh *amante*! I cannot believe it either. You are fortunate among men. I will kiss you for good luck." He kissed both cheeks and sobbed again. Rodolfo was Philip's business partner and Ecuadorian boyfriend; whose features bore the spitting image of a long-haired Antonio Banderas.

"Well I guess I can't be left out," said Dave. Blond and buff, he was with Jamie. He took Skyler in a bro hug, slapping his back. "Congratulations to you both, Skyler."

Keith shrugged. "I couldn't control them. They just burst in here. Where've you been?"

"Well first I went over to Sidney's—the gossip queen, apparently—and then went over to my mom's and told my parents."

Keith only raised his brows in question.

"I'm sorry. I know you didn't want me to tell anyone yet, but I had to tell Sidney. And if I told Sidney, I had to tell my parents…"

"It's okay, Skyler." He smiled indulgently.

"Now sit down," said Philip, "and tell us how this all came about. I'm betting some sort of roofie was involved."

"No," said Keith, sipping his champagne, and winking at Skyler. "Just Skyler getting carried away with the moment."

"Must have been *some* moment," said Jamie.

"We were having sex," said Keith.

As one, the SFC turned to Keith and looked him up and down. No one said anything but all eyes were shining with approval. Skyler's face burst into flame. "Did you have to tell them *that*?"

"They would have gotten it out of you anyway. This way *I* get to see the reaction."

Jamie held up his palm like a traffic cop. "Hold on. This all sounds like *Skyler* asked *you*. And we all know *that* is impossible."

Keith smiled and sipped. "More possible than you think."

They all swiveled toward Skyler. Philip broke from the pack and approached him first, laying the back of his hand to Skyler's forehead. "Are you all right?"

He slapped Philip's hand away. "Cut it out. I'm fine. What's the matter with everyone? Can't I have a change of heart?"

"That's a big change of heart."

"Well…" He gave Keith the once over. "He's a big guy. And look at him. He's like some sort of…Disney Prince."

Keith laughed. "What?"

"Broad-shouldered, muscular, handsome, and suave. Definitely a Disney Prince."

"Oh yeah? So what does that make you?"

"Shut up."

"But seriously, Skyler," said Philip. "*You* really popped the question? It just seems completely out of character."

Skyler's smile faded. "I know. But…" Dropping his gaze, he fiddled with the button on his shirt. "I felt it. I *wanted* to ask him. I wanted him to know how serious I am." Keith, with that black hair hanging over a wide forehead, square jaw covered with cultivated scruff, Greek nose, sculpted lips, ice blue eyes — that face that looked on him so tenderly, was all he wanted to fill his eyes with. Skyler took a deep breath. "It was just time."

Rodolfo let out a loud sob. "It's so beautiful, *amante!*"

Philip patted him gently on the back.

"Wow," said Jamie, sitting next to Skyler on the sofa. "That's a really grown-up thing, Sky. When are you gonna do it?"

He shrugged. "I don't know. I haven't really thought about it."

"What about you, Keith? Have you always dreamed of being a June bride?"

"Can't say I've thought about it too much. But a honeymoon will be tough to schedule in the middle of the school year."

"You're not going to wait a year, are you? I can't stand the suspense that long."

"That's just what I planned to do," Keith muttered, "schedule my wedding around you."

"Well, of course you are! We *are* the wedding party. Am I right?"

There were nods and affirmations all around.

"I never thought of all that," said Skyler.

Jamie sighed. "And surely a nice little weekend honeymoon would suffice until you can take a longer one. That could still be romantic."

Skyler glanced at Keith. His smile always served to calm him. "Yeah, I guess so."

"So, then. When? Someone grab me a calendar."

Keith sat in his recliner, sipping his glass. He looked more amused than annoyed, so Skyler didn't worry too much. Besides, he figured Keith would prefer to do it sooner rather than later, probably so Skyler wouldn't have time to back out.

Skyler's calendar was taken from his desk and thrust into Jamie's awaiting hand. "Now let's see," he said, thumbing through the months. "You still need time to plan. Will it be a big wedding or a small one?"

Keith said, "Big," the same time Skyler said, "Small." They looked at one another across the living room.

"Oh my," muttered Jamie. "A little discussion needs to happen there. How about a compromise? How about October? Three months from now should be enough time to swing either one."

"Three months?" cried Skyler. "Are you crazy? I'd need six months at least."

"That puts you in January. You don't want that. Then if you wait till spring and then summer again it's already a year. No, that's unacceptable."

"Excuse me, but it's *my* wedding."

"*Our* wedding," said Keith.

"Of course," said Skyler. He paused, turning to Keith. "Did...did you want to do it sooner?"

"The sooner the better. Don't you think you and your friends can put it all together in three months?"

"Well..."

"I must bake your cake for you!" wailed Rodolfo between sobs. "It will be perfection!"

Skyler smiled. "Yes, Rodolfo. I wouldn't think of going anywhere else."

"So," said Jamie, pointing to the calendar, "are we agreed on October?"

"What's with the 'we' stuff ?" Skyler muttered.

"The fall would be lovely," said Keith.

The shit just got real. Skyler glanced at his friends, at Keith, at Fishbreath waddling forward and rubbing against his leg. He wanted to pick up the round cat and hold him close for comfort. It seemed it was all getting decided for him. But what the hell? If someone didn't say something, he might never decide at all. He only wished Sidney was here. She was his best man, after all.

"S-so, you think October is okay?" he asked Keith.

Keith moved in, took his hand, and pulled him to his feet. His other arm was around Skyler's shoulders. "Is that what you want?"

Keith's powers of seduction were turned to their highest setting. Skyler felt that dreamy feeling again, looking into those blue eyes. "Yeah," he heard himself say.

Keith seemed to radiate calm and confidence. "How about...October twelfth? I mean, I'll likely have a game that Friday but I think one of the assistant coaches can relieve me for one weekend."

The twelfth. That made it almost exactly three months away. All the projects involved suddenly whirred through his head. Was it enough time? With his mom's help it would be. And with the SFC scouting for a good location, it could work. "But the honeymoon. I don't know that I can swing planning that too."

"I'll take care of that, Skyler," said Keith's rumbling voice.

"You will?"

"Sure. I know you'll want to do everything else."

"I'll ask for your opinion."

"I'll be looking forward to that."

"No, really. Like…how about a kilt…"

"Absolutely not."

"But you've got the legs for it."

"No, Skyler."

"Doves. Are you interested in doves?"

"For the love of God, why?"

"You know. To symbolize our…our…"

"Shitting all over everyone?" said Philip. He was smiling when Skyler glared at him.

Keith kissed Skyler's nose and let him go. "You know I don't like all of that over-the-top stuff."

"A carnival theme!"

"Skyler, what is wrong with a simple, low key wedding with a modest reception?"

"I'm with Keith," said Dave, lounging back on a chair. "Although a barbecue would make a kick-ass reception."

"Not that low-key," said Keith.

"A sit-down dinner?" asked Skyler. "I don't know that I can afford that."

"You're forgetting something, babe. It's *our* finances now. We can combine forces."

"Oh. Uh…how much do you have, finance-wise?"

Keith scanned the anxious faces turned toward him. "I don't really wish to discuss it with an audience."

"Awww," sighed Jamie in disappointment.

"But we're doing okay," Keith added. "That doesn't mean I want to break the bank on a wedding. I know they can get expensive, so I'd rather do some kind of buffet rather than a sit-down."

Our finances. Skyler was still hung up on that. Everything was going to change. Insurance beneficiaries, disclosures, income, debts... What did he really know about Keith? He knew roughly what he made — that was easily discovered through the school district — and he also had some FBI money, but he didn't know if he had bad credit or foreclosures or if he even had life insurance. Skyler's mom was *his* beneficiary. He'd wanted to take care of her if anything had happened to him. But now she was living with his dad and, presumably, if they stuck together, they'd have to change their own policies. Keith was now Skyler's "next of kin" or soon would be.

"Babe, you okay?"

"Yeah, fine." He looked around. Only Keith noticed he had spaced out. Dave was sitting on the arm of Jamie's chair, looking over his shoulder, while Jamie was chatting away with Philip on various potential locales for the wedding. Rodolfo was blowing his nose into his handkerchief as tears continued to stream down his face.

Suddenly, Jamie piped up with, "What about your invitees? Will you invite your students?"

Skyler hadn't thought that far. But Keith was ready with a, "I think that would be great. But you know, just a select few. The GSA, probably."

"With under-aged students, someone will have to monitor the champagne," said Philip.

Jamie patted Philip's shoulder. "And we'll put *you* on that duty, Philip."

"What? Babysit a bunch of teenagers?"

"You did it before. Oh, this is gonna be fun!" Jamie took a pen and made a big circle around October twelfth and drew little hearts and doves fluttering around it.

Skyler took the calendar back and looked at it. October twelfth. Three months. Three months left of bachelorhood. Three months…

He was feeling a little light-headed when Keith took the calendar out of his death grip. "Breathe, Skyler," he murmured. "And talk to your mom."

"Talk to my mom. Good idea."

Chapter Three

CYNTHIA FOXE WAS OVERJOYED THAT THEY HAD picked a date, but when she called him back a few days later, she seemed subdued.

"You know Skyler, I've been thinking. Perhaps a smaller wedding would be more ideal. After all, you've got a lot to plan in a short span of time."

"O-kaaay. What's with the change of heart, though?"

She sighed heavily and paused. He gripped his phone, fingers tapping on the edge of the plastic.

"Well," she said at last, "I started making some calls. And it turns out— I've never been so mad at some of my cousins! My Christmas card list will be considerably diminished this year."

"Mom, what happened?"

"Oh Skyler!" He could hear the tears in her voice, but the anger seemed to override it. "We have some very fucked-up relatives."

"*Mom!*"

"I apologize for swearing. I usually never use that word, but there was no other way around it. I began calling to let them know there was a wedding coming up, and do you know what some of those *bastards* said to me?"

"I think I'm getting the picture."

"'Oh, no offense, Cynthia,'" she said, mocking their voices, "'but I'm against gay marriage. But give him my best wishes.' Ba-loney! Your best wishes for what? For insulting my son? I gave them what for, I'll have you know. They haven't heard the last of this."

"Now, Mom, I appreciate the sentiment, but don't go doing anything you'll regret."

"I'll regret nothing! They can't do that to you. After all those wedding and confirmation presents I've sent to their miserable bastard children over the years. I've a mind to take them all back."

"Mom, it's okay."

"It's *not* okay! Good grief. We live in the twenty-first century, for heaven's sake. They need to get over it."

He couldn't help but smile at his mother's fierce protectiveness. But he also remembered that when she first found out about him, *she* hadn't taken it very well.

"So are any of the cousins coming?"

"Your Aunt Sue and cousin Sean are coming and they were very happy to hear about it. We've always liked them."

"Yeah. I did enjoy visiting them when I was a kid."

"And then there are lots on your father's side who are coming. But it will still be a much-abbreviated list. I'm sorry, dear."

"That's okay. I did want to keep it small. There's still my friends, some of my students, Keith's side… Actually, every time I think about it, it seems bigger all the time."

"Be sure and have Keith send me his list. And then I'll have some sample invitations for you to look at. Your friend Jamie is quite the designer."

"I appreciate your help in this, Mom."

"It's no problem, sweetheart. We don't have much time. If I didn't know better, I'd think that all the rush was due to one of you being pregnant." She laughed.

"Very funny, Mom."

"I told your father that one and he laughed and laughed."

"The both of you are hilarious."

"Well, I'm sorry for the bad news but we are proceeding as scheduled. I'll talk to you soon. I love you."

"Love you, too, Mom."

He clicked off the phone and sat, looking out his bay window at the warm pavement. The dwarf orange trees below his window were heavy with fruit, and the younger kids were outside playing in the late summer heat. He knew most of the older kids and teens were inside in the air-conditioning playing on their X-boxes and phones. He hoped at least some of *his* teens were inside doing homework.

He hadn't really thought too much about his relatives. He hadn't seen too many of them growing up, but he had gone to plenty of *their* weddings and events. It stung a little, but not too much. His favorite relatives would be there at least. And he didn't even have to come out to them now. So there was that.

He was proud of his mom, though.

As the days drew on, he spent his lunches in his classroom, pouring over the interminable guest list. Seems there were about ten to fifteen teachers and office people from school to invite, about fifteen kids, some people from the Lincoln Shrine and from Trixx, his relatives, Keith's relatives — all together it was over one hundred and had to be whittled down to sixty, seventy at the most. How was he to decide?

"Hi, Mr. Foxe!"

Skyler startled in his seat, nearly spilling his water bottle.

"Sorry," said Amber. She had her red hair up in ponytails and sported a cheerleading outfit, clutching her books to her chest. "I just had to get out of the heat and hoped you'd be in your room. Is it okay if I do my homework in here?"

"Sure, Amber. No problem. Where's Heather?" Her Goth best friend—decidedly less Goth these days now that she had a football player boyfriend—was usually never absent from her side.

"She's having a romantic lunch with Drew. They had a tough time there with Sapanigate and they're reconnecting."

"I'm sorry, 'Sapanigate'?"

She chuckled. "It's what we're calling the whole Alex-Ryan-getting-hit-by-a-girl thing." Skyler hoped that Alex—tight end on the football team—was getting over being decked by a girl. Granted, Elei Sapani, the Polk Panther's newest wide receiver, was a *big* girl. Before this, football seemed to bring out the best in Alex. Alex had been angry and aimless before getting on the team. Of course, coming out and being the boyfriend of the class clown Rick Flores had helped him a lot, too.

"Alex seems to have recovered his dignity," he said.

"Yeah. Now he's like bestie's with Elei. It's kind of weird seeing Alex, Elei, and Rick hanging around together at school."

"Yeah, that's something to get used to. It's a good thing, though."

"Totally. So what are you doing there, Mr. Foxe? Doesn't look like classwork. It looks like you're planning a party."

Papers, lists, and business cards were all crammed into his special journal for wedding material. "It kind of is," he said, stuffing in more papers and magazine pictures of table settings he'd cut out. He glanced toward the door. "Can you keep a secret?"

"Of course." She scooted to the edge of her seat, clutching the front of the desk.

"Well, I'm planning a...a wedding."

"For whom?"

"For, uh, me."

She squealed in delight. "You and Mr. Fletcher? Oh my God!"

"Amber, keep it down, okay?"

"I'm sooooo happy for you, Mr. Foxe. He's quite a catch, isn't he?"

"Yeah. He is." Darn blushes. "So I'm trying to keep our guest list down. But we certainly wanted to include the GSA kids."

"Oh my God! We get to come? This is so exciting."

"It is that. But here's my conundrum. If we invite the GSA kids, wouldn't it be unfair if Mr. Fletcher couldn't invite his football team?"

"Oh." She rested her chin on her hand and stared up at the ceiling. "I see what you mean. But that's about thirty kids, isn't it? Of course, some of them may not come. No matter how much they respect their coach, some of them won't want to go to a same-sex wedding."

"Yeah, I had thought of that."

"Still, it would seem like too much favoritism if you didn't."

"I was thinking that, too." He shook his head. "We just have too many people coming."

"Of course the GSA has two football players. That's got to count for something." She leaned forward on the desk, clutching her hands to her heart. "So *we're* on the list? Do we get to bring a date?"

"Naturally."

"Good. Because there may be someone I'd like to invite."

"Would his first name rhyme with Ravi and his last name with Chaudhri?"

"Mr. Foxe! You already know!"

He smiled. "Are you guys dating, then?"

"Sort of. Not officially. We haven't been out solo. Just with the guys."

"But you all get along. That's important in relationships."

"Yes. At first, they didn't seem to like him, but he's worn them down. He has a really wry sense of humor."

"I'm glad to hear it. You guys seem like a good couple."

"Thank you. So are you and Mr. Fletcher. Omigosh! Are you planning on changing your name? It would be weird to start calling *you* Mr. Fletcher."

Skyler's eyes widened. It never occurred to him. Skyler Fletcher? "Why would *I* change *my* name?"

"Oh, it's just that…" There were hand gestures but she didn't seem to know how to finish that sentence.

"He could just as easily change his," he went on haughtily. Keith Foxe? Should they hyphenate? Foxe-Fletcher? Fletcher-Foxe? Shit. Something else he'd have to talk over with Keith. Did all this ever end? No wonder people opted for just living together.

When Skyler got home that night, he slammed the door, faced Keith, and announced, "I'm not changing my name."

Keith looked up from correcting his biology papers at the kitchen table. "Okay."

"And I'm not hyphenating either."

"Anything else?"

"I don't want you to change *your* name. Everyone knows you as Coach Fletcher. Wouldn't it be too weird having two Mr. Foxes at school?"

"Are you done?"

Skyler set his satchel down and sat at table across from him. "Yes."

"Good. I happen to agree with you."

"Oh, thank God!" He slumped back, head tilted toward the ceiling, words rushing out. "I stressed all day that you'd want me to change my name and I just didn't want to. I've been a 'Foxe' a long time—forever—and I didn't want that to change. I know maybe my dad doesn't deserve it, but I'm his only child and I wanted to keep the name, you know. I mean, I was worried about my identity, too. This is who I am. I'm Skyler Foxe. I'm Mister Foxe to my kids. I just didn't want that to change. And you! You'll always be Keith Fletcher to me, the guy who walked into my life and turned it upside down."

Keith chuckled. "That…was a lot. All you had to do was talk to me. I'd never make you do anything that wasn't comfortable for you."

"Really?"

"Skyler…of *course* not."

"Oh…okay. It's just that there's a lot to this. All kinds of changes—"

"And we will take them one at a time. For instance, I was thinking…" Keith suddenly seemed shy. He looked at his papers again as he said, "Maybe we should go look at rings tonight."

"Rings?"

"You will wear a ring, won't you? But…if you don't want to…" He lowered his eyes, looking up at Skyler through his long lashes.

"No. It seems important that we do. Let's look at rings."

"You sure?"

"Yeah. I'm totally into that." Why did his voice seem to rise an octave?

Keith cocked his head at Skyler but assured by his expression, turned back to his papers, shaking his head slightly.

Skyler swallowed hard.

Rings.

They decided to look at a jewelry store and then go out to Taquito Grill for dinner. Skyler stepped out to the landing first, chatting as Keith locked the door. He started down the steps, saying, "I've never worn jewelry. I wonder if it will feel—OW!"

Down he went, bumping his head on the steps, two, three of them before he came to a halt.

"Skyler!" Keith was at his side, cradling him. "Babe, what happened?"

"The step. It broke right out from under me. Ow. My head."

Keith glanced above Skyler at the broken step. "That broke pretty cleanly. We'd better call the landlady about that. But are you all right? Should we go to the emergency room?"

Skyler sat up on the stair, rubbing the back of his head and looking back at the broken step. "No. Only my dignity is hurt. My head's just a bit bruised. Maybe we can patch it ourselves. The stair, not my head. It sometimes takes the landlady a long time to get to things."

"I can handle that. Just be careful of that step from now on. Ready to get up?"

"Yeah." Keith grabbed him by the elbow and hauled him up. No dizziness. There was no excuse not to go ring shopping.

Chapter Four

SKYLER HAD BOUGHT JEWELRY FOR HIS MOTHER over the years, feeling that since she had no one to buy it for her it was up to him. Krueger's Jewelers on State was at least familiar.

Mr. Krueger, the white-haired patriarch of his little jewelry empire, sat behind a glass screen, head down over a piece he was working on, a jeweler's loupe over one eye.

The thirty-ish saleswoman was there who'd helped him many times before. She wore a green cocktail dress with modest jewelry at her neck and ears as if she were going to a genteel affair. "Mr. Foxe, so good to see you. How's your mother doing?"

"Hi, Nancy. She's great."

"What can we find for you today?"

"Well…um, actually, I'm…I'm looking at…wedding rings."

"Oh my goodness! Congratulations. Who's the lucky lady?"

"Me," said Keith, smiling broadly as he stepped forward, laying a gentle hand on Skyler's shoulder. He'd been hanging back, looking around. He seemed to be actually enjoying this. Skyler didn't see anything amusing about it. Especially the look on Nancy's face.

"Oh. Oh, well… Congratulations again." She recovered smoothly and motioned for them to come to a different counter. It was good to know there wasn't going to be any rejection. Her graceful transition told him he'd made the right choice in choosing this place. "You're a lucky man," she said to Keith. "Mr. Foxe has been coming here for years. He has excellent taste. We've been getting in some very lovely dual wedding bands for our LGBT customers. It's a growing business. What did you have in mind?"

Skyler stared down into the glass case and shook his head. "I really have *no* idea."

Keith leaned over and peered into the case. "I'd like to see white gold, I think. I can't see us in yellow gold. Can you, babe?"

He shrugged. The whole thing was surreal. "I don't know anything about men's jewelry."

She grabbed a display of rings and pulled it toward her, plucking a ring from its velvet cushion. "If it's a silver tone you're looking for, then there are several options. Titanium, palladium, tungsten, platinum, and, of course, white gold. Each have advantages and some disadvantages. With white gold, the rhodium plating *can* wear off. Titanium is a good alternative, especially if you have problems with allergies to certain metals. But platinum, since it's so pure, is non-allergenic and permanent." She laid one with a diamond embedded in it on a black velvet square on the glass counter.

"I don't want any diamonds," said Skyler. *Blood diamonds*, he mouthed to Keith.

She put the ring back and picked another.

"And I don't want any rainbow things in it. Or Mars symbols. We already know who we are."

"You're pretty opinionated for someone who doesn't know what he wants," said Keith out of the side of his mouth.

"I guess I know what I *don't* want."

Keith picked up a ring with thumb and index finger, studying it closely. "I guess…they don't have to match…"

"Yes, they do!" said Skyler. His own vehemence surprised even him. "I mean...shouldn't they?"

Keith's eyes crinkled in amusement. "It's traditional. And I'd like them to," he said shyly.

"Okay, then." Skyler leaned into him, just enough to offer a touch of reassurance.

"Then maybe something more permanent," said Keith. "Let's look at platinum."

"It's more expensive," muttered Skyler.

"Let me worry about that."

Nancy smiled indulgently. "So, Mr. Foxe, how long have you and...uh...?"

"Mr. Fletcher," offered Keith.

"You and Mr. Fletcher been together?"

"About a year."

"Oh my. You don't waste any time."

Keith chuckled. "When you know what you want, you go for it. Right, babe?"

"That's about the size of it. Oh, that one looks nice." Skyler pointed to a ring in the case. He was warming up to this. This was all to do with Keith after all. Why was he worrying? Why was this such a big deal? And he got jewelry out of it. How bad could it be?

The ring she placed on the velvet was platinum with a hammered finish and a polished edge. A solid piece with heft, sporting what he felt were masculine lines that were also a bit unique in style.

"What do you think of this, Keith?"

"Why don't you try it on? Here. Let me."

Keith took Skyler's left hand, and reverently placed the ring on his finger. With his hand resting in Keith's, Skyler looked up and swallowed. *Wow*, he thought. *This is...surreal.*

"How does it feel?" Keith asked quietly.

"Heavy." It was a big piece of metal encircling his finger. But it had a nice look to it. When he turned it this way and that, he decided it wasn't all bad. He slipped it off and handed it to Keith. "Shouldn't you try it on?"

Keith gave him a secret smile and forced it on his finger. It looked good on Keith's tanned hand. "I like it. But I think we should look at some more."

They tried on several, even yellow gold ones just to be thorough. He even tried on some with diamonds in a center channel, asking if they couldn't replace the diamonds with other gems. "I bet we could get a cubic zirconia in there instead, right?"

"There are several alternatives, if you're concerned about conflict-free stones," said Nancy. "There's cultured diamonds and moissanite. Moissanite has great brilliance and fire — that's it's level of sparkliness. It's also cultured in the lab and is far less expensive than a diamond. If you replaced the diamond with moissanite, it would knock the price down by a quarter."

"And it's conflict-free?"

"Yes, it is. Unless someone had an argument in the lab." She smiled.

But Skyler's eye kept on returning to the one with the hammered finish. "Could we see that one again?"

Skyler held the ring in his hand, turning it over and over. "What do you think, Keith?"

"I like this one."

"I suppose we should be looking at prices."

Nancy flipped a piece of paper on the tray. "Here's the tag."

He whistled. "Wow. And that would be times two."

"Yes. Did you need something maybe a little more mid-range?"

"No," said Keith. "If this is what you want, Skyler, we can do it."

"I mean it's not down-payment-on-a-house expensive, but it is a-nice-vacation-expensive."

"Don't worry, sweetheart. Let me take care of it."

"Keith, I don't want you to 'take care of it.' We're in this together. We should share the costs."

"Maybe this is my wedding present to you."

"Well, how about mine is your wedding present to me, and yours is *my* wedding present to you?"

"Fair enough."

Nancy shook her head. "You know, life would be better if all couples who came in here were as rational." She leaned in. "You should see what some women guilt their fiancés into buying for them. Not that I mind the commission." She measured both their ring sizes and then glanced over her shoulder at Mr. Krueger. "You know, I bet I can knock ten percent more off the price because it's you. Let me just check with Mr. Krueger."

As she made her way through the maze of display cases, Skyler turned to Keith and said quietly, "You think we should shop around? It's just that I trust this place. I've been coming here a long time…"

"Babe, if this is where you're comfortable, I think we should just go for it. You like the rings, don't you?"

"Yeah, I guess I do. And I really think they'll give us a good deal."

"Skyler Foxe!" cried the booming voice of Mr. Krueger in a thick German accent. "Well, well, well." He strode forward and shook Skyler's hand. Then he turned to Keith and shook his. "Congratulations. So you're getting married. My, my. I remember the first time you came in here. You weren't even driving yet. And you bought a lovely pin for your mother." He turned to Keith. "He's been coming in that long. And now you are getting married. I'm very happy to hear it. You take good care of our Skyler, you understand? He's a good boy. He takes care of his mother."

"I will."

"We give you fifteen percent off. That's a good price. When is the wedding date?"

"October twelfth." He hadn't meant for his voice to crack but his throat was a bit dry.

"That's pretty soon. Don't worry. The rings will be sized and ready in about a week."

Skyler and Keith each paid for the other—Keith's was slightly more for its size—and they left, with wallets considerably lighter.

They climbed into Keith's truck and as Skyler buckled in, Keith casually said, "By the way, I think we should have the wedding and immediately follow with a luncheon reception. Same place, you know?"

Skyler ran through all the venues he and Sidney had been looking at. "Why?"

"Because we'll want to get started on our honeymoon right away."

Skyler drew on a grin as Keith's F-150 engine roared to life. "Someone's anxious to get our own party started."

Keith pulled the truck into traffic and moved slowly down the narrow street. "It's not that. Well, not *only* that. I've got special plans for the honeymoon that require that we get out of here no later than three."

"Plans? What plans?"

"It's a surprise."

"A surprise. I love surprises. What is it?"

"The nature of a surprise is that you don't know what it is until it's sprung."

They turned and headed down toward the restaurant. "I understand what a surprise is, I just want to know what it is ahead of time so I can be properly shocked." He mimed various faces, showing his awe and surprise.

"Skyler, I think you need to go over the concept one more time."

"You're not going to tell me? Really?"

"Nope."

"Till the day of the wedding?"

"Not even then. I'm going to really surprise you, dammit."

"But Keith, how will I pack?"

"I'll have Jamie do it for you."

"*Jamie* gets to know and *I* don't? How's that surprise going to stay a secret?"

Keith frowned. "That's right. That man loves to gossip. Then…uh, I'll get Philip to help me."

He threw himself back in the seat. "Shoot. He's Fort Knox." He scrambled up again, facing Keith. "Come on, Keith! I'm beggin' you!"

"Nope. I'm gonna love watching you squirm for two whole months."

"Two months! Omigod, there's still so much to do."

"Heh, heh. There's the distraction I was hoping for."

"You are evil, Keith Fletcher."

"Heh, heh."

Skyler went about his business teaching, trying not be distracted. But a few teachers had gotten wind of their impending nuptials and there was a lot of back-slapping and congratulations.

When Friday rolled around and the Gay-Straight Alliance met at lunchtime in his classroom, the unusually quiet teens all settled in their places, placid faces turned up toward him. He squirmed in his seat in front of his desk.

"What's going on?" he asked warily.

"Well," said Rob. He was always impeccably dressed like an ivy-leaguer and with his cool demeanor, he looked as if he never broke a sweat. His floppy blond hair was coifed to perfection, and his pouty lips were teased up into a smile. "A little bird told us that you and Coach Fletcher were getting hitched. True?"

Skyler pulled his collar away from his neck and loosened his tie. "Um…yes. That's true."

Stewart, Skyler's scruffy-haired gay-friendly member of the GSA, laughed out loud. "Getting yourself the old ball and chain, eh Mr. Foxe?"

"I wouldn't characterize it like that—"

"Leave him alone," said Rick Flores. As usual, his tall lanky frame sprawled lazily back in his seat with legs stretched out before him. "He found love. Isn't that what everybody wants?"

Evan, a girl with a nose ring and one side of her head shaved down to dark fuzz, cocked her head, letting the long side of her hair drape over one eye. "Mr. Foxe, isn't marriage just a false reflection of a heterosexual culture? I mean, how do two people being together even define themselves? Is couplehood even necessary when pansexuality and gender fluidity are now recognized as valid gender identities?"

"Uh…"

Joyce and Stephanie, his cheerleader couple, waved dismissively at Evan. "We think it's sweet," said Joyce, tossing her blonde hair over her shoulder.

Skyler held up his hands as everyone suddenly seemed to have an opinion. "Hey, everyone! Settle down. Evan has the floor. Let me see if I'm hearing you right,

Evan. So, you think that even getting married is an invalid statement? People should just flow in and out of relationships; this might be the more natural order of the human state?"

Voices rose again to object, but Skyler quieted them once more. "For some in the LGBTQIA community, I think this is very valid. I myself at one time condemned the idea of a steady, monogamous relationship."

"You, Mr. Foxe?" said Alex, with scandalized shock etched on his face, almost to comical extreme.

Skyler steadied himself. This was iffy territory, but he wanted to be as honest as possible with these students. He knew they looked on him as a role model of all things gay, but he also knew that some of them might not be mature enough to absorb what he was trying to convey.

"Yes, Alex. I...never had a steady boyfriend. I just met...lots of men, instead. I was always safe doing it, mind you, but this was my preferred lifestyle. And there's nothing wrong with it."

"Until you met Coach," said a wide-eyed Drew.

"Well, yes. It's funny how your perspective can change for the right person. But, it could have just as easily not. Listen, all I'm saying is that there's a choice. People are who they are, but we can choose to live our own lives authentically. There's a variation of bisexuality that even a few years ago the scientific community didn't recognize. And then there's Genderqueer, a fluidity of gender expression encompassing people who may not identify as male *or* female, but as both or neither, or somewhere in between. Choice. Free to be who you are. And sometimes, that means people pair up. Sometimes briefly. Sometimes for life. And some even choose to triple up, a thruple."

"Like Mormons?" squeaked Amber.

"Not really. A Mormon relationship is one man and many wives, and it's only the man who interacts sexually with each woman. But in a polyamorous relationship, each partner is equal to the other. They're all in a relationship *with* each other."

Reece, the boy with the black-dyed hair who liked to wear rocker t-shirts, sat back in his desk. "Dude, you should teach sex ed."

Skyler rubbed the back of his sweaty neck. "Maybe I've gone off the rails here..."

"No, Mr. Foxe," said Reece. "Who else is going to be honest with us? I mean, I never even would have figured out how to ask that question."

"The *point* I was trying to make" –*before I veered into the weeds* — "was that gay people, LGBTQIA people, have a right to choose marriage if they want to. Choose it or reject it. As long as you and your partner or partners are on the same page."

"But three people can't marry each other, can they?" asked Alex.

"No, Alex. Not at the moment."

After a long, quiet pause wherein many pins could have been dropped and sounded like a cacophony, Heather piped up with, "Well! That was instructive, but well past my pay grade. Still, I'm glad Mr. Foxe and Coach Fletcher can tie the knot if they want to. And even better, that we're invited to go."

Her pronouncement seemed to have broken the ice. Everyone began eating their lunches with gusto and noisy conversation. Skyler flung himself back in his chair and blew out a breath.

Trisha Hornbeck, the calculus teacher and co-sponsor of the GSA, laid her hand on his arm. He'd forgotten she was there. He tried to gauge her face, but her mouth was set and her reading glasses were perched bird-like on the end of her pinched nose. "I'm glad we didn't have any district monitors in here today," she whispered.

"Holy cow, Trish, why didn't you stop me?"

"I didn't know where you were going at first. And by the time I did it was too late. Besides, the kids are right, it was mighty instructive." She gave him a wink and a smile.

He felt only slightly better. He wondered how much trouble he could be in if one of the kids spread around what he had said. Though he was fairly certain that they knew better than to do so. Still, it hadn't shown very good judgment on his part. He had gotten carried away with honesty, wanting the kids to know that they could be who they wanted to be without shame. He crossed his fingers that he'd never have to explain it to the principal, Mr. Sherman.

With days and weeks going by with no blowback, he settled down to schoolwork, teaching, and wedding planning. He felt that he had spent more time with Sidney than he had in a long time. They were making up for the fact that she had eloped and Skyler hadn't had a chance to help her with her wedding plans like they always said they would. He never imagined in his wildest dreams that they'd be planning his.

But boy, did he worry over that stupid guest list!

"Have you chosen a place yet, Skyler?" his mother asked one evening over the phone.

"Sid and I are here hashing it out as we speak."

"Hi, Mrs. Foxe!" Sidney yelled toward his phone.

"Hello, Sidney dear," she said, as if Sidney could hear her. "If you haven't found anything yet, may I recommend the Mitten Building. October can be so iffy. It could be wonderful weather for a garden affair, but it could also be Santa Anas, or even rainy. If you have it all indoors, it's still a lovely venue. One of my bunco ladies has a son who works there."

"Sid, Google the Mitten Building."

Sidney sat on the floor, laptop on her lap, back against the sofa. "Coming up...oh. It's nice. Posh, just like you like it."

She turned her laptop so he could see. "That is nice. Thanks, Mom."

"How's the list coming along?"

"I'm going to kill myself."

"That well? It's always the hardest part about wedding planning. But since you're planning a buffet it will all be cheaper."

"I know, Mom, but we're getting down to the wire. I'm going to have to order invitations soon and mail them."

"I like your friend Jamie's designs."

"He's come up with some...well, off-the-wall things."

"It's the twenty-first century, Skyler. Don't be so stuffy about it."

"What? Look who's talking. You're the one who made me this way."

"I can't hear you. You're driving through a tunnel."

Baffled, he shook his head, though he well knew his mother couldn't see it. "No, I'm not, Mom. I'm at home."

"Can't hear you. Good-bye dear."

Pulling his phone away from his ear, he stared at it as his mother clicked off. "She's getting really weird lately. Have you noticed?"

"I can't hear you. I'm driving through a tunnel."

He gave her a withering look as she sniggered at her laptop. "I love your mother, Skyler. It's high time she finally let her hair down. Who knew your mother was as wild as you?"

He shook his head and put the phone on the coffee table. "I don't like it."

"Get over it. And look at this place." She gestured toward her computer screen. "I think we finally hit the jackpot. Should I call them, see if they're available?"

"Everyone is booked at so short a notice."

"I'm calling."

"They'll probably be booked." He took the computer into his lap and looked through the photo gallery, liking it more and more, but drooped, knowing he'd get his hopes up for nothing. Sidney yammered in the background.

"Yes, I'd like to talk to someone about booking your main room for a wedding. This October twelfth. I'll hold." She leaned toward him. "I'm holding."

"They'll just tell you they're booked. Everyone is booked. I'm beginning to think we'll have to have it at Taquito Grill."

"Can't," she said. "They're booked. Hello? Yes, that's Saturday, October the twelfth. Yes, *this* year. *Oy, they don't listen…* You do? Great!" She leaned in again. "It's available."

"It is?" He nearly dumped the laptop, and quickly set it aside on the sofa.

"We're looking at about a hundred people. Oh, and we want to do the ceremony there. Can they put aside a…yeah? Yeah? Yeah…?"

"What are they saying?"

She shushed him and waved him off. "Yeah? That sounds great. When should we come over?" She looked at her watch. "We can be there in ten minutes. Okay. Don't book it to anyone else. We're coming right now."

She clicked off her phone and turned to him. "Grab your wallet, Skyboy, you've got a wedding to pay for."

They trundled down the steps. Keith was still at school and he'd relegated the venue to Skyler and Sidney anyway, so Skyler didn't worry. Besides, before he signed any papers, he planned on texting Keith. They skirted the temporarily repaired step, and made it to Skyler's Bug and got in. He pressed the brake as usual to start it up but the pedal went all the way to the floor. "Wait. Something's not right here." He tried again but the brake pedal was loose and pushed all the way down again.

He popped the hood and they both got out to look. "Did you remember to put in brake fluid?" she said.

Skyler scratched his head and stared at the various caps, wires, and hoses. "Yeah…I mean I guess so. I always take it in regularly to the mechanic for a tune-up and fluids and stuff."

She dropped to her knees and looked under the car. "Well something is leaking pretty furiously."

"What?" He bent down to look. "I sprung a leak?"

"Probably. Look, we'll deal with this later. Let's take my car."

"Okay." He closed the hood, and glanced back at his car as he got in on the passenger side of Sidney's Honda. Maybe Keith could do something about fixing it. He was pretty handy.

They drove over to Fifth Street and the two-story Mitten Building, turning into the parking lot. It was essentially a giant brick warehouse sitting beside railroad tracks. Sidney jumped out and Skyler hurried after her. "Hurry up, we're late."

They entered through a colonial entry down a long arcade and went inside. "We're meeting Janet Deaver," she said to the receptionist. They were directed to an office and Sidney led the way, knocking on the door.

"Come in!" came the reply in a southern accent. A svelte woman in a tight red dress, made-up to the nth degree with every hair in place in her upswept 'do, came forward, hand outstretched. "Hi, I'm Janet Deaver." Besides the southern twang, she was loud and somewhat brash, smiling with an overabundance of teeth. "Are you Sidney? And is this the lucky man?"

"This is one half of the lucky men," said Sidney, taking her hand and giving it a hard shake. "Let's just get this out of the way. This is my friend Skyler Foxe and he's marrying a man. Is that going to be a problem?"

Janet's wide-eyed face sputtered into a laugh as she turned it toward Skyler. "She's direct, isn't she? And so very loyal. That's a prize. No, we don't have a problem with that. Love is love and we love to bring it all together here at the Mitten. Won't you both sit down?" She gestured toward some seats and she sat on a settee facing them. "Can I offer you wine? We have Chardonnay. Coffee? Water?" When they declined, she picked up a tablet sitting on the cushion beside her, and tapped it. "Now, this is to be the wedding of Skyler Foxe and…?"

"Keith Fletcher," Sidney answered.

"…and Keith Fletcher." She typed. "For Saturday, October twelfth… Are we morning, afternoon, or evening?"

"It's a luncheon," said Sidney.

"Sidney," whispered Skyler. "You can let me answer."

"Is she your best man?" asked Janet, leaning in confidentially, even though her voice was still loud. She widened her already wide smile further. Her teeth were blindingly white and big as a fence. "I love it. And how many guests? Approximately?"

Sidney sat back, looking to Skyler to answer. "Oh, uh, we're looking at about a hundred. And a buffet."

"Excellent. And you'd like the ceremony here as well? Perfect." She set the tablet on her lap and leaned forward. "We do a very nice set-up of chairs and a beautiful arch for the wedding upstairs from the reception in the main room, and then have the tables, dance floor, and DJ space below. In fact, it's set up now and we can go take a peek. Shall we?"

They rose. Sidney held tight to his arm in the expectation that he would bolt. He gave her the evil eye. He wasn't going to do any such thing. But her tight grip *was* comforting, especially since he felt light-headed.

They walked into the barn-like space and Skyler looked around, enchanted. The brick walls, the ceiling beams, combined to give it an old-world look without being tired and rundown. Little white lights draped from the ceiling in long sweeping arcs from one beam to the other. Each round table was set up with lovely centerpieces and electric candles. There was plenty of room for a dance floor. They went upstairs and saw how it was decorated for a wedding, with wooden folding chairs set up in rows, an arch with tulle and flowers standing in the end of a central aisle, and little lights hanging and twinkling all around, like a fairy wonderland. It was pretty but tasteful, and he felt both his mother and Keith would approve.

"I love this," he said breathlessly, hoping it wouldn't all disappear.

"It's lovely, isn't it?" said Janet. She looked down at her tablet. "It's pretty much how you'd see it here, with your special colors for the tablecloths and flowers, of course. Buffet tables over there, bar over there. We have DJ services if you haven't chosen one, and I've got several menus for you to go over. So, what do you think?"

Skyler looked around, liking it more as he checked out each corner. It looked like a fun space to dance in, to have a party, but it was tasteful, too. "Can I just take a few shots and send it to my boyfriend...I mean, fiancé? He's still at work."

"Oh, go right ahead. In fact, I'll leave the two of you here to look around. Come back to my office when you're ready to fill out the paperwork. But I wouldn't wait too long. We're bound to get booked."

She clacked away on her heels and Skyler turned to Sidney. "What do you think?"

"What do *you* think? It's your wedding, sweetie."

"I like it. I really do. And the prices from their website seemed comparable to everything else."

"Then take your pictures and send them off to loverboy."

Skyler did and heard back from Keith promptly with "Go for it!"

"He's so good to you," she said, head shaking.

"I know. I don't deserve him."

"Oh, honey, of course you do." She wrapped an arm around his shoulders. "I'm so happy for you, Skyler. I really am."

"Okay, cut it out. I don't want to cry here."

They both wiped at their eyes anyway and walked arm in arm toward the office to finalize the deal.

Chapter Five

SKYLER STOOD ON THE TOP OF A STEPLADDER AT home, trying to dislodge a platter from the highest shelf of the cupboard when the doorbell rang. He froze, stuck in the limbo between heaven and earth with a heavy platter in hand and a dangerous step below. A doorbell ringing was like an unanswered text and Skyler couldn't let it go. He carefully balanced the plate and the step and made it to safety as the doorbell rang a second time.

"I'm coming, I'm coming," he muttered, placing the unwieldy platter on the dining room table. It couldn't be Keith, because he'd just pound on the door as if he didn't believe in doorbells. Besides, Keith wasn't due back from football practice for another hour. Unless something happened to one of the kids. Skyler kicked into teacher mode, considering all the steps Keith would have to take, and it certainly wouldn't involve coming home from the high school.

But what if Keith was the one going to the hospital? What if he was hurt? Skyler's heart gave a lurch. Big, strong Keith. Nothing could happen to him. His boyfriend had fought off danger and criminals. His FBI training would kick in, even though he was a sort of waiting-in-the-wings kind of agent these days.

The doorbell rang a third time.

Skyler snapped out of his increasingly horrific daydreaming. Why did he do this to himself? This never used to happen before he hooked up with Keith.

He grabbed the door and swung it open.

Two women stood on the landing. The light-skinned one was poised to knock. She had shoulder-length brown hair that reminded him of Sidney. But there the resemblance ended. This woman's face was round, not angular like his friend. Her wide eyes were hazel, and she wore no make-up, but lots of rings and bangles on her hand. Her short nails were painted black and her clothes were loose; cargo pants and a gauzy top. Her companion, on the other hand, was a stunning African-American woman, with short high-top dreads sprouting on her head like a hedgehog, wide five-inch diameter hoop earrings settling over her white tank top, and many necklaces of beads and charms.

They both stepped back and stared wide-eyed at Skyler, who looked from one to the other. Then the women glanced at each other, cracked smiles, and studied Skyler up and down again, a long perusal that made him a bit uncomfortable.

"Um…can I help you?"

The light-skinned woman smirked. "You *have* to be Skyler Foxe."

Skyler clutched the door. "I do?"

"Oh, baby," said the other. "Twink down to the cream filling."

Skyler felt his cheeks heating. "Excuse me," he said indignantly. "But who are you and what do you want?"

The bracelets clanked as the brown-haired woman laughed and moved her hand. "Don't worry, Skyler. We don't mean any harm. We just figured you have to be Skyler Foxe. Keith is pretty…well, *consistent* with his choice of boyfriends."

He frowned. "You're friends of Keith's?"

"Yeah, is he here? Didn't he talk about us? I'm Sheryl Anderson, and this is my girlfriend Tamika May."

It was Skyler's turn to be wide-eyed. Keith had talked about his friends from San Diego and how hard it was for him to get the time to see them. "Oh! Well, Keith isn't here, but you can certainly come in and wait for him." He opened the door wider and gestured for them to enter. This was a first. He didn't think he'd ever had lesbians in his apartment before.

Tamika made herself comfortable on the sofa, tucking her foot under her, while her girlfriend Sheryl sat regally in the wingback.

"Can I get you anything to drink?" Skyler asked.

"That would be lovely," said Sheryl.

"I have iced tea. Is that all right?"

"Anything," said Tamika, fanning herself. "Hoo lord! It's hotter than my mama's oven on a Sunday out there."

He quickly fixed their drinks, offering them on a tray with sugar, lemon, and long spoons. "So," he said, clutching his own sweaty glass, "this is the first time I've met any of Keith's friends."

"He doesn't have many," said Sheryl. "And no offense, but Redlands is a good piece of driving from San Diego."

"I know. I'm just surprised he didn't say anything. We could have gone out to meet you."

"I hear you been busy," said Tamika. "He said you go out and solve crimes. A real Sherlock Holmes."

"I don't. I mean, I did. A couple of times. It's no big deal."

"Keith seems to think it is. Says you pretty clever."

"He did?"

"Yeah," said Sheryl. "He sounded impressed by you. But that's our Keith. We knew by the tone of his texts and emails that he was falling pretty hard, pretty fast."

"He did? I mean, I know." Skyler's belly wriggled pleasantly with the thought of Keith falling for him. It was still fresh and new enough to make him squirm.

"And you cuuuuuuute!" said Tamika. "Mmmm mmm. Keith got him some Twinkie goodness."

"Tamika!" said Sheryl, scandalized. "Ignore her, Skyler. She and Keith used to get into lots of trouble in college."

"I'll bet."

"Oh baby, you don't know the half of it."

"Well, it's really good to finally meet you. Obviously, you're going to be there at the wedding."

"Be there?" said Tamika. "Baby, I'm your officiant."

"My...what?"

Sheryl sipped and put down her tea. "Tamika's got one of those online officiant certifications. Ordained minister from the Universal Life Church."

"Uh huh." She snapped her fingers. "I'm gon' marry you two."

"Oh. Well, okay. Thanks."

"No problem, baby. Now when is that Keith of yours coming home? I have all kinds of shit to give him for being such a girl about all this."

Skyler smiled. He couldn't wait to see that.

"Sorry I'm late, babe," said Keith, kicking the door closed. His arms were full of binders up to his chin. But as soon as he turned, he spied the women. "Hey! You got here." He dumped the binders by the door—ignoring Skyler's sound of disapproval—and took both women in his arms, spinning them to squeals of delighted laughter.

"I can't believe you guys made it at last."

"And I can't believe you're getting married," said Sheryl as he plunked them back down.

Tamika put her hands at her hips and cocked her head. "I can. Parade the best looking blond boy in front of him and he's gone."

Skyler sighed to himself. He supposed this was just as annoying as Keith having to put up with Skyler's past tricks. "Ahem. Said Twink is standing right here."

Keith took two steps and enclosed Skyler in his arms. "So, you met my best friends."

"Finally. And we've had quite a nice long chat."

"Uh oh." He pointed a finger at them. "What have you been telling him?"

"Baby, we been telling him all sorts of tales on you," said Tamika.

"Well, isn't that just perfect." He shrugged toward Skyler. "It's all lies, you know."

"Oh, of course it is."

They decided to go out to dinner. Piling into Keith's giant black truck, Keith glanced across to where Skyler usually parked. "Car still in the shop?"

"Weirdest thing. They said the brake line was broken off."

"Ooooh," said Tamika. "That sounds like a job for Sherlock Foxe."

"No, I don't think so. The garage guy said it could have been mice or even squirrels. Gnawed through. Apparently, they like the taste of brake fluid."

Keith frowned as he settled into his seat and grasped the steering wheel. "Weird, though."

"I know." Skyler buckled himself in and glanced out the window toward the step on their stairwell that had yet to be repaired. He had watched as Keith screwed in a board under it to secure it. The break had been remarkably clean before it had torn and splintered under his weight. If he had a suspicious mind…

"Are you guys staying in town?" asked Keith over his shoulder as he pulled away from the curb. "It's a school night, I mean work week. Did you get tomorrow off?"

Sheryl rested her arms on the back of their seats. "We decided to skip tomorrow, hoping to crash at yours."

"You're welcome to the sofa. It does become a bed."

Keith glanced at Skyler sidelong. "It does?"

"Yeah. Didn't you know?"

He shook his head. "The things I'm still learning."

"Y'all moving fast here," drawled Tamika, "if you didn't even know about your own sofa, homey."

"You know I never paid attention to that stuff."

"Oh baby—Skyler—one time in college, this one—" and Tamika pointed to Keith, "had a slice of pizza stuck to the back of his recliner for a week before he noticed, and that was only when someone pointed it out to him."

Skyler grimaced. "Seriously?"

"Unless it was blond with a cute butt, he never noticed shit like that."

"Tamika!" Sheryl hissed.

"I'm just telling the truth."

"That's not the same recliner?" asked Skyler, trying to keep the bile down.

Keith shook his head in amusement. "No, *Felix*, it isn't."

Skyler looked back at the girls through the rear-view mirror. "So how did you guys meet?"

"Met at an LGBT mixer at school," said Sheryl. "The attendees tend to parse themselves out by gender, but Keith went all over the room. People came up to him, too, because they remembered him from the football team, and were, I think, stunned that a prominent jock could be gay. He helped me open a beer."

Skyler grinned. "Always the gentleman."

"I was probably standing in his way, but he was kind enough to help. I made a joke, he bantered back, and we were off and running. It was all our first time at a mixer like that, and it was such a relief meeting guys that weren't going to hit on you."

"And baby, we were barely together then, but the girls were all over *you*."

Her cheeks blossomed into a blush. "They were not."

"I was beating them back with a stick. But when you were talking to Keith, they didn't approach. So, I heartily approved."

They pulled up to the parking lot of a tiny storefront Greek restaurant and went inside. Amid ouzo, spanakopita, eggplant, and souvlakia, Skyler got to know Keith's friends. He liked their easy camaraderie, something a bit different from the SFC but no less tight. He drank and watched Keith laugh, his eyes sparkling, as he reminisced about his college days. The girls told more tales that sent them all into hysterical laughter, making more than one head turn to look at their table. He liked learning about Keith in this way. Spending time with the man's family in Seattle had been enlightening but brief. After all, family saw you in an entirely different light than friends.

He watched the girls, too. Sheryl was definitely the feminine one. She kept brushing her hair from her face, and touched both Keith and Skyler frequently when she leaned in and spoke directly to them in her soft way.

Tamika was beautiful, with high cheekbones, full lips, and a long slender neck. She was brash and loud, and sat back in the seat like a warrior, as if she was challenging the room, with an arm tossed over the chair back, legs wide. She reminded him a lot of Sidney.

"But enough about us," said Sheryl, pushing her plate aside to grasp Skyler's hand. "Tell us about Skyler Foxe."

"Oh." He downed the last of the wine and set the glass aside. "Not much to tell, really. I've lived here in Redlands all my life. Always wanted to be a teacher, became one, and now teach at my old alma mater." He shrugged. "The boring life of Skyler Foxe."

"Now what about this Skyler Fuck Club I keep hearing about?" asked Tamika much too loudly. People turned their heads and Skyler shrank a little in the booth.

Keith sighed. "Dammit, Tamika."

She shrugged innocently. "I just wanna know. He says he's boring but he was a pretty heavy player in the scene, *and* he solves crimes. That don't sound boring to me." She leaned on her arms. "So how many men have you fucked?"

Keith kicked her under the table.

Skyler knew his face was now scarlet. His eyes darted from table to table, imagining the judging going on from one prim face to another. "Uh…I…"

"Don't answer that," growled Keith.

"He probably can't," said Tamika.

Keith didn't look pleased. "Why are you doing this?"

"All kidding aside…" She looked fiercely at Skyler now, her intense glare holding him rigidly in place. "Players don't become monogamous overnight. And I don't want Keith hurt. Because I've seen him with players before and I don't want to see this man with a broken heart ever again."

Skyler picked up his napkin and dabbed delicately at his mouth before setting it down again. In a quieter voice, he said, "Look, I can appreciate what you're saying. But you don't know me. Yes, okay. I was what you would consider a 'player', but when I met Keith, something changed fundamentally. I never knew I was looking for a relationship. As far as I could tell, I wasn't. But he caught my attention in a way that no one had before. He was…different. In too many ways to count. I found myself attracted to him and only him. I haven't even wanted to hook-up with anyone since meeting him. Maybe I was just looking for Mister Right and didn't even know it. And with Keith…" He touched Keith's arm and that large, warm hand covered his. "I found…home. You don't have to worry that I'll stray. I have no intention of ever doing any such thing. Satisfied?"

"You don't owe her any sort of explanation."

"Yes, I do. These people care about you. And I get it. I would have done the same thing for Sidney."

He gestured toward Skyler. "You see that? That's the kind of man he is. He's amazing. And I love him. And you will not interrogate him again."

Skyler leaned forward toward Tamika and looked her in the eye. "So…how many women have *you* fucked?"

Tamika froze for half a second before she threw her head back and roared a laugh to shake the rafters. "You have balls, Skyler Foxe."

"So do you."

She laughed again.

She reminded Skyler more and more of Sidney. He couldn't wait for them to meet. Fireworks, for sure.

They finished dinner and returned home. They only stayed up till one before Keith and Skyler had to beg off. Skyler made up the sofa bed and left their bedroom door ajar since the only bathroom was through their bedroom. Skyler felt obliged for the sake of propriety to wear his sweats to bed. But as the alarm went off in the morning and he sat up bleary-eyed, a very naked Tamika strode through their room on her way to the bathroom.

"Whoa!" said Skyler, covering his eyes.

Keith hadn't even moved from his place, burrowed under the covers, when he grumbled, "She's naked, isn't she? She does that."

Tamika stopped at Skyler's side of the bed and stood there, one hand on her hip, breasts jutting upward over a slim body and flat stomach. "Baby, you know I got nothing to hide."

Skyler lifted the sheet to cover his face. "But I wish you would," he said meekly.

"Oh, you gay men parade around all the time with your dicks out, and one dyke comes through with her breasts and bush and you go all faint. Baby, you gotta grow up."

"Okay," murmured Skyler, hoping that was the proper response. But still she stood there, like a defiant Greek statue. All she needed was the helmet and spear. Finally, she ticked her head, muttering, and flounced away into the bathroom—*not* shutting the door as she did her business! Skyler cringed down into the bed, the duvet now over his head.

He tried to cover his ears. "Tell me when it's over," he squeaked. Sidney was brassy but never *this* brassy.

Keith chuckled. "She's…something."

"Yeah," said his muffled voice from under the bedding. "Something."

Keith's friends decided to stay for the home game Friday night to watch Keith in action. But after that, they kissed both of them good-bye and wished them good luck until the wedding day, a little more than a month away.

Skyler thought about this joining of friends and family — two people bringing such diverse groups together into a whole new community. It seemed like a lot of responsibility. It felt important, big, scary. Sidney would slap him out of it, and he could hear her voice in his head berating him: *Don't worry about it so much. Jesus Christ, you'd think you controlled the world!*

But still, it *was* a big thing. And mostly…he didn't want to screw it up.

Chapter Six

RIFFLING THROUGH ALL THE RSVPS, SKYLER dutifully checked them off his lists. He was gratified that so many people wanted to come to his wedding. All the teachers, and Mr. and Mrs. Sherman had said they were coming. Most of the GSA kids. Relatives he hadn't expected. But more than that…gifts started arriving on his doorstep. He'd registered Keith and him at a few places and lo and behold, people were actually buying the stuff. He began stalking the registry website, watching as one by one, things began to disappear from the list once purchased. Keith even closed his laptop on him once and shook his head disapprovingly. After all, it wasn't about the gifts and the party…Was it? No! It was about him and Keith.

But it was also a *little* about the party. Skyler loved parties, especially when he could dance at them. And dammit, it *was* a celebration!

But there was also a honeymoon, too, and Keith had kept his word that it was a surprise and there was no budging him. Even buttering up Philip proved impossible.

"Come *on*, Philip!" Skyler wheedled one day before class. "I gotta know!"

"Nope. I have a sacred trust with Keith and I will not break it."

"Just a hint. Are we headed for the airport? What kind of clothes are you going to be packing?" Philip continued, expression unchanged, making Skyler's coffee. "I have fifty bucks in my wallet and it's yours." Philip turned a disdainful eye on him. "Ah, jeez!"

"You might as well give up. You know I'll never tell."

"Will I at least like it?"

There was finally a crack in his façade. He offered a secret smile. "You're going to *love* it."

He threw back his head and waggled his fists in the air. "Philip!"

"Nope. Here's your Ethiopian. Have a nice day, *sir*. Now move along." The last was whispered out of the side of his mouth as other patrons began to stare.

Jutting out his lower lip in a pout, Skyler grabbed his coffee and sulked out the door.

Wedding plans and a secret honeymoon weighed heavily on his mind, but he tried hard not to let it affect his work. He dutifully taught his classes, and when it got to the last class of the day with his favorite students, he felt himself relax a little, even as he passed out their marked-up tests.

"You guys did pretty well," he said, walking down the aisles and handing out the sheets of paper. "There are a few of you having a bit of trouble. So, what I'm going to do, is have you move your desks into two circles. The first circle are the students who 'got it' and the other will be the ones who need a bit more guidance." He called out names, and, led by Amber, they pushed their desks into the first circle. It included Ravi Chaudhri, Heather, Drew, Becky, Elei Sapani, Rick, and a few other students. The students remaining dragged themselves with heavy expressions into the second circle, including Alex, Stewart, and Tyler.

"The reject circle," drawled Tyler. "So great to be here."

"I never said that," said Skyler. "I *said* you just needed more guidance. Now Amber, if you could lead your group in the reading and assignment — quietly — on page thirty-seven, I'll work over here." Skyler threw a leg over one of the empty desks and sat down, passing out worksheets. "You guys, I *never* want you to feel inferior to anyone. Some people just understand quicker than others. I mean, you should see me try to throw a football."

They laughed half-heartedly.

"Now, really. It's just about explaining the work in a different way until it clicks in your head, right? I guarantee that you *will* understand this. Remember, this is very specific stuff. Composition is about being able to be precise in your language, in the words you choose. Now you guys do it all the time when you text each other, right? You use as few words as possible to get your point across. Your brain already works that way, so all we have to do is key into that. To that end, we are going to do an exercise. There is a topic at the top of each of your papers. And I want you to write these as if you are Tweeting — in a hundred and forty characters or less — the topic and opening statement. There are three numbered spaces under each topic, so I want you to try your topic in three tweets. I even gave you a hundred and forty boxes for each character. I'm giving you five minutes. Go!"

Some dove right in, while others, like Alex, lingered, staring at the paper. Skyler watched the faces of his students, eyes narrowed, teeth digging into lips in concentration. They gripped their pens, crossed out, erased if they were using pencils. Stewart even mimed thumbing an imaginary keyboard, staring into space before he wrote down his sentences.

"Time!" called Skyler. "Okay. Read me what you've got. Stewart, start us out and let's go around the circle. It doesn't matter if you were a genius right away or still didn't get it. That's what we're here for."

Stewart read his offerings and didn't do half badly. It went around, landing on Alex, who had only managed one sentence.

"That's not a bad start you guys. Give me some ideas about the topic. What was it about? Alex?"

He stared numbly at his paper and shrugged. "I didn't really get to finish."

"Just one?"

He shook his head. But Skyler could see he had gotten a little something down on his page. He let it go and called on the next one.

Five minutes before class ended, he told everyone to return their desks to their original positions. There was the usual noise of chair legs scraping and screeching, and kids talking among themselves.

"Okay, settle down. You have homework. It's on the board." The bell rang and he swept his arm out to encompass them. "You are dismissed. Oh, Alex? Could you stay a second?"

Students plugged themselves into their phones, loaded backpacks, and shuffled their way out the door. Rick hung back to wait with Alex until Skyler said, "Could you wait outside for us, Mr. Flores. I'd like to do teacher stuff with Alex for a minute."

"No problem, Mr. Foxe. Or will that soon be 'Mr. Fletcher'?"

Flustered, Skyler shoved him gently forward. "No! No, it won't. Wait outside, please. Scoot. And could you please close the door after you?"

With an entire wall made out of mullioned windows, Skyler never worried about calls of impropriety. Anyone could walk by and look through. It was sometimes distracting for his students, however, though kids weren't supposed to linger in the halls near occupied classrooms.

But at certain moments, like this one, he appreciated that extra bit of protection for himself.

Alex clutched the straps of his backpack and dragged it along the floor, slouching before Skyler's desk.

"Have a seat, Mr. Ryan."

"What did I do now?"

"You didn't do anything...*Did* you?"

"No."

Skyler leaned back against the front of his desk and folded his arms in front of him. He studied the stocky teen, recalling Alex's way of participating in class, of his hard work at the teen police academy, even though his report-writing scores were low...and a thought began percolating in his mind.

"Alex...could you read what's on the board for me?"

Alex stared at the whiteboard and moved his lips silently.

"No, Alex. Could you read it *aloud*?"

"Mr. Foxe! I'm not some kid."

"Indulge me."

In a stilted tone, Alex began. "Read... the... ch-chapter... on... writing... about... lit—lit—uh... lit-er..." He paused, staring at the board, face coloring a deep, blotchy red.

"That's enough, Alex. I've been thinking about this for some time. Has anyone at school ever mentioned to you before that you might be dyslexic?"

"Someone said something like that once when I was a freshman."

Wow. Skyler had been shooting in the dark. *My skills at perception must be exceptional!* But his self-congratulation was brief. "Did you get any classes or special tutoring about it? I never noticed anything in your file."

"No. My mom was supposed to talk to the counsellor but she never did."

He dropped his face into his hand for a moment, wiping down to his chin. Alex's parents were a piece of work, all right. He had spoken to them exactly once in two years and that was on the phone, urging them to come down to the school to talk to him, but they had said that Alex was just a slow kid and there was nothing to be done for him. They barely knew he was even involved with football or the teen police academy. He wanted to strangle them.

"Do you know what dyslexic is?"

The teen shook his head on his thick neck.

"Well, it has nothing to do with your intelligence. You are just as smart as the next guy."

"Not if that next guy is Amber."

"Not everyone can be an Amber. But dyslexia is something else again. Plenty of really famous people have been dyslexic. Steven Spielberg, Mohammed Ali, Magic Johnson, to name a few. It only means that your brain has trouble interpreting patterns of letters and word order. It has nothing to do with being slow. You aren't slow. Look at you on the team. You figure out plays and how to do things all the time. There's nothing wrong with you at all. Just this little glitch."

"Great." He hung his head, staring at the floor.

"The good news is we can work on it. Even Rick can help you, if you want."

His head popped up and hope seemed to shine in his eyes. "He can?"

"Sure he can. You can learn a few simple tricks and workarounds, and then practice what you learn. I bet your grades will improve everywhere. Do you realize how far you've come even with this disability? That makes you pretty smart, Alex."

"Yeah?"

"Yeah. Do you know what phonics is?"

He shook his head again.

"It's sounding out words, each letter. Because your brain doesn't connect the look of a letter with its sound, you can't read as well. But if you memorize certain words and what they look like and associate their sound, you can begin to read better."

"You mean all this time I thought I was stupid and it's just because my brain is a little whacked? How come they never told me that before?"

Skyler sighed, annoyed and angry. Why had they let this kid down after they tested him? He planned to ask that of Mr. Sherman. "I don't know, Alex, but we are going to fix it."

"You sure are earning your wings, Mr. Foxe."

Skyler preened. "You think I'd look good with wings?"

Alex laughed, mood seeming lighter by the minute. "Yeah, you would. Big, white, beautiful wings."

Skyler laughed. "Get outta here, you. Have Rick email me and I'll talk to you both about what you guys can do. I'll send him a few website links and you can get started at home."

Alex rose. He had a tentative expression, as if he wasn't sure of his good luck. "Thanks, Mr. Foxe. I mean it. Thanks."

Before the boy launched himself to hug him, Skyler edged away to the other side of his desk. No sense tempting the rumor mill in front of the big window wall.

Before he went to see Mr. Sherman, he'd finally found those records, and according to the brief report, Alex had a mild case of it, and had limped along, unconsciously creating his own tricks to get by all these years. He really was a sharp kid. He just needed that extra boost.

He cornered Mr. Sherman in his office before he left the school and talked at length about Alex Ryan, something the principal seemed weary of, until Skyler laid it out. Alex had been a handful for the last two years he'd attended James Polk High, and he'd warmed a seat plenty of times in the principal's office, but Mr. Sherman also knew he'd been through a lot, what with the former coaching staff and their illegal activities. It hadn't been the kid's fault. He'd been swept up in it like so many others.

Mr. Sherman promised to help, though there was little in the budget, he'd said. Skyler already had a list of websites he'd researched ahead of time, knowing full well the school district was shy of funds where it counted. *Football always had enough, though*, he grumbled to himself. But then he felt guilty. He knew that Keith wouldn't willingly take necessary funds away from students who really needed them. And Alex had really needed football, too, as a home and family replacement. Besides, he knew he could get Keith on board to help out Alex with his dyslexia.

"I'll inform his other teachers, Mr. Foxe," said Sherman. "I appreciate you taking such care with Alex Ryan. I know he hasn't always been an easy young man to deal with. You seem to have found out a lot of things about him. I was especially happy to see the note from the Teen Police Academy instructor. It looks like you've turned the course for Mr. Ryan for the better."

"I consider it my primary job. It's not just test scores and homework."

"Indeed it is not. Have a good day, Mr. Foxe. Oh…and my wife said she's looking forward to your wedding." He grinned, an unusual expression for the usually stern principal.

"Oh, uh, yeah." Skyler realized with some disquiet that he always reacted to mention of his impending nuptials with tongue-tied anxiety.

But thoughts of his spotting Alex Ryan's last significant learning problem had him cheering up as he drove home, and he walked jauntily from his car to his front stoop, wedding anxieties forgotten. Maybe it was those wings, he mused. Climbing the stairs to his apartment, he spied more packages left on the landing. This was one aspect of the wedding that didn't cause any anxiety at all. "We're really cleaning up," he muttered. He'd already sent out numerous thank you notes, and was pleased with the thoughtful gifts from his friends and relatives.

There were two packages from UPS and one large lumpy envelope with a ton of stamps pasted to the front. But no return address.

He unlocked the door, went inside to set down his satchel at the hall tree, and returned out to the landing to bring in the packages.

He set them down in the living room but was intrigued by the pudgy envelope. Turning it over offered no clues about the sender. Strange that there was no return address. He felt its lumps. Nothing recognizable. It was addressed to Skyler alone with big block letters across the front reading "Personal". He shrugged and tore it open.

Something sizzled and smoked and he instinctively tossed it away from him. But nothing else happened. Toeing it with his foot, he leaned down to look at it. A strong smell of almonds emanated from it and he thought for a moment it might be soap or bath salts, but instead, there were wires and silver foil and hunks of what looked like modelling clay. "What the heck is this?" He opened it wide to look inside to see if anything could give him a clue but there were only the things he'd already seen. One of those musical cards? "Weird." He tossed it to the dining room table, dismissing it as he proceeded to open the other packages.

After that, he sat down to work on marking papers. And when Keith arrived home later, he sighed and dropped his bag by the door. Skyler had long ago given up trying to instruct him to leave it elsewhere.

Keith clomped over to him, and even though he was sweaty from football practice, Skyler thought Keith smelled marvellous. He lifted his face to receive a kiss while seated at his desk.

"How was your day?" said Keith.

"Pretty good. I think I've made a breakthrough with Alex Ryan."

"Oh?" Keith was stripping off his shirt in preparation for taking a shower, which momentarily distracted Skyler to silence. "Go on," said Keith, oblivious.

"Oh, uh. Well, it looks as if he's a bit dyslexic."

Keith stopped. "Really?"

"Yeah. I think this might be another thing holding him back. I've put together some lessons, and Rick and I are going to work with him."

"English Lit Man to the rescue," said Keith with a smile.

Skyler smiled back, puffing up a bit. "Just doing my job, citizen."

"So what are you doing over there? As if I didn't know."

"I'm trying to figure out the music—"

"Does it all have to be Motown? Not that I don't like that. It's just…not every occasion needs to be an episode of Soul Train."

"No, it's not all going to be Motown," he said indignantly, surreptitiously scribbling out part of the list. "I was just wondering the kind of music you like. It occurred to me that I've never really heard your playlist."

"I'm not much into music per se."

"I know, but you must like something. We can throw in all kinds of music you'd like." He snorted a laugh. "As long as it isn't country." He chuckled. Then he looked up. Keith wore a pensive expression. Uh oh. "It...*isn't* country, is it?"

"I like a little of that, yes."

"Oh. Well...then, we can...can..."

"You hate it."

"I don't *hate* it, I just..."

Keith folded his arms over his chest, one brow quirked. He seemed annoyed...until he burst out laughing. "Man, I love to watch you squirm. You are so funny when you backpedal."

"So wait. You don't like country western? You're just saying that to fuck with me."

"Yeah, I do actually like some of it, but not that much. Not so much as to ruin your wedding."

"It's your wedding, too. And I want you to have the stuff you want included. Even if it is shitty cowboy music."

"And just what's wrong with cowboys? Hot, sweaty men, with lots of leather and...ropes."

"Oh. Well, if you put it *that* way..."

Keith scanned the table. "More gifts? This is embarrassing."

"It's the proper response to a wedding invitation."

"But we don't need anything."

Skyler drew back, scandalized. "Tablecloths, vases, crystal. I beg to differ."

"Oh. Sorry." Keith picked up the envelope. "What's this?"

"I don't know. I was going to ask you. When I opened it, the thing fizzled and smoked a little. I thought maybe it was a—"

Keith suddenly grabbed Skyler and dragged him toward the door.

"Wait! What's going on!"

Out they went and Keith hurtled with him down the steps. "Keith? What the—"

He planted Skyler behind his truck in the street and crouched down with him. Skyler felt ridiculous as a few cars whizzed past.

"Keith?"

But Keith was on the phone with one hand, shoving Skyler hard against the truck with the other. "This is an emergency," he barked into the phone. "Bring the bomb squad immediately!"

Chapter Seven

MEN IN HUGE PADDED SUITS HAD MARCHED INTO
their apartment, evacuating the other two apartments in
the converted Victorian mansion. Skyler hadn't said a
word, too dumbstruck to believe that someone had tried
to send him a bomb. Thankfully, it hadn't worked, or the
first time he'd opened it would have been his last.

Still shirtless, Keith was talking to another FBI agent
from the look of his suit, gesturing toward Skyler as he
hung back against Keith's big Ford F-150. Just as he was
wishing for the umpteenth time that Sidney was here, he
saw her sedan pull up. Mike was at the wheel, and even
before he could park she had jumped out and ran toward
Skyler. He was in her arms in seconds and he held on
tight.

"Why is this happening?" he murmured into her hair.

"Are you okay, sweetie?"

"Yeah, yeah, I'm fine. But I'm scared, Sidney."

Mike walked up behind his wife and looked down at
Skyler. "You okay there, buddy?"

He gently pushed Sidney back and straightened. "Hi,
Mike. Yeah, I'm fine."

Sidney's face smoothed from its earlier worry and
became all business. "What can you tell me about that
envelope?"

"Nothing. It was just a regular manila kind of envelope.
Padded. With wires and stuff in it. Explosives I guess. It
smelled like almonds."

"C-4," said Mike.

"Did it have a return address?"

"No."

"Cancellation stamp? Where was it from?"

"I don't know. I never looked. The Feds have it."

She glanced toward Keith and the agent before ignoring them again. "I'll take a look later. Have you received any weird phone calls? Hang-ups? Any emails?"

"No…but. Sidney. My car."

"What about your car?"

"Remember how my brakes gave out? The repair place said it was probably mice or squirrels, but now I'm beginning to think that maybe my brake line was cut."

"Whoa," said Mike. "Skyler, are you sure?"

"The guy at the repair place saved it to show me. He said mice or squirrels gnawed through it, but it was a clean cut, like someone took a knife to it. Now maybe a mouse *could* do that, but the more I think about it, the less likely it seems. But I had no reason to believe that back then. I just took the repair guy's word for it."

She whipped out a notebook from her trouser pocket. "Name and address of the repair place?"

She wrote it down as he told her.

"I doubt they'd have kept the broken line but I'll talk to them, see what they say in light of this. Anything else?"

He gestured toward the stairway built into the side of the house that led up to their apartment. Each space in the big Victorian had its own entrance. The other second floor apartment had theirs in the back, and the front ground floor had wide steps up to the wrap-around porch. "My stairs. One of them broke. But it was strange. A real clean break as if someone had sawn through it."

"What? Do you still have the step?"

"It's still up there. Keith gave it a temporary fix, but it's still there. The landlady hasn't fixed it yet."

She gestured to Mike without a word and he trotted away, grabbing a tech. They both walked toward the stairwell.

"Looks like some incompetent killer has been trying to get at you for a while."

He inhaled a shaky breath. "I'm glad he's incompetent."

"Me, too. Can you think of anyone who might have a grudge?"

"I don't know."

"Someone at Trixx you might have dissed? Some parent at school?"

"I don't think so. I always try to be nice to people."

"Not nice enough, apparently."

"Sid, what am I gonna do? I'm pretty scared one of these things might hurt Keith."

"It's all right, hon. I'm on the job." She patted his arm and moved over the lawn toward the other cops in uniform.

Deep in his own thoughts he hadn't even noticed when Keith came up to him. Instantly, he threw himself into his arms. He didn't care that they were standing out in the street. He hugged him tight. "It's okay, Skyler," he rumbled into his ear. "I've got you."

"No," he said fiercely. "I've got *you!*"

Keith looked taken aback when he pulled away. And Skyler clarified. "I'm not going to let anything happen to you."

"Oh, babe." He cupped Skyler's cheek. "My brave man."

Fear receded, replaced by anger. Some asshole was stalking him, trying to off him. Okay. But he was not going to let this lunatic hurt his man. "I'm the target. Maybe I should go away for a while, lure them away."

"No." The word was so firm and final that Skyler blinked.

"I rather think that's up to me."

"Where would you go?"

"I don't know."

"Would you still go to school?"

"I…"

"What about the wedding?"

"I…"

"Look, Skyler. Let's talk to my fellow agents about this before you decide anything. And by the way, I'm not letting you leave."

"But—"

"You're not getting out of the wedding that easily."

"You think I'm trying to get out of it? Why don't we just elope, then?"

"Leave that whole party you planned behind? I don't think so."

"I can't have the fallout from this put you in danger."

"I can take care of myself. Let's have a chat with the Bureau, shall we? Agents!" Keith called, beckoning them over. A woman in a dark blue pant suit and a man in a light gray suit, moved across the lawn toward them. Yellow police tape encircled the perimeter to the sidewalk. Even Skyler's car was now being dusted under Sidney's supervision.

"This is agent Slokum," said Keith, introducing the fortyish woman, "and this is agent Wolf. Skyler Foxe."

Slokum reached out first to shake his hand. She had shoulder-length, blonde hair held loosely by a wide barrette in the back of her head. Her face was attractive but stern, and she wore no make-up. She was older, perhaps older than Keith. "Mr. Foxe. Can you tell us about anyone who might hold a grudge against you?"

"Like I was telling my friend, Detective Feldman" — He gestured toward her talking to a cluster of forensic techs and a few uniforms— "I don't recall anyone whom I could describe that way."

"We understand that you do a little amateur crime-solving," said Wolf. His dark hair was kept clipped short, which accentuated his long neck and patrician nose. His dark eyes would have attracted Skyler in their intense sexiness...had he been looking.

"Yeah. Do...do you think this has something to do with that?"

"You never know. It helps to explore the possibilities. Agent Fletcher here mentioned the step on your staircase, and the brake line on your car. I see Detective Feldman seems to be on it."

"I mentioned those things to her, yes. Do you think those were deliberate?"

"I didn't like the look of that stair from day one," said Keith, sounding just like the FBI agents. He guessed it didn't take Keith long to slip back into the mode. Even shirtless.

Slokum swept the area with her glance. "It's a good thing the suspect isn't very good at it. Cutting a brake line on a car today isn't the same as in the past. In some modern cars, you have to step on the brake to start it. Maybe our suspect has been watching too many old movies."

"I watch a lot of old movies," offered Skyler, and then felt stupid for saying it.

Luckily, Slokum ignored him. "They did a lousy job on the letter bomb, too. Probably got some half-baked instructions from the internet."

"So you have no idea," said Skyler.

"Not yet. We'll dig a little deeper. I tell you what. I'd like to get a list of the crimes you've been involved in, some names."

"I wasn't involved in the crimes. Only in solving them."

"Of course. That's what I meant."

"Agent Slokum, Keith and I are getting married in less than a month. Should we…should we put that off?"

She glanced at her partner. "I don't see that you need to do that. But, uh…I'd like a guest list with addresses, too, if it isn't too much trouble."

"You can't be serious."

She hitched a shoulder. "We're looking at all possibilities, Mr. Foxe."

Skyler commiserated silently with Keith, but he was stone-faced. "Okay." He took the card she offered with its official FBI seal embossed on it and let his hand fall to his side as they wandered toward Sidney to talk.

Keith's hand gripped his shoulder. "Listen," he said quietly, "if you have any reservations about…about getting married, for God's sake tell me now."

He whipped around. "No! I don't. I am *not* looking for an excuse. I promise."

Keith nodded, swallowing hard, his Adam's apple rolling on his neck.

Skyler reached up, pulled Keith's head down for a kiss. "I'm not," he said again.

"Okay," he answered. But Skyler couldn't tell if the concern in his eyes was all about Skyler's safety or about the wedding.

The SFC all leaned in at their table at Taquito Grill, eyes wide, mouths agape, listening with rapt attention as Skyler told the tale of the various attempts on his life. Keith sat beside him, drinking his Corona from the bottle, and offering no commentary of his own, except for the occasional raised eyebrow.

Finally, Skyler sat back, grabbed a chip, dipped it in the salsa, and crunched it, punctuating the end of his story.

"Oh. My. GOD!" squealed Jamie, the first of them to snap out of it. "What are we gonna do? We have *got* to put our heads together."

"We're going to let the Feds take care of it," came the expected reply from Keith.

"Keith," said Philip, shaking his head. "Surely even you have something else to say about it."

Everyone looked at Keith. He was raising the beer to his lips again, when he paused and slammed it down sharply. "Fuck it. You know what? I'm not going to sit around while someone tries to kill my fiancé."

Sitting closest to him, Dave slapped him on the back. "I was worried about you for a moment there, dude."

Keith turned his scowl toward Skyler. "I'm open to suggestions."

Skyler was still flung back in the booth, mouth flopped open in surprise. "Uh…"

Jamie cheered. "The Scooby Gang to the rescue!"

"All right, all right," Keith muttered. "We've got to look at this thing like a detective." He ticked them off on his fingers. "The stair step—clearly sawn in two. The brake line—cut. And a letter bomb. No proof yet, but I'm willing to call that *one* person."

"Oh crap," said Skyler, getting his voice back. "You mean this could have been *three* people?"

"Three people you pissed off that much?" said Jamie. He exchanged glances with Philip and Rodolfo. "There's no way. People love the Skyboy."

Keith snorted. "The people he put behind bars don't. How many is that now?"

Skyler thought back. "Well…Coach Carson is dead…"

"Thanks to Keith," said Philip with chin raised. Skyler supposed he'd never forgotten how Carson had threatened Rodolfo.

"But then there were his two assistant coaches," Skyler continued. "Then that friend of Wesley Sherman, Jr. Then the army guy, then that guy that tried to get Dave…"

Jamie gave his fireman boyfriend a one-armed squeeze.

"Ramone from the Indian Reservation and those two FBI guys, and Denise Suzuki."

"You are so brave, *amante*," gushed Rodolfo in his thick accent.

Skyler felt a weird squirming in his gut. "Boy…that's a lot, isn't it?"

Keith stared at him. "I guess I never thought about it. You did all that in a year. That's…an impressive record even for a seasoned professional."

Skyler puffed a bit. "Really?"

"It's certainly nothing to sneeze at," said Philip. "Not that I'm condoning it."

"So that's nine people who hate me." He frowned. He didn't like people not liking him.

Dave reached into the chip bowl and took a few. "But they're all in jail. They can't do any of this."

"And it's not as if they're mob bosses," said Philip, sipping his margarita. "They can't exactly direct their minions to go after you."

"So it's a whole new person after me? Great."

Keith's arm was around him, a warm presence of safety. "We'll figure this out. We've all just got to be extra vigilant. And Sidney and Mike are on it, too. Nothing's going to get past her…or me."

Skyler took in the intent expression of his fiancé, his friends, and felt a little calmer. It *was* the SFC to the rescue. "Yeah," he said. "Yeah, okay." He raised his margarita glass. "To the Scooby Gang."

They all clinked glasses. Another criminal to foil. Number ten. They could do it. They did it before. They could do it this time.

He drank down his margarita, tasting the sweet lime, tangy tequila, and salt around the glass's rim. Hopefully, they'd get the guy sooner rather than later. He had a wedding to celebrate!

Sidney told him that the envelope yielded nothing forensically. Stamps had their own adhesive now, and she bitterly complained about that. And the suspect had used gloves. But the good news was that the car repair guy still had the piece of broken brake line, and the police techs said that it had been cut, but the bad news was, there was nothing there either. A neighbor's security camera yielded a shadowy person at Skyler's stair sawing it in the dead of night, but the video was so crappy and the person so far away, hiding in a hoodie, that nothing came of that either.

"So someone was definitely sawing your step," said Jamie over the phone. "I mean we knew that but it's creepy to actually see it. Did you see the footage?"

"Yeah, Sidney let me. But I didn't recognize them."

"But nothing's happened since, right? Maybe they've given up. They must have seen the police all over your place. They must know the jig is up."

"I guess. Keith put a motion alarm on my car. I had no idea how many squirrels there were in the neighborhood."

"But that's good. That means it's sensitive."

"My neighbors aren't pleased."

"A little inconvenience to keep you safe. So? How are you feeling?"

"About…?"

"About the wedding! It's one week away."

Skyler was sitting at his desk at school, waiting for the lunch hour to be over. He pushed the papers he was correcting around absently. "I'm…nervous."

"You can't be nervous. You know everyone who's coming. Well, maybe not some of Keith's relatives, but it isn't as if they're coming to protest. It's a day of love."

"I know that. I'm just still…nervous."

"Skyler, you aren't going to take a runner, are you?"

"No…"

"Because Keith is *way* better looking than Richard Gere, and you, sir, are no Julia Roberts."

"I'm not going to leave him at the altar. I swear."

"You'd better not. That would spell the end of Keith and Skyler and we cannot have that."

"No, we can't. It's just… the commitment thing. The… finality of it."

"Oh good grief. Stop clutching your pearls. You've already committed to him, haven't you? And it isn't the end. It's the beginning."

"I know all that. I do. Well…what about you and Dave? Do you think you'll ever get married?"

"Oh, *hell* no!"

"*What?*" He sputtered. "Then what is all this sage advice: 'It's not the end, it's the beginning, blah, blah, blah'?"

"I'm not like you, Skyler. I don't need the trappings. Dave and I are perfectly happy how things are."

"You still live in separate houses."

"And we're fine with that. Honey, we have busy, busy lives."

"Then why are you preaching to me about commitment and beginnings?"

"Because it's true. And Dave and I *are* committed. Just differently. We love each other. But we love our separate lives, too."

"How come *I* couldn't—"

"Honey, you know why. Because Keith wants it. And let's face it, you get all soft and chewy inside when he merely looks at you."

"I do not," he said without any heat to it.

"You so do. And he wants it. The white picket fence, the wedding, the rings, the happily ever after. And I think deep down in your heart of hearts you do, too. Or you would never have agreed to this."

"Well…"

"And look at your parents. A happy ending too. You've got it all, Skyler. Run with it. Not away from it."

"I guess."

"And it's gonna be a helluva par-tay!"

He'd gotten the DJ from Trixx to play at the reception. It *was* going to be a par-tay. He smiled. "I think it's going to be fun."

"It *is*! Now you go back to doing teacher stuff and I'll return to computer stuff and we'll all be in Scotland before ye. Tally-ho! Hey, 'Tally-Ho.' That would make a great drag name!"

"Good-bye, Jamie. And…thanks."

"I am here to serve."

The phone clicked off and Skyler looked at it for a moment before stuffing it back into his pants pocket. Why was he still stressing about it anyway? He'd thought he'd reconciled himself to it months ago. It was just the whole commitment issue in front of everyone that was still a little scary. Saying it. In front of his mother and his relatives. And Keith's friend Tamika there, being the officiant, asking up front and with that brash voice if Skyler meant it. He did, didn't he? Of course, he did! He loved Keith. God, how he loved him. And *he* had asked. *He* had. It wasn't fair to back out if you're the one who asked.

"Sidney's right," he muttered. "Sometimes I *am* too stupid to live."

The lunch bell rang. "No more fretting," he promised himself, shuffling his papers away, and getting the tests out for the class.

Two more classes passed by in a whirr and then his sixth period students started coming in. Rick let a student from the last period leave before he sauntered forward with all the brazenness that had gotten him by for his two years in high school and probably all the years before. He wore a black guayabera shirt with a gold chain at his throat over his tan skin. His black Porsche sunglasses hung on his ears backwards at the back of his head. He swung his arms casually, clutching a notebook in one hand, and smoothly shedding his backpack and catching it with the other.

Skyler marveled at the boy. He wondered what it would be like having such ease with oneself as Rick seemed to have. To be so free with who he was at that age. Skyler would have killed to have that freedom.

"Hey, Mr. Foxe," he said in a slight Hispanic accent. "Only a few days left of freedom. Are you nervous?" He slid into his seat and stretched his legs out before him.

"I'm not nervous," yammered Skyler. "What makes you think I'd be nervous? Do I look nervous?"

"Whoa, whoa." He held up his hands and looked around the mostly empty room. "Of course you're not nervous."

"No." Skyler straightened his tie and pulled at his shirt to straighten it. "I have no reason to be nervous."

Amber bounded in holding Ravi's hand. He let her go to sit in his own desk a few desks down. "Hi, Mr. Foxe!" she chirped. "I bet you're nervous. It's only a few days away."

"I'm *not* nervous!" he said a little too loudly.

Rick leaned over toward Amber. "He's pretty nervous about it. Better go easy on him."

"Oh, Mr. Foxe. You don't have anything to be nervous about. It's only Mr. Fletcher. And you two are the perfect couple."

"O-*kay*, pop quiz!" he announced, turning his deeply reddening face away from the students as they filled the seats. Groans and eye rolls greeted that pronouncement, and some even tried to blame Amber.

Heather and Drew came roaring in and split off to their desks, followed by Alex and Elei, race-walking toward the back of the room as the last bell rung.

Tyler let his hand fall heavily to the desk. "Amber made us get a pop quiz," he told the stragglers.

"I did not! Mr. Foxe has his own schedule."

Skyler didn't tell them that it was partly true that Amber made him do it. He just didn't want to talk about the wedding, and he could tell that they were trying to stall and keep talking about it.

"It's an open-book quiz," he relented, pulling out some Xeroxed pages, and handing stacks to each row. "It's nothing that will kill you."

As soon as he said it he began to wonder again about the person who *did* want to kill *him*.

❖

"Here's what we know," said Sidney, sitting next to Mike on Skyler's sofa. She laid out the file folder of papers and official forms. Skyler picked it up and looked at it. "Foxe, Skyler: Attempted Murder" it read on the tab in typewritten letters. *Wow*. That made it worse. That there was a file at the police station with those words on it. It made it far too real.

Keith snatched it out of Skyler's hands. "You can get into a lot of trouble having this outside the station," he said.

"So? Who's gonna turn me in?" She took it out of his hands and laid it back on the coffee table, taking out some papers and photos and separating them. She pointed to a report. "No decent forensic information from the letter bomb. Although they're still tracing where the C-4 might have come from. It's the best lead we have. I was really hoping the bastard would have gotten sloppy on the bomb because he expected most of the evidence to be destroyed, but thanks to his incompetence, we've got the whole thing. And Skyler, too," she added, patting his hand. "The neighbor's security video is being scrutinized, but the quality is so crappy it's barely worth it. Although, we were able to extrapolate height, weight, and general race—not African American, anyway. But not sex, though the suspect is tallish for a woman, average height if a man, and we weren't able to discern any facial characteristics. So that's a bit of a bust, too. But Mike came across something of interest."

Mike scooted forward, hands on his knees as he turned each to Skyler and Keith. "I decided to concentrate on Skyler's Bug. Someone had to crawl under it to cut the brake line. They knew what they were doing there, but didn't realize that the car wouldn't move or start without the brakes being pumped. It's not like in a TV show where the driver suddenly discovers he has no brakes while they're going downhill. So our suspect is a little knowledgeable and still a little stupid. *And* they left some forensics behind. While under the car, they couldn't help but rub their jacket against the underside of the Bug. After eliminating the guys who worked on your car, we got some threads from the hoodie we saw in the video. The FBI lab came back with a match to fibers found on a particular brand of hoodie that's only sold at the University of Redlands."

"What? Some college kid is after me? I don't even know anyone—"

"Hold on, Skyler," Mike went on. "Who knows if it's a kid? It could be a professor. Or anyone just working there or anyone who's a fan. The point is it's new—not used—so it isn't likely a hand-me-down or something from a thrift store. It's something, anyway."

"Good work, detective," said Keith.

Mike sat back. "Thanks."

"So a hoodie from U of R," said Skyler.

"Yeah," said Sidney. "It's sparse but a lead nonetheless."

He nodded. "That's good. That's good, Mike. Thanks."

Mike gave him a thumbs up.

"Anything else?"

"I've gone through your computer emails," said Sidney. "The older ones before you met Keith proved…interesting." She waggled her brows.

Skyler shifted and laughed uncomfortably. "Do I still have those?" he said as innocently as he could.

"And your Grindr account was also—"

"Ha! Sidney! I don't have that anymore. I deleted the app!" He turned to a stern-faced Keith. "I deleted it a long time ago."

"Your FBI friends were able to retrieve it. Such colorful language. And some real hotties. Anyway, we're keeping our eye on some of those guys. We'll need you to fill us in on them. Some of the details about them. I take it you remember your hook-ups?"

Painfully aware of Keith's eyes on him, Skyler rubbed his face, trying to hide it. "Yeah," he mumbled. Behind his hand, he pointed at Keith. "Later, okay?" he mouthed.

"Okay. Oh, and we've been looking into all the people you've put in jail. You've been to a lot of trials lately, haven't you?"

"Yeah. I kept forgetting that they'd want me to show up as a witness. Mr. Sherman's been a saint about it all."

There was a pause as they considered Mr. Sherman's own involvement because of his son's murder.

"Was there anyone at the trial that might have threatened you, even in a subtle way? Passive aggressive stuff, too?"

"I don't recall."

"Okay, just checking. But if you ever remember something, no matter how trivial, let us know." She glanced at Keith. "How're you holding up, Big Guy?"

How was **he** *holding up*? thought Skyler. What about Skyler? But then he saw Keith's face. He was obviously worried sick, but he hadn't let it show in front of Skyler before. Yet as soon as he realized he had let slip his vulnerable side, he tugged the mask back in place again. "I'm fine. Keeping an eye on this guy." He grabbed Skyler and pulled him close.

Poor Keith. Skyler was scared but it was only a sort of buzz in the background. His anger often won out, anger at some turd trying to ruin his life. But for Keith, he probably worried every moment that Skyler might be taken from him.

Skyler put his hand on Keith's thigh and squeezed. *I'm still here. Nothing's gonna happen to me. I love you.*

Keith turned his attention to Skyler. "And we're getting married Saturday."

Sidney smiled and gathered the file, trying to hide it under her satchel. "That is for sure. And *we* have a date Thursday night with the girls. Your bachelor party."

"Oh, do we have to do that, Sidney? I think Keith —"

"Keith can have his own party. But Trixx wants to give you a send-off. If we don't do it there, they'll just bring it here."

"What do you know? Trixx it is!"

They all rose and moved toward the door. She hugged him. "Don't worry, Skyboy. We'll get this guy."

"I know you will. Thanks for all you've done. And you, too, Mike." He hugged the tall, Filipino detective.

"Don't worry, Skyler," he said, drawing back. "We're closing in."

It didn't much sound like that to him. A couple of fibers that led to a U of Redlands jacket? Hardly a tight dragnet, but he didn't want to say that out loud.

Once Sidney and Mike left, the apartment fell to uncomfortable silence. "I'm sorry this is happening. We should both be more excited by this weekend."

Keith visibly relaxed. He moved forward and slipped his arms around Skyler. "I'm still pretty excited. I'm marrying you. I really am."

"You really are."

He leaned down to kiss Skyler. The stubble from Keith's scruff, the subtle notes of his cologne, soothed in their familiarity. They rubbed noses for a moment before

Keith pulled his face away, but not his embrace. He held Skyler loosely, casually. His affection was easily readable in his eyes. "This is us. We don't have to worry about anything else. Just us."

"I'm not worried." He tightened his hold on Keith, feeling the muscles under Keith's shirt flex and constrict. "I can't think of anything I'd rather do than marry you." And he meant it. With Keith looking at him like that, with Keith's arms around him, it was absolutely true.

Keith smiled. "*Nothing* you'd rather do? I can think of at least *one* thing…"

Skyler smiled, too. He slipped out of Keith's hold but grabbed his hand, dragging him toward the bedroom. "Let's see if we're both on the same page for that. I predict we are."

Chapter Eight

RIGHT AFTER WORK, SKYLER GOT THE ITCH TO *DO*
something, investigate something somewhere. And since
the only clue they had was the jacket, he didn't feel there
was any other choice but to get over to the university and
check out the bookstore.

He hadn't been back since graduating two years ago,
and going up the drive on Colton Avenue was as familiar
as his own apartment. He'd lived on campus, even
though it was only seven miles from his mother's house.
He had sworn up and down to his mother that it would
be for the best so he could get in some deep studying. But
what he had wanted most was to study his sexuality,
something he didn't feel comfortable doing still living at
home. He had gone a little crazy in that department but
he had managed to do his homework and projects while
staying up late, discovering Trixx, getting laid, and
making friends. He'd met Philip there after all, and many
more men before he'd gotten his degree. Good times.

The sky was blue without a hint of smog, and the
mountains were clearly visible, sitting as a ragged blue
crest beyond the tall stalks of palm trees; as perfect a day
as California made them. There was the administration
building with the words "Redlands" done in carefully
coifed topiary, and in the distance, the memorial chapel,
looking like Independence Hall in Philadelphia with its
colonial architecture and clock tower.

He found a visitor parking lot, a decent hike to the bookstore, but he hoofed it with no problem, eyes scanning the campus with students riding bikes and hiking from here to there, backpacks heavy on their backs.

He'd worked in the bookstore for a number of years while going to school. He'd had his scholarships, and the help of his old friend, mentor, and boss Lester Huxley. He'd worked for Lester in the summer at the Lincoln Shrine in Redlands, even up until three months ago when Lester, too, was murdered…

Jeez, for a smallish town, we sure have our share of intrigue, he mused.

Walking through into the bookstore, it was definitely a sense of déjà vu. There were the walls of mugs, plush bulldog mascots, t-shirts, and maroon hoodies, along with the shelves full of over-priced text books.

He couldn't resist running his hands over the hoodies with their white silk-screened school logo. Who was trying to kill him? A student? But he wouldn't even know any students here anymore. Some kind of prank? That was pretty heavy duty, especially with the letter bomb.

"Skyler Foxe!"

He turned. A plump woman in her mid-forties, stood with arms akimbo, with a ridiculously wide smile on her face. "Are you still looking for a job?"

He enclosed her in his arms. "Debbie! Oh, man. How are you?"

"I'm fine. Still managing this joint. And look at you. Always cute as a button. Please tell me you're teaching somewhere?"

"I am. My bookstore days are over. I'm teaching at James Polk."

"No shit. That's your old high school, isn't it?"

"Yup. It was a miracle but there was actually an opening. I'm in my second year."

"That is so awesome, Sky. I'm so glad to hear it. So what brings you here? Are you applying for a professorship?"

"Oh, no way. I'm pretty happy with my high school kids."

"I'll remind you of that in five years. What are you doing here, then?"

"Well…" What was he to say? He hadn't anything to go on but the hoodie. *So tell me, Debbie, who bought a hoodie in the last few weeks? Just hand over the thousands of names.* "It's kind of a…I really don't know how to say it."

Her smile faded. "Is something wrong? Look." She checked her watch. "I've got my dinner break coming up. Let's head over to the Bulldog Cafe. Give me less than five." She scurried off and disappeared behind the checkout counters to the back room.

Skyler took those minutes to look around, to gauge the students there, some little older than his own kids at James Polk. Going to college had been his freedom to explore his sexuality, his moment to finally find himself. He had nothing but good memories of the place. He wanted to tell those students around him to grab life by the balls, to take chances, to see the world differently…but he didn't want to come off as a crazy person. He supposed not all of them lived such sheltered lives at home as he had.

Briefly, he wondered what Keith's life in college had been like. But, of course, he'd gotten a look at that, what with his old boyfriend Ethan and that woman Laurie Henderson with whom he'd slept that one drunken night. He shivered. Maybe that was more than enough to know about Keith's past. Except that he recalled the stories Sheryl and Tamika had shared. It wasn't all bad, he supposed.

Debbie popped up beside him. "Ready?"

He walked with her across the campus to the café, marveling at the improvements in the décor and menu. He guessed a lot could happen in the intervening years.

She ordered a taco salad and Skyler grabbed a yogurt, just to hold him till Sidney snatched him away for his bachelor party.

Debbie watched him steadily as she picked at her salad with a plastic fork. "Something about you, Sky. Definitely a new kind of confidence. And something else I'm having a hard time identifying."

"Oh, well…it could be that I'm getting married. This Saturday, in fact. And now I feel stupid that I didn't invite you. Will you come? Are you available?"

Her fork stopped in mid-rise to her mouth. "*You're* getting married?"

"Yeah. Hard to believe."

"*You're* getting married?"

He got in close. "I know. The last person in the world you'd expect, right?"

"I gotta say, the last time I saw you at graduation, you seemed to have a trail of men dogging you. Was it one of those guys? Was it that business major with the glasses? He was pretty cute."

"That was Philip. And no. But he's still one of my closest friends. He owns The Bean in town."

"I'll be darned. So who?"

"One of the teachers at James Polk. He's the biology teacher and head football coach."

"A jock. Nice. I bet he's a handsome fellow."

Skyler whipped out his phone and showed her a picture of Keith, one of his better ones, shirtless and smiling.

"Oh my God. Is he ever glorious."

"I know." He put the phone away and sat back.

"I realize you probably didn't have my email or home address, so I'll forgive you for not sending me an invitation. I'd be happy to go." She grabbed her phone and said, "What's your number."

They exchanged numbers and email addresses, and once phones were put away again, and respective forks and spoons were taken up, Debbie studied Skyler once more. "But I'm betting you aren't here because you wanted to look me up."

He shook his head. "Ah, Debbie. Besides teaching, I've kind of got this other hobby. I sort of solve crimes on the side."

"What? Like a private eye?"

"No, more like an amateur sleuth. Like Miss Marple."

"And does that really work?"

"Yeah. A little too well, really. I've solved something like seven murders in the last year."

"Skyler! Are you shitting me?"

He shook his head. "Uh uh. It's for real. And... uh... apparently, there's someone after me. The FBI think it might be because of those murders I solved."

"The FBI? You're pranking me, right?"

"I'm afraid not."

"Wait. There were some detectives here a few days ago, looking at the —"

"Hoodies. Yeah, I know. That's why I'm here. Though I don't really know how it's going to help me."

"Skyler." She scooted closer to the table, her salad forgotten. "Are you serious? That was all because of you?"

"Uh huh. They think the suspect was wearing a University of Redlands hoodie, and it was a new one.

Which means they must be a student or a worker or, I guess, even faculty."

"That's crazy."

"You're telling me. Frankly, I didn't know what I expected to find here today. I just felt I had to do something. My best friend is a police detective. Maybe she was the one who came here."

"Long curly hair, pretty; Asian partner?"

"Yeah, that's her and her husband Mike."

"Wow. This is nuts. Well, if there's anything I can do, you know to call me, right?"

"Yeah, I will. It's stupid, but I bet a lot of people have been buying those lately."

"Not in the summer. I mean, the weather is still pretty hot, even at night. So we haven't sold too many yet."

"Really? Is there a way to go back over your sales records to see who they were?"

"The detectives are already having me do that. It's tricky. But we've gone back to the beginning of the school year. New students started arriving end of August, then orientation, then the school year started over a month and a half ago."

"You don't think *I* could get that list, too, do you?"

"Well…I wouldn't ordinarily do it, but seeing that it's you, yeah. I'll send that to you as soon as it's put together."

"Thanks, Debbie. That's a weight off my mind."

"Seriously, Skyler. This is crazy."

"You don't know the half of it."

❖

They finished eating after reminiscing a bit, and then Skyler, checking his watch, had to take his leave. He gave

Debbie a parting hug. "I really do hope you can make it to the wedding."

"I'll make it. I *have* to see this guy in person that managed to trap you. He was probably beating all the rest of those guys off with a stick."

Skyler raised a brow and she slapped his shoulder.

"You know what I meant."

He left her at the bookstore and then looked around surreptitiously, just to make sure he wasn't being followed or spied upon. Back in his car on his way home, he thought about who it could be. Who *could* it be from U of R who could have that big a grudge against him?

Chapter Nine

SKYLER HURRIED, SPLASHING ON SOME COLOGNE, and rushed across the apartment to answer the door. "Sidney! You're early."

"I wanted to make sure you weren't late. Are you actually ready?"

"Yes. Shall we go?"

Sidney and her bachelor party, even though he was pretty sure he had specifically told her *not* to do that. And apparently, Mike, Keith's brother, and his brother-in-law, were taking care of one for Keith the very same night. They could commiserate on hangovers together tomorrow. That's why Sidney suggested there be at least a day between now and the wedding.

Sidney pushed him into her car and drove too fast— as always—to Trixx, the local gay bar hangout. Ever since Skyler had come out in college, he had ventured into Trixx and he'd been going ever since. He'd hooked up with Jamie there, and Rodolfo, and Dave, come to think of it. The roots of the Skyler Fuck Club. And he'd slept with a majority of the men who still frequented the place. He both dreaded and looked forward to what the night had to offer.

When he walked in, he saw that the place was decorated with a banner stretched across the dance floor that read, "Congratulations, Skyler!" Everyone burst into cheers, and a few threw confetti. He gasped. He couldn't believe that the whole place had stopped their regular business to throw a party just for him.

Men, one after the other, came up to him and kissed his cheek, did a little groping, and offered congratulations. Tyrone, the statuesque black drag queen in full regalia and extra tall pink wig, picked Skyler up, tears in her eyes. "Skyler, honey," she whimpered. "I'm so happy for you!"

A great big smack on the lips from Tyrone punctuated her cry. "Thanks, Tyrone. But…your make-up's gonna run."

"Not this make-up, honey. It's permanent as the Rockies."

Tyrone's make-up was always tasteful, never over-the-top—more "Ru Paul than Rue Morgue," as she used to say. She managed to look darned good to Skyler. Sidney always said she was jealous of Tyrone, that Tyrone looked better than *she* did. And even though Tyrone favored a pink mile-high wig, it had a nice sweep to it. Of course, being as tall as she was only made her that much more imposing, but remarkably graceful on her size elevens.

"Could you—" Skyler motioned toward the ground at least a foot away.

"Sorry. I just get emotional. It's such a fairy tale, you finding your man like that. And he's such a gorgeous hunk of man. Where is he, anyway?"

Skyler adjusted his shirt as he hit earth again. "He's having his own bachelor party at a different location."

"Well that's a shame. I love me an eyeful of Keith Sexy-Scruff Fletcher. But I guess I'll see him at the wedding."

"I can't wait to see what you'll be wearing."

Tyrone gushed and hitched a bare shoulder at him. She was wearing a cold-shoulder blouse made of a black lacy material. "Just you wait. But I promise not to upstage you."

Was that even possible? he wondered. But it didn't matter. He was glad some of the men from Trixx would be there.

Sidney slipped in to talk to Tyrone, and as Skyler moved away, he heard her plea of, "You promised to help me with my make-up Saturday."

"*Gurl*, you know I'll help out. You have the best cheekbones. Are you finally gonna let me put your hair up?"

Gil the blond, buff bartender slipped a drink into his hand. Grey Goose on the rocks with a twist. Skyler hefted the drink in salute. Gil gave him his million-dollar smile. His exceptionally white teeth shone from a California-tan face. "Congratulations, Skyler. I regret that we never had a chance to hook-up. I mean…I take it that's off the table now?"

Skyler grinned. "Sorry. It's definitely off the table. But, uh, I appreciate the offer."

"No sweat. I've heard tales about you, of course, from the other patrons. You've been a pretty popular guy over the years."

"Yeah. It's not Keith's favorite thing about me."

"But he gets it, right? Don't go marrying anyone who tries to slut-shame you."

"Oh, no! He doesn't do that. It's just that he's a bit possessive. Not weirdly so, but…you know."

"I know. I've watched you and your friends in here. It's nice to see a young guy like you settling down. Usually I see our older clientele. But, to be fair, they hadn't been allowed to marry before."

"That's something, isn't it?"

"It is."

"What about you, Gil? I mean, let's face it, we haven't really talked much outside this place and not much more than what we're going to drink on any given night. Have you got someone special?"

"As a matter of fact, I do. We've been together over ten years."

"No kidding! Any wedding bells in your future?"

"We've been talking about it. We'll see. But we're pretty happy with the way things are with us. We've lived together for most of those ten years."

"But you propositioned me all the time."

"It's an open relationship. Sometimes I'm off with someone, sometimes he is, sometimes he brings someone home and we share. Open."

Skyler had thought in the past that if he ever got a boyfriend—in the distant future of his brief meanderings—that he'd probably have to have an open relationship. He hadn't ever imagined settling down with one man. And yet now, he couldn't imagine sharing Keith with anyone. It made his stomach curdle with jealousy. Probably how Keith felt.

"That's awesome," he said, squeezing Gil's hard bicep.

"Well, if ever you and Keith want to change things up, just tap me."

"Will do."

Gil moved off, offering his tray of cocktails and pints to the others. Skyler watched him move away, eyes sliding down to the man's firm ass in those tight, artfully shredded jeans before he shook himself. He reminded himself it was okay to look, even fantasize, but he was with Keith. And as soon as that thought crossed his mind, the image of Keith arose and he didn't wonder why he eschewed extracurricular activities with other men. Keith was definitely enough for him.

He roamed about the room and had just lifted his drink to his lips when someone slammed into him. Vodka spilled all over the dance floor. He didn't even have to turn around to know who it was.

"Jamie!"

"Sorry, Skyler. I'm just so excited." He grabbed him by the shoulders and nuzzled cheek-to-cheek. "Our little Skyler's getting married."

Philip and Rodolfo helped peel Jamie off of him and took their turns giving him a hug. Rodolfo did his best to stifle his tears but he was obviously having a tough time of it.

Dave grabbed him and pressed his lips to Skyler's in a long slow kiss. Everyone stopped to stare as Skyler staggered back. Dave shrugged. "Hey, I figured it was my last chance."

Skyler ticked a finger at him before gesturing with the half-empty glass. "I can't believe Trixx agreed to all this."

"But Skyler," Rodolfo purred, "everyone loves you."

"Or at least had a chance at you," said Philip, hiding his smirk behind his bourbon.

"Well, I mean I guess you're right." He took a closer look at all the men gathered, dancing, leaning on the bar, partaking of the free appetizers Gil had laid out. He did know everyone there, either casually or more intimately... No, he knew them *all* intimately at one time or another. Good grief. Palm Springs was bad enough, parading his conquests for Keith to see at the White Party, but *this*. This was Skyler's whole history in miniature, complete with the SFC. Though, sweeping his glance over the crowd again, he had to admit, they were all a nice bunch of guys. Not a sour note among them.

He lifted his glass to them. Some noticed, and lifted their beers right back, cheering.

Sidney sidled up beside him. "Having a good time? I thought of getting someone to jump out of a cake, but didn't think it was necessary… Or *did* I?"

A slow jazz rhythm started up. And in came two muscled men in leathers, parading around the dance floor. One was a bald African American man, and the other was a Caucasian man with shoulder-length black hair and a closely cropped beard and mustache. The audience started to catcall and moved out of the way, giving them room.

Hips began a slow gyration to Aretha Franklin crooning *I Never Loved A Man The Way I Love You* and the two men slowly helped each other out of their leather vests, leaving toned and oiled torsos on display, hands running down each other's six-pack. The dark skin on white mesmerized. Both their bodies were shaved, the better to oil them up and show off the muscles twitching and flexing; arms and legs sinuously intertwined.

Jamie yelled in his ear above the music, "Oh I think I'm gonna like this."

Sidney hung an arm around Skyler's neck and kissed his temple. He held on to her wrist as they all watched the men strip each other, hips and bodies undulating to the sensuous song. They were down to leather G-strings, but it didn't stop them from frotting their protruding bulges against each other. Skyler lowered his hand from Sidney to adjust himself. *Was it getting hot in here?*

The strippers were still sort of dancing, if one could call it that. They were moving against the other's body, hands roving, torsos sliding, flesh on flesh, and kissing with a generous use of tongues. Their bare asses were also slicked up, and the disco lights raked over their skin, illuminating one interesting landscape after another. Just as Skyler didn't think it could get any raunchier, they peeled down the front of their jocks, rubbing their erect dicks skin to skin to a surge of cheering. Phones were whipped out and videos recorded.

Skyler tore his eyes away to stare at Sidney, amazed she would condone such a thing, but her eyes were just as avidly on the two dancers as everyone else's were.

Dollar bills, fives, tens came out, and the boys of Trixx stuffed them in the little straps still holding the dancer's jocks on. As the music settled, they finished their routine with a kiss, and snapped their jocks back into place, though not as easily as they had before.

"Jeez," said Skyler, wiping the sweat from his brow. "I thought you were going to have to raid the place for a minute there, Sid."

"Wha…? Do what?" She seemed glazed.

He smiled wickedly. "I am so gonna tell Mike what you set up."

She grinned back and winked.

Men were pairing up after that display. Once the dancers collected their tips from their jocks, they came over to Skyler. "Hey, you the groom?" asked the African American man.

Skyler's gaze fell automatically to the man's covered erection until he consciously brought it up again to his eyes. He shook the man's hand. "Thanks for that, guys. That was… something."

Joined by the other stripper, the black man slipped his arm around his partner's waist. "Yeah, we like getting it on with an audience."

"I can see that." He blinked, willing his gaze to stay up at eye level.

"Leaves the audience with a problem, but we're happy to give the groom a happy send-off with a congratulatory BJ. Either one or both of us."

Skyler swallowed. "That's part of the deal?"

"Naw, we just figure we might as well." He rubbed his hand over his considerable bulge. "We're just givers that way."

"Oookaaay…but I can't. Love to, but can't."

"I get it." He glanced at Sidney. "Hey, pretty lady."

"Hey yourself. Skyler is off limits as the groom. He's the monogamous type."

"I feel you. Well, from me and my boy—" He squeezed the man still clinging to his side, "we wish you congratulations. But we gotta go and get rid of these boners."

"Bone away!" said Sidney blithely. Her eyes were glued to those bare asses as they wandered off. "I have a lady boner you wouldn't believe, but there isn't a soul here who can help with that."

"I dare say," said Philip, looking a little flushed himself, "there's a few of us retreating to the bathroom and their cars to take care of business."

Jamie poked Sidney's shoulder. "You are such a naughty girl. And a terrible cop. You should have busted those guys."

"What, and be the most hated person here? No way. Besides, I knew what their routine was."

"You are so bad! Did I mention that I love you?"

She elbowed Jamie as other men came up to chide Sidney… and probably to get the strippers' business card.

Skyler accepted more well-wishes, lots of drinks, and finally sat back to enjoy the view. But the hour was drawing late and it was still a school night, so around one o'clock he begged Sidney to take him home.

She gave him a hard hug in the car. "Mmm. Love you, Skyler. I hope that was a good send off."

"It was perfect. Thank you, Sidney." He tried to pull away to leave but she held fast to his shoulders, eyes fixed to his.

"You're still going through with it, right?"

"Yes! Jesus! Why doesn't anyone trust me?"

"Because you have a spotty record where commitment is concerned."

"I do not. I was committed to Keith from the very start."

She tilted her head and narrowed her eyes. "I guess. But you sure waffled a lot."

"My waffling days are over. I'm in all the way."

She brayed a laugh. "That's what *he* said!"

He shook his head. "You should *not* be driving."

"I'm fine. Do you want me to walk you to the door?"

"I'll be fine. If there's a sniper after me they're liable to hit you."

"Hey, don't kid about that."

"There's no sniper. If they could do that, they would have tried it first."

"Are you sure?"

He kissed her again. "Good night, Sidney."

He got out of the car and stood a bit unsteadily on the curb. A little buzzed. He'd be fine. He waved as he made his way up the stairs and unlocked the door. Keith was inside, watching the television with his feet up on the coffee table.

"He arrives in one piece," Keith declared.

Skyler flopped down on the sofa beside him and turned his face up to accept a kiss. "How was your bachelor party?"

"Van, Tim, and Mike took me to a cigar and whiskey bar. It was all very civilized."

"Eww, cigars!" He waved his hand at the air, even though he only caught the merest of whiffs from Keith's skin. He'd already shed his clothes and was wearing sweats and a tank top. "You didn't *smoke*, did you?"

"Maybe one. Just to be sociable."

"If you think mouth cancer is sociable, then far be it from me—"

"*One*, Skyler. In my entire life."

Skyler was still muttering under his breath when Keith asked, "And how was yours?"

"Well, it didn't involve any smokes. Sidney talked Gil into turning Trixx into 'Skyler Night'."

"I'm almost afraid to ask."

"My virtue was not compromised once, though there were many offers."

Keith grunted non-committedly.

"And there were these two strippers—"

"Two? Wasn't one enough?"

"Not for what these guys were doing. Honestly, there wasn't a limp dick in the house."

"I can imagine. Wish I'd seen it."

Skyler grabbed the clicker and shut off the TV. He turned toward Keith. "Well, if you're very polite to me, I can see my way into giving you a replay."

"Oh? Well. In that case…"

He dragged Skyler against him and planted a deep kiss. Soon Skyler climbed up into his lap, stripped off his shirt and trousers, and did his best to recreate the scene.

The next day at school, Skyler sleep-walked through the day. Teachers who ordinarily gave him a wave in passing, now stopped to talk to him and wish him well.

Ben Fontana, the big sheepdog of an art teacher, cornered him in the teacher's lounge; Skyler with his coffee, Ben with his small bottle of orange juice.

"Now explain this to me," said Ben. "Is a same sex wedding different from a straight wedding?"

Skyler burned his tongue on the hot coffee, giving it a quick, bracing gulp.

Trisha Hornbeck was at the fridge and paused in the door. "Ben! Don't be ridiculous."

"I'm not being ridiculous," said Ben. "I'm inquiring."

"For goodness sake," she said. "You were the first sponsor of the GSA. How could you ask such an insensitive question?"

His face fell. "Oh, gee, Skyler buddy, I didn't mean anything by it."

"It's okay, Trish," said Skyler. "Like he said, he just wants to know. I wish more people would ask questions. So, as far as I know, Ben, a same sex wedding is just like any other wedding. Or it can be very different. The only difference is it's a same sex couple. But I suppose there's a lot of bride and groom things we won't be doing. We're going down the aisle together, escorted by both sets of parents, for instance."

"Oh. Well, that's...that's great."

"You are coming, right? Then you can see for yourself."

"Darned right I'm coming. Wouldn't miss it." He swigged his orange juice and made a hasty exit.

"Trish, you shouldn't shame him like that."

"Maybe *I'm* too sensitive," she said, removing her glasses and letting them hang on their chain on her chest. "It just seemed too ignorant for someone like him. He should know better."

"Down, girl."

She smiled and patted his arm. "Are you getting nervous?"

He stiffened. "Only because everyone keeps asking me if I am."

"Oh dear. Speaking of ignorant. I'm sorry. You'll be fine. There's nothing to be nervous about. Unless you don't like public speaking, and this would be a pretty stupid profession to get into if you're that shy."

"You're right there."

As the day went on, he spent the time obsessing over the wedding and what it would be like, and if everything was going to go off without a hitch. They had rehearsed it Wednesday night with all the parents, with Tamika officiating, and had even had fun that evening, with families meeting, lots of laughter, and perhaps a little too much drinking all around. But it hadn't been the actual wedding. Not yet. That was tomorrow.

In each class, someone had brought a bouquet for him and cards signed by each period's students. His classroom was beginning to look like a flower shop. He was grateful that the kids seemed to care and offered their heartfelt congratulations. It made him feel better about the world in general and about his small world of school and job in particular.

Once his last period class left for the day, he looked around the room at his collection of flowers and cards, and sighed. He knew he was going to be staying late to get work done. After all, they weren't getting back from their honeymoon till Wednesday, and he wouldn't be back in class till Thursday. He wanted to make sure to leave detailed instructions for his sub, get all the papers and tests corrected before he left, and leave instructions for the janitor to dispose of the flowers—though he was sure to take a sample from each bunch and carefully pack it with its card.

He corrected paper after paper, marking down each grade in the computer as he went. And then he settled in to read some essays. Some moved along at a good clip, while others were covered in red marks and notes.

He came to Alex Ryan's essay and was cheered by the upward progress he was making. He and Rick were working on his dyslexia with assignments and exercises and it appeared to be working. He was surprised himself when he marked a B- on his essay. That was surely the best grade the teen had ever achieved. "He's going to be shocked with that one," he muttered happily to himself.

Stretching his achy back, he glanced at the clock. "Wow. I didn't realize how late it was." He looked up at the noise in the hall to see that it was Mr. Bashir with his floor polisher. He waved when the janitor looked up, and the man waved back, earbuds firmly in place, playing his music, no doubt.

Skyler worked on, filing pages into clearly marked folders for his sub and adding a long note to each manila folder. He reached for his travel mug but it was empty. Glancing across his desk, he could see that he was far from finished, and there was no way he could take it home, especially because he had to file them and leave notes. Reluctantly, he rose and exited the room to go to the teacher's lounge to make more coffee.

The school was dead quiet. It seemed that every soul had left and even the sounds of Mr. Bashir's cleaning machines were silenced. He knew that Keith was probably here in his own classroom in a bungalow across the campus, or maybe in his office in the boy's locker room. He'd be just as busy as Skyler, getting papers ready for his biology substitute. But Skyler was in the main building, an old 1930s monolith with two staircases to his second floor classroom; one centrally located and one on the other end of the long corridor.

He tromped down the central staircase to the teacher's lounge, not too far from the office. Didn't look like any personnel were still there. The office lights were dark. He poked his head toward the glass wall. Even Mr. Sherman had gone, and he was usually the last to leave.

The school always felt ghostly when all had gone, when the sunlight of the day had turned to unfamiliar shadows. The sound of his footsteps was lonely on the polished floors, and echoed in a solitary reverberation off the lockers lining the corridor, the glass trophy cases, the myriad of posters and flyers pinned to the walls. The colors of the sunset streaked through the glass front doors and left a rainbow of reds and golds stretching across the linoleum in front of him, like a carpet. He crossed over it to reach the lounge and pushed open the door, flicking on the light. He set to the automatic job of filling the coffee maker with his own stash of ground Ethiopian from The Bean, far better than the usual fare in the lounge. He hummed to himself as he waited for the brew, the rich aroma of the coffee filling the small room. He ticked off in his head all that needed to happen tomorrow. The flowers, the photographer, Rodolfo with the cake, the string quartet for before and during the wedding, the DJ for the reception, the families, the friends, everything to happen and go off without a hitch. Both grooms in place, of course. Keith was excited and ready to go. Skyler was…hmm.

Skyler was being Skyler. Yes, he was ready. Yes, he would be there. No, he didn't want to back out of it. Much.

Married. To Keith. It felt as if they had always been together, but in reality, it hadn't been that long at all. He looked around the little lounge and remembered the first time he laid eyes on him right in this room. In his head, he had called him a "Walking Wet Dream," and that assessment had not changed since he'd known the man. The mere thought of him made his heart flutter girlishly. And his dick surge. "You are so smitten, Skyler," he murmured, chuckling. He hadn't even known if Keith was gay when he had been trying to get his attention…and nearly spilled hot coffee in his lap.

"That got his attention, all right." He still reddened upon thinking about it. He had been such an idiot, too, insulting football players before he was told Keith was the new assistant coach. It should have ended right there. Yet Skyler had been attracted to him and had tried to apologize, but Keith was being an asshole about it. Little had Skyler known that he had been working undercover for the Feds and was trying desperately *not* to be attracted to Skyler. "So much for that," he said, cheerfully. He rinsed out his tall travel mug and poured himself a cup of the steaming brew.

He remembered their first kiss. Keith had dragged him into an empty classroom and kissed him right there in the school. He hadn't been sure about Keith up until that moment. The kiss had been sexy and exciting and dangerous and…wow. There had been no going back. That was a year and a month ago.

And now he was getting married to him.

He turned off the coffee maker, cleaned it, and switched off the light as he left. He started down the hallway when all suddenly fell dark.

"What?" He looked at his watch. Six thirty. Were the lights on auto? He headed down the hall, but it was darker than he thought. He reached in his pocket for his phone when he realized he'd left it on his desk. "Peachy."

He could have sworn he was here late before without the lights going out. He reached the stairwell, groped for the light switch on the wall, and flicked it on. Nothing. Flicking it several times, he looked around and noticed some lights that should have been on all the time in the corridor in front of the main entrance weren't. "Oh, great. The power's out." He grabbed the railing with one hand, griped his coffee mug with the other, and carefully made his way up the stairs.

But once he'd reached the top landing, he stopped. Footsteps? "Mr. Bashir?" His voice echoed and died away but there was no answer. The footsteps were faint and then stopped. "Hello?" The security guard? But shouldn't he be answering? "H-hello?"

The footsteps started again. He looked down the corridor one way and then down the other. In the dimness, he couldn't see anyone. He stood frozen. What should he do? Run to his classroom to the phone? Down the steps to the outside? But there was the gate and he had left his key back in his room, too. Sprint to the gym and hope that Keith was still here?

Decision made. He ran.

His classroom was nearly the last down the end of the corridor. The footsteps pursued. He raced to his classroom, stopped himself by grabbing the door jamb, and flung himself inside. Slamming the door, he threw the lock, then stared out through the little window in the door to the darkened corridor.

No one.

Were they scared off? Gave up?

He wanted to open the door to look and almost did. Instead, he threw himself against the windowed wall and with his face pressed against the glass, stared down the corridor. Was that a shadow receding? He couldn't tell.

Two steps to his desk in the dark room and he snatched his phone, poised to call 9-1-1... and hesitated. What had really happened, after all? The lights had gone out, he heard footsteps... and then nothing.

Instead, he called Keith.

Keith told him to stay where he was. And it wasn't long until the lights came back up. Heavy footsteps again, but then Keith's figure appeared in the slim window in the door.

"Skyler, it's me."

Skyler threw the deadbolt open and flung wide the door. Keith engulfed him in his arms. "Are you okay?"

"I'm fine. Just...a little shaken."

"I checked on the main panel. Someone cut off the lock. I've already called maintenance, Mr. Sherman, and Sidney."

"We'll be here all night."

"No, we won't. I already told Sidney we were leaving and that anything they needed to do, they could do without us."

"Are you sure?"

"We have a wedding to celebrate tomorrow, and *nothing* is getting in the way of that."

"Well...okay." He gathered his things and followed Keith out the door.

Looking back at the school as they entered the parking lot, Skyler wondered when — and where — this would all end.

Part Two

"A man in love is incomplete until he is married.
Then he's finished." – **Zsa Zsa Gabor**

Chapter Ten

I'M NOT PANICKED, I'M NOT PANICKED, I'M NOT panicked.

And yet there he was, breathing into a paper bag, and hiding in the bathroom.

This is ridiculous. I love Keith.

"Skyler? Are you okay in there? Why have you locked the door?"

"Did I?" He stuffed the bag into the trash bin, took a deep breath, and flipped the lock, letting the door fall open. Keith looked him up and down.

"Babe, you're still in your underwear."

"So are you."

With a deep sigh, Keith pivoted, strode to the bedroom, and sat on the edge of the bed. "Here we go."

Get a hold of yourself, Skyler. He marched out of the bathroom and stood before Keith. "I have something to say."

"Fuck. I *knew* it. I tried to talk myself out of it, that it wasn't going to happen. But there it is. I fell for it again. At least you had the grace not to leave me there alone at the altar."

"No! Shut up. Listen to me. This is not what you think it is."

"Isn't it?"

"No." He spread out his hands. "Keith, it's no secret I've been...scared."

"None whatsoever."

"Wow. A little hedging could have gone a long way," he muttered.

"Skyler, just pull the goddammed Band Aid, already."

"Okay. I've been hesitant, scared, numb, questioning. In fact, I was just in the bathroom having a panic attack." He swallowed. "I'm over it now. But." He crouched in front of Keith and took his cold hands in his. "I've never doubted you and your feelings for me. And you know what? You must never, ever, doubt my feelings for you. I love you. I've never loved anyone like this. And I panicked a little. One last time. Panicked about my decisions and what might happen. But you know what? Today, we're getting married."

"Are we?"

He still had that hang-dog expression. It stung Skyler's chest with a dull ache. Why did the man torture himself like this? "Are you saying that you've gone all these months with all these wedding plans going on around you, under the assumption that I *wouldn't* go through with it? What kind of sadist are you?"

"The kind that loves you."

Ouch. "Keith, look at me." It took a while, but those blue eyes finally rose to his. Still wary, as wary as that first night that Skyler proposed, they nevertheless looked at him straight on. "I'm just trying to tell you, that as scared as I am, I know this is the exact right thing for me. And I'm gonna marry you."

"You are, huh?" Keith didn't look any happier and Skyler's whole chest felt as if his heart might die of it.

He poked Keith in his carefully coifed furred pecs. "Yeah, mister. That's right. I'm gonna marry you *so* hard, you're gonna feel it the next day. You are gonna be *so* married."

A smile cracked at the edge of Keith's formerly downturned mouth. "I am?"

"Oh, let me tell you. I'm gonna *pound* that marriage deep into you. I'm taking this marriage to the extreme. This is going to be the biggest dildo of marriages."

"Okay, this metaphor is getting away from you."

"But do you believe me? Do you?"

He pulled Skyler closer. "Why are you still so scared?" Fingers stroked the side of Skyler's face. His skin tingled where Keith touched. He kissed gently, just the merest touch on his lips. "It's just me. We'll go on as we have before. We'll have rings and a certificate this time, and I guess we'll be more than we were, but still us. Right, babe?"

Skyler nodded. A little of the fear receding. He licked his lips. "And *you* won't leave, right?" he said quietly, almost too quietly for Keith to hear. But the look of astonishment on Keith's face told Skyler he *had* heard.

"Oh, sweetheart. Is *that* what's really bothering you?"

Skyler hadn't realized till that moment that…well, maybe it was. His father's leaving had left an indelible impression, far more than he'd realized. Damn Freud!

"You know *I'll* never leave," said Keith softly.

"But you did…once."

"And I was an idiot. Never again, Skyler. Never."

Something lifted off Skyler's shoulders. It seemed to fly away, leaving a lightness that eased the darkness in Skyler's soul. "Okay, then."

"Okay." Keith's quiet affection turned to playfulness. "So, are you going to get dressed already?"

Skyler looked down at himself. "I can't go like this?"

"It's not that kind of wedding."

He rose. "Then I guess it's time for the tux. Are we, uh, all packed for the honeymoon that you still won't tell me about that's sort of stressing me out?"

"Yes. Philip was here yesterday packing. He even bought a few new items for you that he thought you might find necessary."

"That's even more mysterious."

"Get. Dressed."

"Okay, already. So, this is how it's gonna be? You think you can boss me around just because of some rings and a certificate?"

"So help me God, I think I'm going to shoot you for the insurance money."

"Dres-*sing*!"

They had both agreed to buy their tuxes; designer, black, slim fit, one button. But Skyler insisted on an orange-gold bow tie to add a splash of fall color.

They dressed, with Skyler primping in the bathroom mirror. Skyler poked his head through the doorway and spied Keith. "Oh my," he sighed. "You really are one handsome hunk of man."

"I was just thinking the same thing about you."

He moved into the bedroom and couldn't help sliding into Keith's arms, lifting his face, and opening his lips to him. They kissed for a long minute. Skyler's cheek was burning from the scruff, but he didn't care. He inhaled deeply of Keith's cologne, savoring this suspended moment between them, of just them, with nothing else in the way of it; no ceremonies, no rings and certificates, no stress and anxieties.

Both breathing heavily, they rested foreheads together. "Have I told you in the last five minutes that I love you?" Skyler whispered.

"If that kiss was any indication…"

With a shaky breath, Skyler drew back, hand smoothing down the hard chest of his soon-to-be husband. A small sigh of regret, and he knew this delicate moment all their own was over, like a burst soap bubble. "We'd better go. Sidney's going to be calling me any minute—"

The phone rang. He grabbed it out of his pocket and clicked it on. "Hello, Sid. We are walking out the door right now. Right *now*. We're walking through the door, Keith is locking it—*you've got the suitcases? The rings?*— and we're going down the stairs. And we're walking... we're walking to the truck and... goddammit!"

"What? What, Skyler?" asked Sidney over the line.

"My tires! All the tires on my car are slashed. Sidney, you've got to get this guy."

"Don't worry. I will. You just get over here. Don't worry about anything. I'll take care of it later."

"We're coming." He clicked off the phone and stared at his car. "Why do they keep doing this to my car?"

Keith touched his tux jacket near his underarm, jaw squaring, searching the neighborhood with hooded eyes. "It's okay, Skyler. Just get in the truck."

Was there a bulge under the man's jacket? "Are you *armed*?"

"Shh. Of *course* I'm armed."

"You're armed on your *wedding day*?"

"When my fiancé is threatened I am. Now would you please get in the truck?"

"It's getting more and more surreal." He climbed into the truck and buckled in, searching out the tinted windows for anyone hiding in the bushes.

Keith got in and slammed the door.

"You aren't going to wear the gun when we actually get married, are you?"

"No. Sidney will be armed, though."

"Oh well, that's *much* better!"

"Skyler, this is still an ongoing investigation. Anything could happen. I'm not risking you."

"Chiffon and a swag of shantung silk with just a hint of Glock. That will make a pretty bridesmaid photo. Will we all have matching Kevlar vests?"

"I'm not going to argue with you. This is not up for discussion." He started the engine and pulled away from the curb.

"So you and Sidney had this planned."

"Yes. Look…babe…it scares the hell out of me that someone is trying to hurt you. It scares me even more that I can't be the one to protect you. Please let me handle this."

He sat back and pondered it. Skyler certainly felt helpless, not knowing who it was and why they were hunting him. But it must have been worse for Keith. Keith was a solver, a man who took charge of things. How must it feel to him to not be able to do the solving for the person he loved?

Skyler laid a hand gently on Keith's arm. "Okay."

Keith glanced at him, his tense jaw relaxing slightly. "I need to protect you."

"I know. It's okay."

They rode silently to the Mitten Building, pulling up in the space marked for the groom. "We're here," said Skyler unnecessarily.

Keith didn't move. He turned to Skyler. "Last chance."

Affronted, Skyler jerked his head back. "Fuck you. I'm not running out on you."

"All right then." He unbuckled and opened the door.

Skyler slipped out and stood on the asphalt, waiting for him when he was assaulted by Sidney. She grabbed and spun him. "You okay?"

"I'm fine. My tires, on the other hand…"

"Those we can fix. You, we can't."

Sidney was wearing a knee-length chiffon spaghetti-strapped number in wine red. Her hair was piled up, with a few escaped ringlets artfully framing her face, which Tyrone had glammed up with make-up. "Sidney, you're beautiful."

She twirled. "You like?"

"I like very much." She smiled and fell into his arms, hugging tightly. "Still going through with it?" she whispered to his ear.

"Yes, goddammit. I wish everyone would stop asking that."

She glanced at Keith, standing by patiently. She grabbed him and hugged just as tightly. "You are marrying my very best friend, and if you *ever* do *anything* to hurt him, I have a bullet with your name on it."

"Happy wedding day to you, too."

"Sidney," said Skyler, "I understand you are being Annie Oakley in this ceremony."

She glanced at Keith. "Let it out of the bag, did you?"

Skyler looked her up and down. "So, where is it? Do you have a special exploding orchid?"

She smiled and lifted her skirt until her thigh was exposed...as well as the holster strapped to her leg.

"Kinky. It's a real wild west wedding."

She dropped the skirt and shook it back into place. "You can't be too careful. And Keith insisted on removing his own holster for the ceremony. Mike won't, though."

Skyler shook his head. "That's something at least."

She gestured behind him and he turned. Uniformed cops patrolled the parking lot on foot. They saluted him and he waved limply back.

"Wow. This sucks."

"No," she said. "This is protection. There might also be a few plainclothes FBI agents inside as well."

"Wait…are we paying for their food?"

"Skyler! They're here protecting you. Are you gonna begrudge them a little pork loin?"

He kicked the gravel. "No. I guess that's a bit disingenuous."

"That's *right*." She grasped them each by an arm. She had a hard grip, Skyler noted. "Well, gentlemen. Let's go in and see to it. You have pre-wedding photos to take before the guests begin arriving. I suggest you don't open the bar till after the ceremony. I'll make sure the doors are kept closed until eleven sharp." She pulled them along and they followed, the three of them arm in arm.

Mike was the first one they saw as they entered the building set up for their affair. He was decked in a tux, dark hair combed back from his wide forehead. "Has she threatened either of you yet?"

Skyler and Keith both raised their hands.

"That's my demure wife. Come here, wife." He grasped her hand and pulled her toward him. Skyler noted the string quartet above in the gallery, tuning. "It looks like all is ready," said Mike. "Oh! This is my part of the job." He turned to a small table with the guest book and offered a wooden tray laden with boutonnieres of olive leaf, seeded eucalyptus, passion vine tendrils to match their bow ties, and silver brunia, all wrapped tight in linen strips.

"Allow me," said Keith, taking Skyler's and pinning it to his lapel.

A little breathless, Skyler pinned Keith's to his.

Sidney pinned Mike's to his dark suit. The others were for Skyler's dad, Keith's dad, his brother, brother-in-law, and the SFC.

Sidney looked down into the tray and shook her head. "It's gonna be such a sausage fest."

Skyler narrowed his eyes. "Sidney," he warned, "there's going to be lots of family here. Behave."

"I know. That's why I'm trying to get it all out now."

"Shall I give you the ring?" asked Keith.

"Oh, yeah, gimme." She took the small box and looked inside "Simple, elegant, masculine. Good choice, boys. Now, where did I put my fucking bouquet?"

Off she went to search as Mike watched her depart. "Don't worry, Skyler," he said. "I'll make sure she tones it down when family is present."

"Thanks, Mike."

Just as he wandered off, the SFC arrived. Jamie was stunning in a dark blue trim-fit suit sporting a subdued floral design in splashes of color, with a small white polka dot pattern on the pocket flaps. "Jamie, wow."

Jamie twirled, and smiled, eyes hooded. "I don't think it's too much. You don't think so, do you?"

"On you? Never." He hugged him, they exchanged kisses, and then Skyler offered him the bowl of boutonnieres.

"These are awesome, Skyboy." Skyler pinned it on him but it soon disappeared among the floral pattern. "And may I say, Keith," Jamie went on, "you look absolutely stunning in that suit. You should always wear black." He gave Keith a kiss and then giggled, rubbing his cheek. "Scruff. Skyler, I don't know how you do it."

"It's how *he* does it."

He slapped his shoulder. "Naughty thing. Come here, I need to ask you something." He pulled Skyler aside and gave him an earnest gaze. "Are you still going through with it?" he stage-whispered.

Skyler looked back at Keith who was trying to pretend he hadn't heard.

"Dammit, Jamie, for the last time YES!"

"Okay. Don't get your trousseau in a twist. We've had more than our fair share of Skyler meltdowns."

Feeling guilty, Skyler lowered his gaze. "Not lately."

"That's true." He switched gears from serious to giggly, rubbing his hands together. "So, are you excited?"

"Yeah. And strangely calm. Just enough of both to enjoy it all."

"Well, that's exactly how it should be. Oh! Come look at my Dave. Isn't he a charmer?"

Dave was decked out in a classic Armani suit with peaked lapels. He wasn't quite as buff as Keith, but his tailor was worth his salt making his arms and shoulders look balanced.

"Skyler! And Keith! Mmm mm. You are two handsome dudes. Give it here." Dave opened his arms to the both of them and there ensued a three-way hug.

"Are we too late to enjoy the frotting?" said Philip coming up behind them. Skyler seldom saw him in a suit, but he was reminded all over again why he chose to hook-up with the handsome man all those years ago. He wore a sexy, naughty smile, and though he wore glasses, the playful expression in his eyes wasn't hidden at all. But those eyes were only for Rodolfo these days, and *he* was wearing a slick blue shark skin suit and magenta shirt, sans tie, open at the throat. Skyler could well remember why he took him home, too.

Skyler hugged each in turn, but Rodolfo looked on the verge of tears again.

"Rodolfo," soothed Skyler, rubbing his back. "It's okay. Shall we look at your cake?"

"Oh yes, *amante*. And bring your wonderful Keith with you. Come!" Rodolfo led the way, and Skyler was pleased when Keith slipped his hand in his to walk side by side. He supposed that was to be their natural state from now on, and it wasn't a bad thing.

They arrived at the cake table, decorated with flowers and greenery. Rodolfo's cake was a thing to behold. Understated, but executed to perfection, Skyler peered around it, at fondant laid down with the artistic skill of a Renaissance sculptor. It was three tiers high, and looked exactly like birch logs hewn right out of the forest, with flourishes of birds, twigs, and flowers, all made with fondant and sugar. "Rodolfo," he said breathlessly, "I don't know what to say. It's amazing."

Rodolfo bowed.

Keith laid a hand on his shoulder. "No kidding, Rodolfo. This is really magnificent. Thank you so much."

"Keith, I think this is the first time you've said more than two words to me."

Keith considered. "Really? Well, I apologize for that. Maybe I just didn't know what to say. But this... Skyler and I appreciate it, and we are honored to have you here."

Blinking furiously, Rodolfo suddenly burst into tears again. "It is *I* who is honored," he wailed.

"Okay," said Philip, steering his boyfriend away. "I think that's enough of that."

Janet Deaver, the wedding coordinator, clacked forward, and put her hands on her hips. "This is as handsome a wedding party as I've ever seen! Every one of you is so good looking! Mr. Foxe, Mr. Fletcher, your photographer would like to take some pre-wedding photos so I'll let y'all get to it."

The photographer greeted them and explained some of the shots. More would be taken after the ceremony but others would be taken now. The wedding party was gathered, including Keith's brother Van, and Sheryl and Tamika. Rodolfo wiped his face and pulled himself together long enough for the photographer to get in some good shots of all the SFC.

Thinking they were going to be cliché, Skyler was pleasantly surprised when the photographer had them in some more non-traditional poses.

Excused for now from the photographer, Skyler was dying for a glass of champagne and excused himself to make his way over to the bar when Philip grabbed his arm and dragged him away from the others. "How are you holding up, Skyler?"

"So help me God, Philip, if you ask me if I'm going to go through with it…"

"I'm not. Not now, anyway," he said, muttering the last.

"I'm fine. I'm more than fine. I'm… determined. I mean… look at him." They both angled toward Keith who was laughing with his brother. Van was just as tall, with gray sideburns and a full beard. There was no mistaking the resemblance. When his father, Howard, joined them—his youngest son the spitting image—it was plainly a vision of Keith in the future, and it was not a bad look at all. His mom Helen was on Howard's arm, a tall, stately woman with short gray hair who reminded Skyler of Glenn Close. And then the rest of his family gathered; his sister Bree, her husband Tim, and their daughter Toni. Van's wife Sarah was nudging her twin sons—both with the best of the Fletcher features—Jon and Mick. He'd never be able to tell them apart now that Jon wasn't wearing his ubiquitous baseball cap.

Keith, in Skyler's mind, was breathtakingly handsome. Tall, muscled, just the right amount of hair on his body, a square jaw covered in scruff, black hair teased into a casual style, and ice blue eyes. He carried himself with the ease of an athlete, and spoke with a deep baritone and a twinkle of amusement in his eye. And he'd only ever had eyes for Skyler.

Skyler sighed.

"Do you need a moment?" asked Philip softly.

He chuckled. "No."

"You know, Skyler, I thought I knew you. Painted myself this stereotypical picture, I guess. You were always going to be the slutty bottom. Boyfriends were not on your radar. I mean, if it wasn't going to happen for the two of us together, it wasn't going to happen."

He shoulder-nudged Philip. "I know. It was tempting."

"We got along so well. I was very disappointed at the time."

"I know. I'm sorry."

"You don't have to apologize. Look who I have now. I never did think you'd settle down. But the first time I saw you with Keith, I had my suspicions. You couldn't keep your eyes off of him. Like now."

"What?" He whipped his head around toward Philip, who was chuckling at him.

"It's okay. You're allowed to look. Today more than ever."

"But isn't all this out of character for me?" A spike of heat made his neck break out in a sweat. He flapped his coat.

Philip shook his head. "No. Our characters change, mature. They have to, with circumstances. This is perfectly in line with who you are today. You jump in feet first with everything you do. I couldn't see you with a long engagement. You were ready. And whatever Skyler Foxe decides, he's in it all the way."

He couldn't help glancing at Keith again. And just at that moment, Keith turned and zeroed in on Skyler. His eyes crinkled and his mouth curved into a gentle smile.

This is my life, he thought. "He's what I want, Philip."

"I know. You're lucky. And I'm very happy for you."

They hugged. When Philip drew back, he sighed and wiped suspiciously at his eye. "I'd better go see what Rodolfo is doing. He's going to bore those poor people to tears talking about that cake."

"It's a great cake. Too pretty to eat."

"He loves hearing that."

Just as Philip walked away, the string quartet started playing. That meant that guests were now allowed in.

Skyler flapped his coat again.

Toni, Keith's thirteen-year-old niece suddenly stood before him, hands behind her back, rocking on her heels. She was wearing a white mini party dress with black scrolled designs on it. He noticed the top was separate and bared a bit of midriff. She had seemed so young when he'd first met her a year ago, but kids grew up fast, and with just a touch of make-up, she almost looked ready for high school.

"Wow, Toni, you look fabulous."

She smiled and twirled, no sense of the emo attitude he'd first seen on meeting her. "So do you and Uncle Keith." She sighed. "I guess now I really do have to call you Uncle Skyler."

"Please don't. Call me whatever you'd like."

"I think Uncle Keith made a really good choice."

"I think so too."

"Are you nervous?"

"A little. Mostly because everyone keeps asking me if I'm nervous."

"I guess people do at these things. This will only be my second wedding. I was a flower girl at one of my mom's friend's weddings a long time ago."

"Well, you can relax. No wedding duties…unless you want one."

"It's cool," she said.

"Well, I'm glad you're here. I hope it won't be too boring for you."

"No. There's a boy my age over there I'm sort of cruising."

He coughed, choking a bit.

"I *mean* I'm checking him out."

"Oh. Well, that's my cousin Bill. You can go introduce yourself. Tell him how we met."

He assumed she would demure, but he should have known better. She was a Fletcher, after all. "Okay. Will do. Good luck, Skyler. I'll see you on the other side."

"Okay." Off she went, her long legs taking her quickly toward the unsuspecting boy.

But before he could even process that, he was swept up by Sheryl in a flowery gauze floor-length dress. Tamika wore a long dress with an African print with gold embroidery and a low-cut neckline. Her headwrap was tall, accentuating her angular features.

"You are stunning," came out of his mouth before he could think on it.

"Why thank you, baby. So are you."

Sheryl kissed his cheek. "Don't be nervous," she said softly. "It'll all be fine."

Yet, as each successive person told him not to be nervous, and as the time drew closer, his nervousness doubled.

Sidney suddenly appeared and he grabbed her hand like a lifeline. "Sidney! Where've you been?"

"Doing best man stuff. Hey Sheryl, Tamika."

The three had met the other night when they had had their rehearsal, but hadn't seemed to have time to talk.

Sidney had been eyeing them most of the night and now they actually circled one another. Skyler shot a worried glance toward Sheryl, but she was placid and gave him an encouraging smile.

Sidney sidled closer to Tamika, narrowing her eyes. Suddenly, she blurted, "I *love* this dress. Where did you get it?"

"Oh, baby, this old thing? I whipped it up in my free time."

They walked away arm in arm, discussing fashion, of all things. He had never in his life heard Sidney talk about clothes.

He needed a drink.

But there was no drinking till after the ceremony. What barbarian had come up with that?

He looked at his watch. It was almost time.

Cynthia Foxe and Dale swept in and grabbed Skyler in a hug. Too busy with a tissue in her face, Cynthia let Dale do the talking. "Today's the day, Skyler."

"Yeah. This is it."

"Oh, Skyler!" His mother clutched at him again and he rubbed her back.

"Okay, Mom. You've got to keep your make-up intact. We're all going down the aisle any minute. Think of the photos."

"Of course, you're right." She stood back and blotted her eyes carefully with the tissue. She snapped a compact out of her purse and proceeded to try to repair the damage.

"Cyn, you look fine," said Dale. "More than fine."

"How is everything?"

Skyler startled at the sudden appearance of Janet Deaver, the wedding coordinator.

"Pre-wedding pictures all taken? Everyone here who needs to be?"

"Looks like it, Janet."

"That is awesome. Then I think we need to get into our places and get ready to begin. I'll announce that guests should be making their way upstairs and to their seats. That will take about twenty minutes." She gave him crossed fingers, and clacked away to do her thing.

Skyler whipped his head toward his mom in a panic. She gazed at him with her calm mom expression and approached, taking his arm in a gentle grasp. "It's all right, Skyler." She tucked in close and, smoothing out his shirt, said in a whisper, "This is *your* marriage, sweetheart, not mine. Look."

He raised his head, and with her words still ringing in his ears, he spied Keith coming toward him. He had an entourage—his parents and siblings—but Skyler saw them as if in a fog. He only saw Keith, striding toward him in slow motion, a heavenly light shining golden upon him.

"Huh?"

Well, a recessed light from above, as it turned out. But by that time, Keith stood beside him. He leaned over and kissed Skyler and his whole being warmed from it. "Are you ready? Please say yes."

Skyler released a breathy laugh. "Yes. I'm ready."

Keith squared his steady gaze on Skyler's and took his hand in a firm grip. "It's just the two of us, remember?"

Skyler smiled back, his heart pounding, but not with nervousness this time. "Just the two of us." He held Keith's gaze a moment longer before he said, "But where's Sidney and the guys?"

"We're right here," said Sidney, race-walking up behind him, her bouquet dragging behind her. Jamie was tugging Dave, and Philip had his arm in Rodolfo's.

"Oh dear," said Cynthia, reaching for Rodolfo's face with her hanky, and wiping away a tear. "You're in worse shape than I am. Buck up, boys. And lady," she said, with a head tilt toward Sidney, arranging Sidney's ringlets for a moment. "We've got a wedding to celebrate. Smiles, everyone. Don't look directly at the cameras until later."

At the wedding rehearsal, a coin toss initially decided which side each groom would stand on, but when Skyler made it known he wasn't happy about standing on what would traditionally be the bride's side, Keith offered to stand on the left instead. "It doesn't matter to me, as long as you're at my side."

The wedding party assembled up the stairs and waited as the string quartet finished their song. There was a pause before one of the violin players set down his instrument, took up a ukulele, and started strumming the Israel Kamakawiwo'Ole version of "Somewhere Over the Rainbow." The cello player began to sing.

Sheryl, with her bountiful bouquet draped over her arms—made of dahlias, tuberoses, scented geranium, yellow trumpet lily, seeded branches, eucalyptus, and leafy vines—walked out first in slow, sedate steps. She was smiling broadly, gazing at her girlfriend Tamika who was waiting for her under the arch ahead.

Then, two by two, the SFC walked out, resplendent in their various suits, striding proudly down the aisle, and finally positioning themselves on both sides of the arch.

Van and Sidney proceeded next, she on his arm. She bore the same bouquet as Sheryl and artfully arranged it to fall as designed over her arm and down her dress.

Both sets of parents came down next and stood on either side of the arch, Keith's parents fairly tall, Skyler's fairly short. Much like the happy couple, Skyler mused.

With a deep breath, Skyler looked up at Keith. It was no longer a question of *if* he would go through with it. That wasn't even on his mind any longer. The music of the ukulele was played as soulfully as when Israel Kamakawiwo'Ole first played it, and the cello player's voice soared over the notes, over the rainbow. The rest of the quartet picked up the melody line and jammed it with all the heart and joy of the original.

Skyler took the moment to smell the sharp fragrance of his own boutonniere with its eucalyptus, and the pungent aroma of the chrysanthemums on the banquet tables below. He absorbed the look of the twinkly lights, the warm generous lighting around the wedding party and guests, the rustle of fancy fabrics, his friends all dressed up, his students in their best garb with wide smiles on their faces, and even a few tears...and then Keith.

Keith gazed at him with already glistening eyes, hope and happiness stirring in them.

Skyler breathed. He clutched Keith's hand and didn't let it go an inch as they moved together, walking down the white runner laid out before them.

The music concluded just as they reached Tamika, stunning in her African textiles and perfectly made-up face.

She wore a placid smile and addressed the assembled guests. Her voice, though loud enough to be heard without a mic, was more mellow than Skyler had been used to from their brief encounters. "Welcome, loved ones. I am Tamika May, and it is my honor and privilege to be officiating at my best friend's wedding. I am also required to say that I am a certified officiant by the state of California, so when I say it's official, it's official." Soft laughter rippled through the assembled. It relaxed the tensed muscles in Skyler's shoulders. "A wedding is such a special place to be," she went on. "It's a celebration all about love. And families coming together; strangers becoming one. Keith and Skyler have come together today to proclaim to the world of their love, a love to last to the end of time."

Rodolfo wailed into his handkerchief. Philip hugged him one-armed as Tamika paused to glance at him before she continued.

"They met in a place they weren't supposed to meet. Skyler was a new teacher and Keith was there for a different purpose, even temporary. But when love meets, it isn't a brief passing. It opens wide to the universe for all time, etching itself in the stars."

Rodolfo gave another muffled sob. Jamie dabbed at his eyes as well, and, sniffing, leaned his head against Dave's temple.

"Who stands up for this couple?"

"My husband and I do," said Cynthia in a strong voice that surprised Skyler.

"And my wife and I," said Howard Fletcher.

"And I do," said Sheryl, clutching her bouquet.

"And I do," said Sidney with a sniff, softening her gruff voice.

"And I do," said Van, looking every bit like a Fletcher man.

"And we do!" said the SFC in unison, broken only by another sob from Rodolfo.

"Isn't that a fine assembly of people? Aren't you all proud of yourselves for being here today?" she said to everyone else in their seats. They turned to each other with smiles and a low buzz of conversation that soon died away. "*Is the light vanished from our golden sun,*" she began again. "*Or is this daedal-fashioned earth less fair,*

That we are nature's heritors, and one
With every pulse of life that beats the air?
Rather new suns across the sky shall pass,
New splendour come unto the flower, new glory to the grass.
And we two lovers shall not sit afar,
Critics of nature, but the joyous sea
Shall be our raiment, and the bearded star
Shoot arrows at our pleasure! We shall be
Part of the mighty universal whole,
And through all Aeons mix and mingle with the Kosmic Soul!

"Now that was righteous! That was Oscar Wilde, and he knew about love in all its golden fragments. And here's another who knew about love, one of my favorite sonnets from Mr. William Shakespeare:

"*Let me not to the marriage of true minds*
Admit impediments. Love is not love
Which alters when it alteration finds,
Or bends with the remover to remove:
O no! it is an ever-fixed mark
That looks on tempests and is never shaken;
It is the star to every wandering bark,
Whose worth's unknown, although his height be taken.
Love's not Time's fool, though rosy lips and cheeks
Within his bending sickle's compass come:
Love alters not with his brief hours and weeks,
But bears it out even to the edge of doom.
If this be error and upon me proved,
I never writ, nor no man ever loved."

Shakespeare. That did it. Skyler felt his throat close with a hot lump, and his eyes prickled with moisture.

"Now I love poetry, and I could go on and on," said Tamika, "but I don't think these boys could stand it, do you?"

She turned to Keith and Skyler. "Keith Aaron Fletcher." He looked at her once, but then turned his gaze to Skyler and kept it there. Mesmerized, Skyler was now unable to look away. He felt the people in their seats rustling, and the sounds of a beam settling, and a quiet waiter scurrying on softened feet below. And just like that, it all fell away, and it was just him and Keith — just as Keith said it was — just them. *Just us*, he thought breathlessly, and he couldn't help but send his gaze all over that face, taking in his misty eyes, the gentle smile teasing his sensuous mouth. There had never been the like. He didn't think he would mind being suspended in that one moment, dipped in amber for all time.

"Do you take this man to love, honor, cherish, devote your life and time to, through sickness, health, wealth, or poverty? Do you give yourself to him with your whole body, soul, and life till the end of time?"

Keith's usually strong voice cracked, and when he opened his mouth to reply, his eyes glistened suspiciously. "I do."

"That's good, baby. I can see the love. Now. Skyler Leslie Foxe. You are marrying my best friend. Do you take this man to love, honor, cherish, devote your life and time to, through sickness, health, wealth or poverty? Do you give yourself to him with your whole body, soul, and life till the end of time?"

Skyler licked his lips and inhaled a shaky breath. Half-sob, half-spoken words, Skyler said, "I do." A tear trickled over his cheek and made its way down…until Keith reached over and caught it with his thumb.

"That's fine," she said softly. "Will your guardians present the rings?"

Van stepped forward and handed Tamika Skyler's ring. Sidney rummaged and finally plucked it from the back of the bouquet. Tamika raised both rings so that the assembly could see them. "Y'all know the symbolism of the ring, right? It's a never-ending circle. It can't be broken. It goes on and on, and it wraps around the finger at the pulse point, where the heart beats. Is it necessary? No. But when present, it is a visible sign every day of this special kind of love, this togetherness. Each wearing the symbol of the love of the other. Now Keith you take this ring and you *slowly* put it on Skyler's hand. Repeat this: With this ring…"

With eyes fastened on Skyler's, Keith took up his hand. Keith's hand trembled a bit even as he poised the ring over the tip of Skyler's finger. "With this ring…"

"…I thee wed…It is the symbol of my love for you…my life with you…a never-ending circle of my faith and devotion."

Keith repeated it and gently pushed the ring on his finger. It was a solid presence, foreign at first, until the metal warmed and seemed to become a part of him. *Weird*, he thought.

She took up Skyler's ring and handed it to him, urging him to repeat the same message. Skyler flashed back to an afternoon about a month ago:

Working at his desk, Skyler suddenly looked up, realizing he was alone. He rose from his chair, looked around as if the cat would say something about it, and moved softly into the bedroom, sneaking through his own house. Opening the closet door, he carefully slid the dresser drawer open and reached inside for the satin-covered box that held their rings. The hinge was wound tight and he had to push hard to open it.

There they were.

He reached for it and removed it from its velvet lining, and held it up. The silver color gleamed in the closet's light, the polished edge, the stylishly hammered core. It was a solid and expensive chunk of metal. Platinum. Like his hair.

He circled the tip of his left ring finger with it, paused, and then slipped it on, turning his hand this way and that. Shaking his head, he slipped it off again. Was he really going to do this?

A key jiggled in the front door lock. His heart clutched. Scrambling to shove the ring back into the box it slipped through his fingers. "Shit!" He dove down into the depths of the closet amid shoe boxes and stored items but couldn't lay his hands on it. The box with the other ring was still in his hand and he vacillated as to whether he should put it down to search or keep it handy to pop it quickly back in before Keith found him —

"What are you doing?"

Double shit. "Uh…"

"Caught you, huh?" Keith was all smiles, cocking his head at Skyler positioned on all fours on the floor.

"I dropped it."

"Oh Christ." Keith knelt to help when Skyler suddenly felt it.

"Found it!" He held it up victoriously and then with a sheepish expression, tucked it back in the box. He almost closed it but Keith stopped him.

"I've looked at these a few times when you were in the bathroom."

"You have?"

"Uh huh. Wondering if I'd really get to wear mine."

"Why were you wondering that?"

"You know." He shrugged and snapped it closed. The drawer was still ajar and he tucked it inside, sliding the drawer closed.

"We're going to wear them. We are."

He smiled and reached for Skyler, pulling him in against his chest. Skyler inhaled the man's sweaty scent. "I am marrying you, you big galoot," Skyler mumbled into his chest hair.

"I can't wait."

"I really am. And I love our rings."

"I love them, too. It's gonna be the best moment of my life when I get to put that on you."

Skyler nuzzled his collar bone, licked at the base of his throat. "Yeah. Me, too."

And here it was. The moment, in the flesh. Skyler held up Keith's left hand and placed the ring at the end of the digit. "With this ring…I thee wed…It is the symbol of my love for you…my life with you…a never-ending circle of my faith and devotion."

Tamika held both their hands and placed one upon the other. "Today is all about love and about joining. About new couples and new families. It has been my honor to officiate at the wedding of Keith Fletcher and Skyler Foxe. And now, babies, I get to say my favorite thing. By the powers vested in me by the State of California, I now pronounce you spouses for life! You may kiss your husband. And make it count."

Skyler didn't wait for Keith. He leapt up, threw his arms around Keith's neck, his legs around his waist, and pressed his lips hard to him. Keith kissed chastely at first, but soon he opened up. They kissed as if they were alone. They held on for a long time, until Skyler took a deep breath and finally came back down to earth. And it was then that he finally heard the cheers.

They were the first ones to walk back down the aisle amid applause, grasping their hands. The string quartet sawed sprightly on "Origin of Love" by Mika, while the cello player sang it.

Van and Sidney followed on their heels. With a whoop, Sidney reached up and tossed her bouquet behind her. It arced upward for a breathless moment…before Jamie startled when it landed in his hands. But it lighted there barely a moment before he tossed it like a hot potato, bouncing into Rodolfo's arms. He stared at it dumbfounded for a moment before his mouth curved into a smile, and he turned his head shyly toward Philip. Philip's eyes widened but he said nothing as Rodolfo kissed his cheek, grabbed his arm, and marched triumphally after Jamie and Dave.

The parents were last and then everyone rose and started making their way down the steps.

At the bottom of the stairs, Keith and Skyler were alone, but they knew it was fleeting. Keith took the opportunity to grab Skyler and kiss him again. They hugged tight, and Keith whispered in his ear, "We did it. We did it."

"We really did. I'm so proud of us."

"I'm so grateful."

Skyler smiled. "I love you."

"I love *you*…husband."

"Oh my God. I've got a husband, too!"

"Break it up, you two," said Sidney. "There is plenty to do. First, you've got to greet your guests in the reception line, then the photographer wants us all again, and *then* you can party down. But first…" She grabbed Skyler and drew him into a tight embrace. "You did it, my Skyboy. You're married. Did you ever imagine?"

"It was like Tamika said — it was love."

She moved on to Keith just as Mike swept up with two glasses of champagne. "In the meantime," he said, "I thought you could both do with a bit of a pick-me-up."

"What are you doing?" said Sidney. "They're not supposed to do that yet."

"Sidney, give the guys a break."

Keith and Skyler clinked glasses and drank. Boy, was that refreshing! Skyler didn't realize how dry his throat had become. And tonight, he wanted his throat to be able to do whatever he asked of it.

Chapter Eleven

SITTING TOGETHER AT THE HEAD TABLE, SKYLER found he was famished. He dug into his pork loin with relish, and scarfed the many salads decorating his plate. Keith—though not too much of a salad guy—took to them too, especially the crab salad.

"Skyler, this is delicious. Good food choices, babe."

"It is, isn't it. I'm so glad…"

The sound of a fork hitting a glass again. He looked across the sparkling room and sure enough, it was Tyrone once more, happily pinging her glass. Her pink wig wasn't as high as normal—maybe it was her straight crowd wig?—but she was just as glamorous as always. Some of Keith's cousins had been hovering around her until Keith had to mention to them quietly who Tyrone was. They had all quickly moved away…except for one who, without much fanfare, seated himself next to the tall drag queen. You just never knew.

Keith leaned over and kissed Skyler as the glass pinging requested, and the tables cheered.

"These people are hungry for blood," said Keith.

"Well, one thing's for sure. I'm getting over my kissing-you-in-front-of-a-crowd embarrassment."

Sidney stood, raising her champagne. "As the best man to my best, *best* friend, Skyler Foxe, I enjoin all of you to fill your glasses for a toast."

Waiters scurried about filling glasses and Sidney waited, her own held high. When it looked like most had theirs at the ready, she cleared her throat again. "I have known my bud Skyler here since we were nine years old. We'd just moved into the neighborhood, and here was this tow-headed kid, skipping over to me—"

"I was not skipping."

"*Skipping*, mind you, and I thought to myself, 'Oy, what's this? Am I going to have trouble with this one?' But he was all smiles, and cheerily said, 'I noticed that you just moved into the neighborhood and you seem to have excellent taste in shoes.'"

Skyler hid his face in his hands.

Keith leaned in. "You didn't?"

Without taking his hand away, he nodded. His face flamed with heat. "I'm gonna kill you, Sidney," he hissed out of the side of his mouth.

Ignoring him, she trundled on. "Well, it went on from there. We became fast friends and got into our own kind of trouble. I always backed up Skyler when his mom asked what he was doing—"

There was a sound of indignation from Cynthia.

"Sorry, Mom!" he cried.

"And he backed me up with my mother."

"I knew it!" came the call from Sidney's mother Esther from across the room.

"Even before we got to high school, though, *I* was the one to break the news to Skyler that he was one of those boys who seemed to prefer guys."

Resting his chin on his hand, he slurped his champagne in surrender.

"And thankfully, that turned out all right. I kept an eye on him at school because there are idiots and bullies everywhere and I wasn't about to allow them to hurt him."

"Way to go, Sidney!" yelled Jamie.

She bowed. "We shared our mutual interest in all the boys in our year. There was even a football player her really liked—"

Skyler rose halfway from his seat. "Don't you dare!"

"No names. But I'll just say, he comes by his preference for buff football jocks honestly."

Keith, grinning from ear to ear, knocked him hard with his elbow.

"God, is this over yet?" Skyler muttered.

Sidney grinned. "We haven't even gotten to the college part."

"Please don't."

"Now Mrs. Foxe, perhaps you'd better cover your ears for this one."

Jamie, being helpful and sitting next to her, did that for her. She was reddening as much as Skyler.

"College was where Skyler really got his wings, if you know what I mean. First thing he did was find any LGBT groups in school…and became a joiner, if you catch my drift."

"Sidney," groaned Mike, head hiding behind his hand.

"Hey, I'm just telling it like it was. …And then he discovered Trixx."

The Trixx tables cheered. Someone threw confetti.

Sidney waved at them. "And I was there for *practically* all of it." There was some oooos from the room.

"Is this what you're really supposed to be doing?" asked Skyler weakly.

"Shush, I'm almost done. But through it all—through all the ups and downs and all the heartaches—and yes, you did have them, because I saw when a guy or two wasn't as into you as you seemed to be into him—and all the times you stood by *me* when some asshole *I* was dating broke *my* heart—when I had to leave you on your own when I joined the police academy—you were always there for me. Oh, how many late-night phone calls did we make to each other? How many texts? We never lost touch."

That familiar prickle watered his eyes again and he pressed his lips tight, nodding.

"And now, after all this time of Skyler being Mr. Solo out there, he runs into this guy and smack! He goes insane. He falls for him right away—"

"I did not! I mean…I…I didn't. Not *right* away." Looking at Keith's moue, he sunk down in his seat.

"*Right* away. He couldn't stop talking about him and I thought, 'Uh oh. This guy's different. Skyler never goes on about anyone'."

Keith's hand slipped into his and squeezed. Skyler's embarrassment vanished. After all, it was true. Jamie had called him Hunk-on-a-stick, and Skyler had called him a Walking Wet Dream, and he was. He was all of those things. He squeezed back and grinned sheepishly.

"And then *I* met him. And then I really knew our Skyler was falling. Because, just like now, he couldn't keep his eyes off of the man. And then I was scared. Because I didn't want to lose my best friend."

Skyler snapped his head up to gaze at her. She had tears in her eyes now and tilted her chin up to hide them.

"But thank God I didn't. I just gained a new one. One who loves him as much as I do. So here's to the happy couple. And to love!" She raised her glass and drank, and then everyone else did, too, before they clapped and whistled. She leaned over and kissed Skyler, and he hugged her tight.

"Love you, Sidney," he whispered. "As if you could ever lose me."

Van, sitting on the other side of Keith, stood as she sat. "So I'm supposed to follow that? I'll give it a try. My little brother Keith was always a pain in the ass."

"Van!" said his mother Helen, swatting toward him but didn't come close to striking distance from her place at another table.

"No, seriously Mom. He was the baby. He got away with everything. He liked football, he liked Scouts…he liked boys. He got away with everything." The crowd laughed. "Except he was *good* at football. Really good. For me, football was a fun pastime and us kids always played it at home, but for Keith he almost went all the way. It would have been great if he had had a chance to go pro and he would have been the first openly gay player, I'm sure of it. That injury screwed that up, and I'm really sorry, bro."

Keith shrugged unabashedly, but Skyler couldn't help but rub his hand up his arm condolingly.

"But then you went on for that biology PhD — one-upping the rest of us *again* — see what I mean? A pain in the ass. And as if that weren't good enough, he ends up at Quantico as an FBI agent. I mean, seriously!"

Keith threw up his hands at the good-natured ribbing.

"And then one winter day," Van went on, "he tells us that he met someone and he wants to bring him home to Seattle for New Year's. And I said to our sister Bree — remember, Bree? — I said, how blond and how young is this one?"

The crowd burst into laughter while Skyler pursed his lips and stared at the table. Keith threw his arm around him, his turn to placate.

"Our Keith had a type, you see. And sure enough…" He gestured toward Skyler.

Keith gave Van the finger.

"I'm not the one with a type, bro. Anyway, Skyler turns out to be this really sweet guy that everyone couldn't help but like. I guess the family fell in love with him, too. And I'm really glad my little brother found the love of his life. So here's to Keith and Skyler, and a long and happy marriage."

Everyone cheered and drank, and then the DJ began rolling out some music.

Relieved the toasts were over, Skyler stood. "Dance with me?" he asked Keith.

Keith dabbed at his mouth with the napkin, tossed it down, and rose, taking Skyler's hand.

They stepped out to the dance floor alone under the sparkly lights as the DJ blended the background music into the first jazzy strains of Etta James belting out, "At Last." Keith pulled Skyler in tight as he led him into a slow, swaying dance.

Skyler listened to the words of the song, and it was for him as much as it was for Keith, because Skyler's love *had* come along, and Keith had gotten his hard-worn love "at last."

Skyler couldn't believe it. He truly couldn't. How had he spent so much useless time worrying about this? It was just Keith. It was only just them. And oh, how he loved slow dancing with the man! Keith held him just so, and with his hand at the small of Skyler's back, led with such easy precision. The man was solid and strong, and oh-so-graceful, his athleticism coming to the fore and producing steps so smooth it almost made Skyler jealous. But he knew he was good, too, and he followed Keith's lead with his own supple grace and style. Resting his head against Keith's scruffy cheek, he closed his eyes. If this was marriage, he could get used to this.

The song ended and they sealed it with a kiss.

The DJ came on the mike and said, "How about the moms dance with their sons?"

Skyler turned to his mom and strode toward where she was sitting.

She rose, scooted around the edge of the table, and approached. She wore a peach chiffon dress with three-quarter sleeves. Still slim, his mother looked like a mature woman with her silvered blond hair, but she was still stately and beautiful. At least in his eyes.

He took her hand and led her to the floor. And as Keith danced with his own mother, Skyler gave Cynthia a little twirl before bringing her in. He smiled. "You look beautiful, Mom."

She blushed. "Don't be silly. This is *your* day."

"Can't everyone look as beautiful as me?" He smiled and fluttered his lashes. She slapped his shoulder.

"It was a lovely wedding, sweetheart."

"Yeah, it was."

"You know something, Skyler. I have a confession to make. I had always wanted a little boy."

"I think you've told me that before."

"Now let me finish." He turned her, smoothly avoiding the photographer. "I wanted a little boy because I thought they would be easier. And you were. You were the perfect little child."

"Of course."

"So precocious. So smart. You seemed to love everything I did; art, museums, culture."

"I was raised well."

"And we were a team. I'm sorry I was gone to work so much in your teen years."

"You couldn't help it. You had to make a living. I totally understood that. Besides, I was pretty busy with friends. But you and I always made sure we had dinner together."

"Something that's hard to forgive your father for. But I have tried."

He kissed her cheek. "You're a saint, Mom."

"No, I wasn't. Listen, Skyler. When you told me about being…about being gay, I was very upset at first." She raised her hand to his cheek and gently stroked it, countering, perhaps, the time she slapped it when he'd told her. "And then…I was glad, for such selfish reasons. I didn't have to share you with another girl. Isn't that terribly shallow of me?"

Wow. Was it? Who was *he* to judge? "I don't know."

"I mean there was always Sidney, but that was different. When I met your Keith…well. It was so strange at first to see you…see you…*kiss* a man. Now it's old hat."

He bulged his eyes at that.

"But I like Keith. I have since the beginning. He seemed like someone special. And now here you are."

"Here I am."

"I'm so very happy for you, sweetheart." She kissed his cheek and he hugged her tight. He held on even as the song ended and another began. The DJ announced that all the guests were welcomed to dance, and he put on another slow dance, though it had a bit more energy to it.

Cynthia eased back. "Well, it looks like someone else would like to dance with you. I'll beg off. Skyler, do you think that fellow in the dress with the pink wig would dance with me? I'd like to ask him."

Blinking, Skyler stared at his formerly staid mother. "Uh… no, Tyrone wouldn't mind at all. I'm sure she'd love that."

"Good. I always wanted to lead."

She moved away, heading straight for Tyrone's table. Skyler hoped the photographer would be all over that.

When he turned to greet his next partner, he jerked back. "*Dad?*"

Dale Foxe, blond with a cascade of gray blending together, and with blue eyes instead of his son's gray, hastily took Skyler's hand and curved his arm around him seemingly before he could change his mind. He jolted with him on the dance floor before their steps smoothed out.

Skyler glanced about, and though people were looking at him, it didn't seem as if it was with anything but happiness. "Dad, what are you doing?"

"Well, I'm dancing at my son's wedding."

"A-aren't you supposed to be dancing with the —"

"There is no way in hell I'm dancing with Keith." Dale rolled his shoulders and stared off over Skyler's ear. "I'm just trying to fit in here. Sidney's toast was certainly...interesting."

He knew his pale cheeks were coloring again at the thought of what she'd said in front of his parents...and *Keith's* parents. His *in-laws*.

Skyler's hand felt clammy in his dad's.

"Frankly, I don't know the protocol at a gay wedding," Dale went on. "I don't have any experience with them."

"Neither do I."

"I just — holy hell, will you look at your mother?"

He turned Skyler and they both watched as she tried vainly to lead the statuesque Tyrone in her four-inch heels across the dance floor. People gave them a wide berth, and many raised their phones for photos and video. But Cynthia was smiling and looking as if she was having a good time.

Skyler shook his head silently. He never imagined this. Not in a million years.

He and Dale continued dancing for a few more quiet moments. All the while, Skyler kept screaming in his head, *This is weird!*

"Look," said Dale, breaking the awkward silence at last. "I suppose while I've got you, I should impart some advice."

Warily, Skyler watched his father's face. "Yeah?"

"Listen. Listen to the other person. Skyler, I spent years not really hearing your mother and she spent just as many not hearing me and my needs. Listen to each other, son. Hear what the other is truly saying. A lot of grief can be spared."

"Okay," he said softly.

"And if you ever have kids—"

"Dad!"

"If you do…" He swallowed, blinked wet lashes, and started again. "If you do… hug 'em and kiss 'em every day. Because… believe me, you'll be sorry if you don't."

Skyler's vision blurred before the tears spilled over, running down his cheeks. "Okay, Dad," he whispered.

Dale nodded, lips mashing and trembling. He raised his arm awkwardly and wiped his eyes on his sleeve. "You know," he said unsteadily, "you're a darned good dancer. I think I'll try and tear your mother away from that tall fellow. You go find your…your husband, son."

He released Skyler, patted him on the shoulder, and left to retrieve Cynthia, who was doing a step touch while holding on to Tyrone's fingers with one hand.

He wiped at his eyes. Wow, this party was certainly doing a number on his emotions. He looked for Keith, who graciously left his partner and hurried toward Skyler.

"You all right, babe?"

"Yeah. My Dad and I…we just had a talk."

"And a dance. That was pretty ballsy of him."

"Yeah, I guess it was. Us Foxe men are known for our unorthodox moves."

"He's all right, Skyler."

He held tight to Keith. Yes, he was beginning to see that.

Chapter Twelve

THERE WAS MORE DANCING, GUESTS LAUGHING AT the photo booth, and a pause to cut the cake and pass it around. It was a chocolate almond cake with a raspberry mouse filling, and chocolate ganache frosting under the fondant. Skyler moaned as he slipped the cake from his fork into his mouth. "Rodolfo," he said when he could speak again. "This, my friend, is divine."

Afterward, he made his way through the room sometimes with Keith, sometimes without, greeting his guests. Finally, he had a chance to slide into an open seat at the GSA table. "Hey, you guys."

"Congratulations, Mr. Foxe," said a red-faced Alex, who had just gotten off the dance floor with Rick. Rick draped an arm over the boy's shoulder and nuzzled the buzz cut of his hair.

"Thanks, Alex. How did you like the ceremony?"

"That was dope," said Drew. "I mean that lady who did the ceremony, she rocked."

"She's something else, isn't she? There she is on the dance floor with her girlfriend."

Drew turned and shook his head. "A lesbian, too. Dude, you throw an awesome party…"

He stopped talking as Tyrone swept up to the table and glanced at all the faces looking up at her. "Skyler, who are all these amazing young people?"

"They're from my Gay-Straight Alliance club at school."

"And all these precious faces are gay?"

Drew raised his hand. "Not me. I'm just an ally."

Tyrone strode toward him and crouched down, batting her long, fake lashes. "Honey, you are not *just* an ally. You are my brother. When you sit with my brothers and sisters here, when you stand with them in their times of trouble and times of happiness, you are not 'just' anything. You are a superhero. And we love you. Y'all take care of this one, my pretties," she admonished the table, ruffling Drew's hair, before she stood upright again, and swept away, skirts swishing after her.

Drew watched Tyrone depart with a slackened jaw. "Mr. Foxe, who was that?"

"*That* is Tyrone."

"That was a dude, right? A real life Ru Paul."

He chuckled and turned back to Alex and Rick. "So, did we do okay?"

Rick twined his long fingers together on the table and cocked his head with a thoughtful expression. "Mr. Foxe, I think it was beautiful. What that black lady said, the poetry she recited, the things she had you say to each other…it was all beautiful. You made this one cry." He motioned toward Alex.

Alex shoved at Rick. "I did not."

"Well, *I* cried," Rick admitted. "I think someday I'd like to get married and have a ceremony like that…since I'll never get my wedding mass."

"Well, you never know Rick."

"Oh, I know."

"Amber was balling her eyes out," said Heather.

"Omigod," said Amber, "was I ever! That was *amazing*, Mr. Foxe."

He felt shy suddenly, and toyed with the greenery around the candle. "Thanks. I'm really glad you guys came."

"It's an experience I'll never forget," said Amber with a sigh.

Skyler turned to her date, Ravi Chaudhri. "And what about you, Ravi? Did it leave a good impression?"

"It was fascinating. I've only ever been to an Indian wedding, and a lot of the same sentiments were said. Of course, I suppose all weddings are the same in that respect."

"They would be, wouldn't they? I haven't been to very many myself. But to tell you the truth, this is my first same sex wedding."

"Well you did it right," said Rob, holding his hand up for high five.

"What are all these troublemakers doing?" said Keith coming up behind him and sliding his arm around Skyler.

"Oh, the usual. You know these characters."

"Hey, Coach," said Stephanie. Skyler barely recognized her without her cheerleading outfit. Instead, she wore a flowery short-length party dress. Her girlfriend Jennifer wore a similar one. "So what are the plans for the honeymoon?"

Keith opened his mouth and then stopped himself. He turned to Skyler. "Why you dirty, underhanded scoundrel. Using children like that."

"Who, me? I don't know what you're talking about." But to Stephanie he mouthed, *Nice try*.

"Who's a children?" said Evan. She wore a dark shapeless dress, more like something that Lisa would have worn, only Lisa was wearing an out-of-character boho handkerchief-hemmed gauzy number.

Before he could answer, the DJ eased in Micro's "Inside of Me" and all the kids jumped up from the table to dance.

"Come on," said Rick. "Rest time is over, Alex." Reluctantly, the teen rose, and shrugged at Skyler. The

GSA kids took over the center of the dance floor, and were soon surrounded by Trixx boys, the SFC, and Keith and Skyler's younger relatives.

Skyler watched it for a bit, marveling for the umpteenth time at all these different people coming together.

"It's pretty amazing," said Keith in his ear above the pounding roar of the music, seeming to read his mind.

"I was just thinking that."

Keith had long ago abandoned his tie, and his shirt was opened by three buttons, exposing the first trimmed hairs of his chest. Skyler couldn't help but start to think about the honeymoon. Maybe it was the muscle memory of the beat of the music. It always reminded him of hooking up, so a hard-on was the natural result. He'd left his jacket back at his chair and now he felt a little trapped sitting at the kid's table.

"You wanna dance?" Keith asked.

Or he could dance and hope the low light kept him hidden. He opted to dance.

Dancing with Keith, either fast or slow, was one of his true joys in life. And it would all have been perfect, if he hadn't glanced to the edge of the dance floor and caught sight of Special Agent Slokum and Special Agent Wolf.

Wolf was not out of place in his suit, but Slokum was wearing a modest pant and top ensemble in a boring fabric with a terrible drape.

It all brought home that—oh yeah, someone was trying to kill him.

Of course, Keith noticed his change of mood immediately. Skyler answered his questioning expression by tilting his head toward the agents. That scruffy jaw set immediately. Obviously, he too had forgotten, at least briefly.

When his gaze returned to Skyler's, he tried to blow it off with a small smile. But the spell was effectively broken.

And then Keith looked at his watch. He motioned for Skyler to leave the dance floor away from the loud music.

"I hate to say this, but it's almost time for us to go."

"And we'll have to shut down this party. We only have the room for so long. I think there's an evening affair in here tonight."

But even with the specter of some killer on the loose, there was also the promise of his surprise honeymoon, and he truly did love surprises. He grabbed Keith's arm. "You can tell me now, right? Where we're going?"

That sly smile Keith was so good at appeared. "Nope. Surprise to the very last."

"You are so mean to me."

He turned and gathered Skyler into an embrace. "Oh yeah. I am going to be so mean to you…you won't be able to sit down for this whole weekend."

Squirming in Keith's embrace, Skyler perked up…and so did his cock. "Oh my. I like the sound of that."

The DJ turned down the tunes so he could announce, "This is going to be the last dance, you happy campers. Our lovely couple have to scurry off to their honeymoon, but the rest of you can continue the party down at Trixx on Citrus. I'll be playing all night. It's been a privilege being your Controllerist today. Let's get the groom and groom up here to dance away the last of their party."

Everyone cheered as Keith and Skyler moved to the center of the dance floor again. The beat began, and then it was obvious that it was mash-up of the Village People's "YMCA" and Madonna's "Like A Virgin." Skyler cast a withering glance to the DJ, who saluted with his beer bottle, laughing.

The SFC wormed their way across the dance floor and joined Skyler and Keith, dancing all together. Skyler tried to look over the heads of everyone. "Where's Sidney?" he yelled.

"Right here!" she hollered from behind him. She and Mike joined them, and they formed a big circle, dancing with each other. Skyler threw his hands in the air. Everything fell away. There was just this. Music, lights, his friends, and his lover. It couldn't get better than this.

The gang got themselves presentable again, with Skyler and Keith making a quick change in the bridal room after the leaving pictures and video were shot. And then Skyler spotted Debbie talking with his cousins. He rushed toward her. "Debbie! You made it!"

She gave him a hug. "That was really something, Skyler. I was so glad I could be here. And don't worry. I'll email you that list tomorrow."

He'd almost forgotten. "Okay, Debbie. Thanks. Of course, I have no idea where I'll even be tomorrow. Keith is keeping the honeymoon a secret."

"How exciting! Well, I'm sure it will be amazing. I'm so happy for you, Skyler. You keep in touch now."

"I will. Thanks, Debbie."

More people came up to greet him and wish him well. But always in the background, were the shadows of the special agents, circling the pack like wolves.

It didn't matter. What mattered was Keith. And Skyler began to feel the excitement of their going away. What the heck had Keith planned? A little getaway in the mountains? The beach? It was maddening not to know.

The SFC had gathered for their good-byes and well-wishing. Philip was the last to give him a hug. "It's going to be wonderful."

"And you're the only one besides Keith who knows what it is."

"That's right."

"Still not going to tell me?"

"Have a happy honeymoon, Skyler."

Sidney seemed distracted but Skyler tugged her into an embrace as he was going through the door. When he let her go he noticed an envelope that seemed to have his name on it that she was gripping hard. "What's that?"

"Nothing. Something for later. Have a very happy honeymoon, sweetie. Fuck your brains out." She gave him a loud kiss on the cheek.

The SFC walked them out to Keith's truck when Skyler paused.

All over the black truck was painted the words "Just Married." And some rather considerable dildos were tied to the back bumper on ribbons.

"Jamie!"

"How did you know it was me? Besides, they all helped."

Keith reached into his pocket, drew out a Swiss Army knife, and snapped open the blade. He sawed off each dildo and left them sprinkled on the asphalt. "Souvenirs for you," he said to the boys, and plunked the knife back in his pocket.

Skyler gave the dildoes a perusal. "Now let's not be hasty…"

"Get in the truck, Skyler."

"Bossy. He's married now. Thinks he can boss me around."

"Could you please get in the truck?"

"That's much better. Bye, everyone! And thanks. You really made it a special day! I love you guys!"

"Good-bye, Skyler and Keith!" called Jamie. "Have a good time fucking!" Dave elbowed him so hard he stumbled.

Skyler waved at his crazy friends and watched them as he and Keith pulled out of the parking lot. As the truck hit the street, he saw Sidney gather them close.

Chapter Thirteen

SIDNEY WATCHED SKYLER DRIVE AWAY WITH trepidation. The envelope in her hand felt like a razor.

She motioned for the SFC to come together. Thank God for them! But what could they do that the cops couldn't? She needed their advice. And with Mike at her elbow, she felt the panic ebb and her confidence lift. "Guys. Guys! Shut up for a minute."

All eyes were on her even as she glared down at that stupid envelope. "Mike, have you got a handkerchief?"

"Yeah. Why? Are you gonna cry again?"

"Just give me the handkerchief."

He plucked it out of his breast pocket and shook it out before handing it over. She took it and covered her hand with it, and carefully, with the handkerchief-covered hand, extracted the paper from the envelope again. "I found this on the table. Here's what it says:

Skyler,

I know where you're going.

I'll be there to join you.

Bon Voyage."

Philip gasped. "Is that from the suspect?"

"I have every reason to believe it is." She tucked the letter back in and covered the entire envelope with the handkerchief.

"Well...what do we do? Shall we call over those agents?"

"I've had this for ten minutes already. Most everyone was gone by then. I've been trying to figure out what exactly to do."

"What do you mean?" said Mike, slipping his hand in his trouser pocket and retrieving his phone. "You stop Skyler and Keith right now. We clear the place and get surveillance footage. We —"

She put her hand on his phone. "I know all that. But goddammit, this is Skyler's honeymoon. This is his once-in-a-lifetime thing. He was already nervous as hell, ready to back out. I can't ruin this for him."

"But he's in danger."

"I know!" She gritted her teeth before lifting her face to Philip. "Philip, where are they going?"

"I promised not to say —"

"You promised not to tell Skyler. This isn't a joke, Philip. Tell me where they're going."

"Oh hell. Okay. They're going on a cruise."

Jamie squealed. "That's so romantic! Oh, I wish I'd known."

"Where Philip? What ship? How long?"

"Out of Long Beach. Till Wednesday. The Mexican Riviera. Oh my God, Sidney," said Philip, "you've got to stop him from going."

"I can't ruin his cruise. Shit!" She clutched at her hair.

"Then there's only one solution," said Jamie. "We'll go and make sure nothing happens to him."

Philip tapped his shoulder. "What do you mean 'we'?"

"It's simple. We just go on the cruise with him and protect him."

Dave pushed forward. "Jamie, we can't do that."

"Of course we can. For Skyler."

"Right. You mean buy a ticket on a *cruise* ship. At the last minute."

"Yes! I'm willing."

"But honey, I have to go on shift."

"You don't have go to till next week. We can do this."

"Wait," said Philip, "besides how stupid this is, he'll see us. I don't think he wants a group honeymoon."

Jamie folded his arms over his chest. "We just make sure he *doesn't* see us."

"Jamie," said Rodolfo, pointing his finger at him, "are you saying that we go on this cruise and sneak around to watch out for Skyler?"

"Exactly."

"I think this is a brilliant idea!"

"Now wait a minute," said Sidney, cutting through all of them. "You are *not* doing this. *I* am doing this. I'm going to call the cruise line now and explain that this is police business."

"We aren't doing this," said Mike.

"You're right. *You* aren't. *I* am." She had her phone in hand, jabbing at the keypad with her thumb.

"Sidney —"

"I need you to watch Fishbreath. I told Skyler I would."

"I can't check on Fishbreath. My allergies, remember?"

"Then wear a surgical mask — Hello, this is Detective Sidney Feldman with the Redlands Police Department, badge number one forty-two. I am following a suspected felon who is traveling onboard one of your ships scheduled to sail this evening. The —" She snapped her fingers at Philip.

"The Exaltation."

"The Exaltation. Yes, this is a police matter and the utmost emergency. I'll hold."

Mike raised his hands in frustration. "The station will never pay for this."

"I don't care. I'm going."

"And we will go with you!" Rodolfo declared.

"You're not."

"You can't stop us."

"*I* can," said Philip. "We are not going."

"We are. You know, Philip, sometimes our friends are more important than common sense."

"Yeah," said Jamie. "And besides, this isn't a fun trip. We won't be able to lay out in the sun or go to the dance parties. We have to lay low."

"Wow." Dave looked at Jamie anew. "I thought…well, I thought you were just looking for an excuse to get in on this cruise deal."

"How can you say that to me? This is about Skyler and Skyler alone. And we can all share a room."

"I'm not sharing a room with all you goons," said Sidney, sighing into the phone. The operator got back on the line and connected her to a supervisor. "Yeah. Yeah. Only one room left?"

Four pairs of eyes stared at her anxiously.

"Shit. How many people does it sleep? I have a *team* going with me. Five? Well isn't that just perfect. Okay. Book it. We'll be there before you sail." She clicked off the phone and dug her hand into her hip. "Everyone go home and pack *very* lightly. I mean it. Anyone brings a trunk and I'm chucking it overboard. And grab your passports. I guess we're going on a cruise."

Part Three

"I never knew what real happiness was until I got married. And by then it was too late."
– **Max Kauffmann**

Chapter Fourteen

SKYLER BUZZED WITH EXCITEMENT. AND SOMETHING of relief. Whoever this stalker was, Skyler felt better knowing that there was little chance of the guy following him and Keith on their honeymoon, especially with Keith driving the way he was on the freeways. No one could keep up with that!

Glancing out the windows, Skyler followed their journey and tried to come up with exactly where they were going. They had hopped on the 10 and were going in distinctly the opposite direction from the mountains. *Strike that off the list,* he thought. Unless they were headed for northern California. But at the juncture at the 605, they headed south. *Okay, where does that go?*

"Having fun trying to guess?" said Keith, grinning like a Cheshire cat.

"It's frustrating. I have to confess I can't imagine where we're going at this point. Unless..." Maybe the beach? But what beach? If they were going to San Diego they've been off course from the start. Long Beach? That's what it looked like. Well, there was a gay area in downtown Long Beach. Maybe they'd be staying there.

He scrutinized the freeway signs. "Commodore Schuyler F. Helm Bridge Terminal Island? Where the hell are we going? Wait, are we going to the Queen Mary? It's a hotel now, right?"

"It is but that's not quite where we're heading."

"Well what the hell. It now says Piers F to J and it clearly says the Queen Ma— Wait. Wait. You didn't?"

"Didn't I?"

Trembling hands clutched the arm rests, and he stared slack-jawed out the windshield. "Keith. You aren't…you didn't…are we…going on a…cruise?"

"Bingo!"

"Oh my God!" He jumped up but was yanked back by the seatbelt. "Oh my God!" He grabbed Keith's arm.

"Hey, watch it! I want to get there in one piece."

"I'm sorry. I just can't believe it. Are we really?"

"Yes, we really are."

"You are the best! Oh. But isn't that too expensive?"

"It's really not that bad, what with coupons and triple A discounts."

"I can't believe you. You're taking me on a cruise. Me, on a cruise… Oh no. Do I have sunblock?"

"Philip made sure that all that was there. And if it isn't I will personally walk you around the deck with an umbrella."

"Keith, I love you so much!"

"And I love you, babe. I wanted something memorable."

"As if anything with you wouldn't be. A cruise. Where?"

"Well, we spend a day in Catalina—"

"Oh my God, I've never been there!"

"And then Ensenada—"

"But Keith. I don't have my passport!"

"Oh no, why didn't I think to pack your passport? Oh wait. I did."

He slapped Keith's shoulder. "I can't believe you."

"And then there's a day 'out to sea' just cruising around, I guess, and then we're back early Wednesday morning to Long Beach."

"And there're buffets and restaurants and dancing and stuff like that?"

"All of that."

"You are too good to me."

"I do like my arm candy."

"Oh, I guarantee you. I will be *such* arm candy! Oh! So that's why you insisted we buy our tuxes. You rascal, you."

"So you're surprised?"

"*So* surprised." He sat back in the seat and bit his lip, grinning. His heart pounded with a new excitement. That meant that Keith would be in his swimsuit, and he loved Keith in that tight, sexy swimsuit. And there would be fine dining, and wine, and travel. He turned his head along the headrest to gaze at his…his husband. "This is like a dream."

"It is, isn't it. I can't wait to get you into our cabin."

"Is that all you can think about? Sex, sex, sex?"

"That's a lot of what I'm thinking about."

"Ooo. Good."

They took the long, curving overpass toward the terminal and Keith maneuvered the truck into the correct parking area. When they both got out and began pulling out luggage and garment bags, other people in the lot cheered and whistled. Skyler couldn't figure out why until he remembered the "Just Married" painted on the side of the black Ford.

Keith glanced at it with a frown.

"Well, you knew Jamie was going to do something."

"I suppose it's better than dragging dildos down the freeway."

Skyler laughed and wheeled his bags behind Keith.

Once in the enormous terminal, Keith handed Skyler his passport and they went through the process of checking in and going through security. As soon as they got past the checkpoint, photographers were there in numbers, snapping shots of arriving passengers. "I feel like a celebrity," said Skyler, as he pocketed business card after business card. But soon the flashes started to annoy as they waited to move forward.

"I suppose everyone's gotta have a job," he quipped.

"An annoying job," grumbled Keith, pushing his way through some particularly tenacious paparazzi.

At last they embarked up the wide gangplank, wheeling their luggage behind them. "When does it sail, Keith?"

"Five-thirty tonight. We'll see our room first, have some time to hang around, and then they'll instruct us about the lifeboats."

Skyler shivered. "I don't want to think about that."

"Safety first."

"You are such a cop." He shook his head, laughing, until he noticed his surroundings. Soaring ceilings lit up like a casino; mirrored walls, glass-fronted walkways, sparkling mosaic floors, shops… "Wow."

"Not bad, huh? We're on the upper deck."

"Not steerage?"

"Not for this honeymoon."

Skyler followed Keith into the glass-walled elevator and up they went. He planted his face to the glass, watching as they passed each floor laid out like some elaborate layer cake. "Have you ever been on a cruise before?"

"No. I thought this would be something different for the both of us. There's plenty of shopping, and even an old movie night."

Skyler sighed. "You must really love me."

He slipped his arm around Skyler's waist and squeezed. "I really do."

The elevator opened to the Verandah deck and Keith led the way down the long corridor to room 8202. "You seem to know your way around."

"I looked at a map."

Skyler couldn't stop smiling. Not only were they on a cruise ship, but here was Keith being...well, Keith. Without even thinking, his hand slipped into Keith's.

"Here it is," he said. "Shall I carry you over the—"

Skyler put up his hands. "Don't even think about it."

Keith chuckled as he fit the card key in the lock, and then opened the door, offering Skyler entrance first.

Walking in, Skyler stopped. "This is a suite."

"Yup."

"Keith, we can't afford this."

"Yes, we can. Trust me. I didn't break the bank."

A huge basket of fruit, chocolates, cookies, and cheeses, along with a bottle of champagne sat on the desk. A note read, "Compliments of the Crew to the Newlyweds." There was also two towels on the bed set up like swans with heart-shaped necks.

"Keith, look at this!"

"That's awesome."

When he looked up, the drapes were wide open, revealing the Long Beach Harbor. "We have a *balcony*? Are you insane?" Without waiting he ran to the door, jiggered with the lock a moment, and then threw it open. The salty spray and breeze tossed his hair back, but he felt the warmth of the sun on his cheek and inhaled the fresh air. The balcony wasn't huge, but had a small table just big enough for cocktails with two chairs, and looked to be completely private. He turned around, back to the railing. "I can't believe this!"

Keith watched him, eyes moving over him, until those blue eyes seemed to darken. "Come here."

Walking slowly, Skyler did. They stood toe to toe for a moment, simply looking at one another, before Keith reached for him. Hands cupping Skyler's face, he bent down for a kiss. His lips teased at Skyler's, and Skyler could feel the man holding back, trembling with the effort to keep under control. But Skyler didn't see the point. He reached up and slid his arms under Keith's and tugged him closer, chest to chest. He angled his face and opened his mouth, kissing deeply, welcoming the scratchy sensation of Keith's scruff against his own smooth jaw. He sucked on Keith's tongue until the man groaned, grinding his groin against Skyler's, proving that Keith was just as hard as he was.

He tore himself away and unbuckled his own belt before he dropped to his knees and worked on Keith's zip.

"Oh babe," he moaned, fingers combing through Skyler's hair.

Skyler made fast work of the zipper and pulled down Keith's briefs enough to release his thick beast of a cock. His nose filled with the warm musk of him before he opened wide and sucked it in. One hand stretched up under Keith's shirt to glide up that furred belly, while his other hand was busy releasing *his* dick and he took himself in hand, slowly stroking.

Keith widened his stance, allowing Skyler access to his balls. Slipping his hand into Keith's briefs, Skyler gently fondled them. He slurped the fat meat of his cock, running his tongue up and around the head, tasting the first bitter fluid of pre-cum, and laving the crown before closing his lips just at the underside near the tip and flicking his tongue.

"You're teasing," gasped Keith.

"Mm hmm," Skyler admitted, closing his lips fully around the head again and sucking him in deeper. He opened his throat and took him down.

Keith rolled his hips and thrust at Skyler's face. "Shit. Wound so tight. Gonna come."

Skyler sped his efforts on his own cock, bringing himself as close as Keith was. He sucked on the up stroke, and covered him deeper, letting that dick hit the back of his throat just as Keith unloaded. He kept it there, nose deep into the man's sweaty pubic hair, throat open to take his release, lips tight around the pulsating dick.

Keith's fingers clutched hard at his hair, and he thrust once, cock so deeply embedded Skyler wondered if he'd ever breathe again. But he loved the feel of it, the loss of his man's control, that thick cock unleashing its load that he would soon taste — and he couldn't hold on anymore. He couldn't shout with a mouth and throat full of Keith cock, but he shuddered and spurt in a puddle on the carpet. He milked himself, easing his fingers over his quivering flesh until he released his cock, sticky hand reaching for the floor to steady himself as he pulled off of Keith's softening meat.

He sucked in air with flushed cheeks, and his eyes felt bleary, but he looked up satisfied at his lover's face, who was looking down at him with an equal measure of gratification and tenderness. "That makes it official," said Keith dreamily. He didn't pull up his pants as he swung around and sat on the edge of the bed. "Need a hand?"

He grabbed Skyler's waiting hand and pulled him up to sit beside him.

Skyler left his trousers open too, and they both sat, pants hanging open, silly grins on their faces, staring at each other's limp dicks. Keith leaned in and kissed Skyler with a loud smack. "Mm. Tastes like me."

"The best flavor ever invented." Skyler flung himself onto his back, toying with his softened prick. "I could take a nap, what with all that champagne from the wedding, but I don't want to. We have a ship to explore."

"Yeah," said Keith, lying beside him. "We should get up." Except that neither of them moved for about five minutes. Finally, Skyler sprang up.

"Come on, lazy bones. I know you're old, but try to keep up with your young husband."

"We aren't starting with that, are we? That balcony is looking mighty useful about now."

He grabbed Keith's hand. "Come on! Should we change?"

"We'll run out of clothes if we change at every opportunity. These are fine. Didn't get any cum on my pants, did I?"

"No. And neither did I. So we're good to go." With his trousers and underwear around his ankles, he waddled to the bathroom, sponged himself off, tucked in, and drew everything back up into place.

"I think we should take a walk, get to know the ship. See where the bars are," said Skyler.

"You young whipper snappers, always looking for the bar scene."

"Come on!"

"All right, all right." He gave Skyler a quick kiss. "Let's go."

They wandered the ship, poking their heads into bars and shops, strolling up along the Lido deck, investigating the pool, the theater, the lounges. They decided to head to one of the bars and took a seat by the window to watch the goings-on at the pier. Just to be in the spirit of the thing, Skyler ordered a colorful rum drink with an umbrella and scads of fruit on a skewer, which he dared Keith to order. Not taking the bait, Keith ordered a beer.

It wasn't long until the signal was given that all were aboard and they would set sail. The gangplank swung away and the ship's horn blew a long, loud drone.

Skyler was disappointed that there was no other fanfare of streamers and confetti with the passengers at the railing, but they made their way outside anyway and stood with the others, waving to the shore. It wasn't long after that that all the passengers were called to go to their separate lifeboat drills. For Skyler, it was a long hour standing in his lifevest, though he was sure to listen carefully, check his vest, and where he would sit if they had to abandon ship.

And after that, they were free to do what they wanted.

"What shall we do?"

"Well, I was thinking we should probably get our dinner reservations."

"That would be nice. Let's make it for the later seating, huh? I think I'm still full from our reception."

A flash. Skyler blinked.

"Sorry, gentlemen," said a young women in a blue pantsuit carrying a camera. "My card. If you'd like your photo."

"Thanks." Skyler took it and tucked it in an ashtray when she wasn't looking. "More paparazzi."

"It's a different life aboard ship."

Exploring the ship took them to the purser's, where they looked over the activities for Catalina. "Skyler, have you ever kayaked?"

"No. I'd like to try, though."

"We can sign up for that, too."

"I could get used to this. Do we really have to go back home?"

"I suppose we could get jobs here. I could be security and you could be...hmm. Cruise director?"

"I'd be fabulous at that. And then I could wear a jaunty outfit…"

"Shorts?"

"Hmm. If people loved lily-white legs."

"I love your legs. I could lick one of them right now."

Skyler plucked the brochure from Keith's hand. "I've got a suggestion."

"I know. But I was actually thinking maybe change to our trunks and do a little Jacuzziing. After the stress of the wedding, we deserve to relax."

"And order more drinks."

"You really like those fruity drinks, don't you?"

"No comments, please. I just figured when in Rome. And I don't want to get plastered on Grey Goose. I have a whole evening planned, after all."

"Oh really."

"Yes, really. And I think you might know what I have in mind."

"I have an idea."

He grabbed Keith's hand. For some reason, he didn't feel that they were being judged, that they could be themselves. He swung his hand as they walked, shielding his eyes from the sun streaming in through the windows.

They changed into their trunks, threw on their shirts and shorts, and headed out.

There was plenty of room in the hot tub and Skyler got to order his drink poolside, which made him feel decadent. Soon, a young couple in their thirties joined them.

"Hi. I'm Brian Cherry, and this is my wife Macy," said the man.

"Hi," said Skyler. "I'm Skyler, and this is my new husband Keith."

Macy's eyes crinkled when she smiled. "Your *new* husband?"

"I guess that sounds weird. What I meant was, we just got married today."

"This is your honeymoon! Oh, congratulations. I hope you'll be very happy."

"Thanks. It's our first cruise, too."

"Oh, we've been on tons of them, haven't we, Brian? And we just wanted a quick getaway from the kids, you know? Do you have kids?"

"Not at the moment," said Keith. "But we're both high school teachers, so we still have kids to get away from."

"That's funny," said Macy in her bubbly way. She elbowed Brian. "Isn't that funny?"

"Yeah." Skyler got the impression that he wasn't as enamored of being in a Jacuzzi with a couple of gay men. But Skyler was feeling too good to care. He concentrated on Macy.

"So what do you do, Macy?"

"Well, I teach Sunday school at our church, and I homeschool the kids — we have two, a girl and a boy — but grandma will do the honors till we get back. Brian owns a construction rental company, Cherry Rentals. That's our name, Cherry. You know, he rents out equipment? Diggers and tractors and stuff."

"That must be pretty interesting," said Keith. "Nothing like boy's toys, huh? As for me, I'm also head football coach for the school."

Brian perked up at that. Skyler wanted to shake a finger at Keith, but he knew why he mentioned football. Suddenly, Keith was no longer a gay guy in the hot tub. He was a regular football-loving guy. "No kidding," said Brian. "How's your school rank?"

"Actually, we're doing real good this year. We've made it to the CIF."

"I played some ball in high school."

Skyler nudged Macy with his elbow. "And they're off and running," he said to her. "Whenever he gets to talk football with a true believer, I just get out of the way."

"Isn't that the truth! I can't stand sports myself. But Brian is into everything to do with football, even our local college games. Wears the shirts and everything."

He got in close. "I'm not one for it either, though I do go to our high school games to support my students."

"Isn't that nice of you. You could not pay me to go."

They laughed, and Skyler waved over the waiter to get Macy a drink. Soon they were laughing like loons over their fruity drinks, while Keith and Brian were going at it about percentages and point spreads. Brian said that the pool big screen often showed the games, and Keith seemed interested in that.

"You two are real cute together," said Macy.

"Why thank you, Macy. So are you two."

"We are not! We're just an old married couple."

"Is it good, though? I was a little anxious making the commitment at first."

She sipped her strawberry drink down to the bottom, sucking loudly. "Oh yeah. Everyone has their ups and downs. We've had some loud fights for sure. But in the end, it's still just us being us. When you have your first fight, you'll know."

"We've had some fights."

"But you made up. Just take it in stride. I mean, you are two different people after all. There are bound to be disagreements." She took the strawberry off its skewer and began eating it. "You know, I know Brian doesn't know very many gay guys, and our church isn't big on it, but I've always liked gay people."

Here comes the drunk part of the evening, Skyler mused.

"People are just people, you know," she went on.

"I know."

"I'm real glad your Keith is a football player. Cause that will shut up anything Brian'll have to say about it later."

"It will?" he asked innocently.

"Oh yeah! I bet you anything, the first thing he'll say to me is, 'that queer guy wasn't half bad,'" she said, mocking her husband's voice. "And then he'll say something like, 'he was real macho, too. Not like I expected at all.'"

"That's good."

"I know. You try to open a person's mind, but it's hard."

"Tell me about it."

She pushed at his shoulder. "Like *I* have to tell *you*. But cruises are real good places for LGBT people. There's so much partying to do, no one has time to be a bigot about it."

"That's good to know."

"No, really. Hey, I know I'm talking out of my you-know-what—alcohol always loosens me up—but I mean it. This is going to be fine. Listen. I better get out of here before I totally wrinkle up. Brian, you've talked that poor man's ear off enough. Let's get cleaned up for dinner."

Brian shook Keith's hand. "It was sure nice meeting you, Coach. Hope we can watch the game poolside Monday."

"I'd like that."

"All right, Macy. I'm coming." He climbed out and toweled off, and before he got too far away, Skyler just caught his saying, "You know, Macy, that queer guy wasn't half bad—"

He looked at Keith who was drinking his beer and nearly spat it across the hot tub.

"They weren't so bad," said Skyler.

"They weren't half bad for straights."

Now it was Skyler's turn to spit his drink.

A flash and Skyler got his picture taken again. He looked up and saw a man in a Hawaiian shirt. "Hey! I'm Mark. I didn't mean to disturb you, but this is what I do. Take pictures."

"I suppose you have a business card."

"Look, I know it seems like a pain, but if you do connect with a photographer, then the other ones leave you alone. Maybe I can do a few. You're under no obligation to pay for them. Just a few here and there, at dinner, that sort of thing."

"Well…we are on our honeymoon."

"That's awesome. Congratulations."

"Mark, leave your card. And yeah, you know what? Why don't you snap a few. We'll be in the Poseidon Room tonight for the later seating."

"Dude, that's awesome. Okay. I'm leaving my card on your towels. See you later. I'll be discreet, too. Tell me to scram and I will. Don't want to be keel-hauled. I'll shoot one more, then leave, okay?"

"Come on, Keith, scoot over." Keith floated over, put his arm around him, and they both smiled for the camera.

"Beautiful. So you are Keith and…"

"Skyler. We're in room 8202."

"Catch you later, guys."

Once the man left, Keith gave Skyler a peck. "Everyone is so friendly here."

Skyler agreed. "I know. It's too good to be true."

Chapter Fifteen

SIDNEY WAS ON HER LAST NERVE. THEY WAITED in the huge terminal as far away from Skyler and Keith as they could get. She'd spotted them right away and managed to herd his friends behind a counter and made them plunk themselves down.

"Honestly, you are like a bunch of children. This isn't a pleasure cruise."

"Well, actually," said Philip, "that's exactly what this is."

She speared him with a poison stare, and he shrank back. "For a minute there I thought your hair was going to turn into serpents," he muttered.

"Okay, listen up," she said as people started to board. "We check into our room and you *stay* there until I tell you to come out again."

"What?" cried Jamie. "I'm not going to be stuck in a tiny room until *you* say we can leave."

"I am in charge of this. What I say goes. If you don't like it you can stay behind."

"It's just that more eyes are better, aren't they? That's why we're here. No." He postured, hand on his hip. "We won't stay in the room."

"Jamie is right," said Rodolfo. "More eyes to watch Skyler. That is our primary goal."

"Jesus, all right! But honestly, you have got to stay out of the way. And for God's sake, don't let him see you."

They let the couple get far ahead of them before they moved *en masse* to the gangplank. Once checked in they headed for deck four, traveled down the long hallway, and found their room. It was just as she expected. No window, two bunk beds, two twins, and a pullout sofa. "I feel like I'm in a Marx Brothers movie," she sighed, "and all of you are Zeppo."

"No, he was the bland one," said Philip. "We are all far from bland."

"I'm going to tell all of you right now. There is to be no hanky panky. No masturbation, mutual or otherwise."

Rodolfo made a scoffing noise.

"I'm not kidding. I don't want to listen to any of that. And no nudity. I do not want any of that burned into my retinas."

"Well, then likewise, missy," said Jamie. "Keep the tits incognito, *capice*?"

"I don't mind," said Rodolfo.

"You don't mind about breasts?" asked Philip.

Rodolfo shrugged. "We are all friends here. And we are here for Skyler. And these are tight accommodations," he said, looking around with a scowl.

"All right," she said. "Suit yourself. I'm getting back out there. I'm calling one of the twin beds," and she tossed her small bag onto the one on the right.

"I want the bunk," chirped Jamie. "Dave, get the other one!"

"I feel like I'm back at the station," he grumbled, throwing his small gym bag up on the bunk opposite. He put Jamie's up on the other one.

"Sweetheart," said Philip to Rodolfo, "do you want the other twin, or the sofa?"

"Oh no, my Philip. *You* choose."

"I wouldn't dream of imposing."

"But I don't want you to be uncomfortable…"

"Oh for fuck's sake!" Sidney grabbed each of their bags and heaved one at the twin, and the other at the sofa. "All sorted. Let's go!"

"You know," said Philip, arms crossed over his chest. "A little courtesy goes a long way. We are just as worried about Skyler as you are."

She paused in the doorway, recalling a similar conversation with Mike. "You don't always have to be so brash," he'd told her. "Rudeness doesn't always help."

She took a deep breath and blew it out. "Okay. You're right. I'm sorry. And I appreciate you guys all coming. Thanks for doing that."

There were sighs all around and then they maneuvered into a group hug before she squirmed out of it. "But we really need to go."

With her badge, she had ascertained Skyler's room number, but with the configuration of the hallways, it would be impossible to stake it out without being seen. "Let's split up. Everyone take a section of the ship. See if you can find them. And stay out of sight. That won't be easy."

"You're telling us," said Dave. He kissed Jamie. "See you later."

Rodolfo kissed Philip as if he wouldn't see him again till the end of the voyage. They parted, and Sidney was finally alone.

She appreciated them. She really did. But it was times like these that she wished she was with Mike or some other police partner. She might have to move fast, and she didn't want to worry about their safety either. But when you've got friends as determined as that…well. It was probably best just to let them help. She had to grudgingly admit that she was proud of those idiots for insisting.

She decided to stake out the glass elevators. After all, she doubted they would take the stairs from the eighth floor. It didn't take long from her vantage to spot them. She counted the decks. Looking down at the map of the ship on her phone, she realized they were on the Lido deck. The pool. Seemed a bit brisk for the pool so they were likely headed for the Jacuzzi.

She took the elevator up and texted the others.

They're headed for the pool area. Likely the hot tub.

How were they going to do this for four days? Was it practical? She'd talk to their cabin steward, see if she couldn't get him to keep an eye out, too.

According to the map, the elevators on this end, opened nearly to the hot tub. She turned her back as the lift opened and hurried out, skirting around the Jacuzzis. She needn't have worried. They were raised up on a platform above the pool. Now to settle in and patrol the area.

She spotted Philip and Dave arriving from the other end of the pool.

Philip spotted her, and like Paul Newman in *The Sting*, he flicked his finger alongside of his nose to indicate he'd spotted her and them.

Another couple joined them in the hot tub and it all seemed friendly enough. Sidney took a seat at the outdoor bar and ordered a plain tonic. She watched the pool, the people milling and finding seats. She didn't notice anyone, man or woman, who seemed to pay them any particular attention.

When the other couple left them, a photographer came over, took their picture, talked for a moment, and then moved on. He and Keith stayed side by side, even kissed a little in the hot tub. Skyler looked so happy. She'd never seen him look quite like that. And then she felt like a perv watching them. This was a private moment. They never expected anyone to be watching them. She felt like a heel...except that that note kept her on edge. Mike had waited for the forensic people. They looked at the footage, saw a little girl—one of Keith's relatives, she thought— place it on the table. She was probably asked to by the would-be killer. They'd have to find her and ask her what they looked like. She was glad Mike was on it. He'd turn up something. And then, looking around, she wondered if Mike would like to take a cruise. She'd have to look into it when all this was over.

Philip made his way over to her and sat on a stool beside her. "This is hard work."

She toyed with the straw in her untouched drink. "Yeah, I know. A stakeout is never easy."

"Have you noted anything suspicious? I haven't seen a thing."

"No, I haven't."

"Any word from Mike?"

"Nothing."

They both watched the happy couple, touching and kissing, eyes only for each other, and Philip sighed. "You know, I never thought I'd see the day where Skyler fell for anyone, let alone marry him."

"You and me both. Except that...he really did want someone for his own. He would just never admit it."

"Was he lonely?"

"I think in a way he was. He was just too busy to notice. Until he wasn't."

"I see what you mean. When I knew him in college, he was a very busy boy indeed. There wasn't a night where he was sleeping alone."

"By that time I was at the academy. Hoo, how I worried about that kid."

"And you still worry."

"Who wouldn't? Why and how he got himself into this mess I will never know."

Philip grabbed her glass, took a sip from the watery drink, grimaced, and put it down again. "Do you really think this person is on board?"

"There was every indication. The cruise line just emailed me the passenger list. We can go over it tonight."

"But we don't know if we're looking for a man or a woman."

"I have a gut feeling it's a woman. Just the way everything was done; the stair step, the car brakes, the letter bomb. It's distant. I feel like a man would have done more already, moved on it more personally. And if she did get on this ship, that meant she did more than just watch Skyler's house. She had to have hacked into their wifi somehow. How else did she know Keith was making these reservations?"

"This is pretty elaborate."

"But it's just the thing an obsessed person would do. I'm really worried, Philip."

"Well, she'd have to get through Keith first."

"Yeah. That worries me, too. We'd best keep an eye out on anything food and drinkwise that comes to them. Follow it from bar or kitchen to table. Let's find out what they're doing for dinner tonight."

"Isn't it group seating?"

"Yes, but there are restaurants now on cruise ships, too. Mr. Romance might have reserved one of the restaurants tonight so they could dine alone."

"Wow. Have you profiled all of us?"

"Of course. God, you people are the easiest in the world."

"Well thanks. So much for feeling like an original."

She squeezed his arm. "I'm sorry. It's just a cop thing. I'll bet you anything Keith has done it for you guys, too."

"I don't know that I'm encouraged by that."

"So what do you think of all this, about Skyler getting married?" She studied him earnestly. For a while in college, she was almost sure Skyler might start dating Philip, and was slightly disappointed that he hadn't.

"Do you mean do I think it was a good thing that Skyler got married?" said Philip. "Yes. Yes I do. Of all the men I'd seen Skyler with—and God knows that list is long—I'd never seen him act like he did when Keith showed up. Talk about obsessed."

"He was, wasn't he? He was well and truly caught. It was something to see. And encouraging. I think it's what made me make a move on Mike. That was such a delicate thing at the station. You are definitely not supposed to fraternize with your partner, let alone marry him. Fortunately, my captain is a mensch and it all worked out. I can't see working with anyone else but Mike."

"I'm glad it worked out for you both. Mike is a great guy."

"Thanks. Oh! They're on the move. Can you watch them to the elevators? I'm sure they'll be returning to their room. I'll contact the others and we'll rendezvous back at whatever restaurant."

She watched Philip leave, almost a little sorry Skyler didn't choose him. But she liked Keith. He might be a little pushy but she couldn't help liking the cop in him. He was definitely a take charge kind of guy. Maybe that's what Skyler had needed most. Not that Skyler wasn't a take charge kind of guy, too, just with a different kind of priority.

God, but she hated watching him.

They all met back in the lobby, keeping an eye on the elevators at the aft of the ship. She'd found out that they had made reservations at the Poseidon main room, not a restaurant after all.

"What about us?" asked Jamie. "I don't know about anyone else but I'm feeling peckish."

"Tell you what," said Sidney. "Two of you take off and eat in one of the dining rooms or the bar and grill, and two of you can watch with me at the main dining room."

It was decided that Jamie and Dave would get to the pub first, and Philip and Rodolfo hung with her.

"So you think we are looking for a woman?" asked Rodolfo, glancing around.

"I think so. I mean, let's not rule out a man, but my instincts say it's a woman. Listen, after they retire for the night, I have an appointment with security and I can go over the tapes, see if we missed anything."

"That will be useful," said Philip. "But they might go dancing or something."

Sidney gave him a side-eye, and Philip conceded it. "Of course you're right. They'll be fucking like crazed weasels."

Rodolfo lifted a finger. "Weasels?"

"It's just an expression, darling."

Sidney's stomach growled. A few appetizers wouldn't go amiss about now. But either way, she was looking at a long night.

Chapter Sixteen

KEITH AND SKYLER GOT READY FOR DINNER, putting on their tuxes. Their cabin steward, Guillermo, had left a note welcoming them aboard and letting them know that he would provide ice twice daily.

Skyler watched Keith getting ready. "Have I mentioned how romantic this whole thing is."

"I am nothing if not romantic."

"Actually, you're pretty amazing."

They got to the main dining room at the aft of the ship, and were seated immediately at a table for eight. An older couple was already seated there and they greeted Skyler and Keith.

Keith ordered the T-bone, while Skyler went with a fish dish. He noticed Mark with his camera and waved. Mark was slender and wore a dark suit. He arrived at their table and took his shots, and then left them alone to dine.

The man seated across from them looked at them over the rim of his glasses. "What's the story with you fellas? Looking to find some sexy women on this voyage?"

Skyler placed his napkin in his lap and toyed with it. "Uh...no, actually. We—Keith and I—are on our honeymoon. Together."

"Well, I'll be darned. Beverly, they're on their honeymoon."

"I heard him, Francis."

"Well how about that. So let me ask you fellas. How does that work?"

Beverly dropped her face in her hand.

Skyler looked from one to the other. "How does what work?"

"You know. You're two men. Do you love each other? Does it work like that? Hope you don't mind my asking."

Skyler was relieved. He didn't know what he expected, but it wasn't that. "Yes, it works just like that. Just like you and your wife. We're in love."

Keith grabbed his hand on the table.

"That's terrific. I said to Beverly, when all this gay marriage was on the TV, I asked her, 'Now why is there all this fuss? If they love each other like normal people, what's the big deal? Just let them get married.' And you do. Son of a gun. I never knew any gay people."

"Oh, I bet you do. You just don't know it."

"You know young man, you might be right. I always wondered about my lieutenant when I was in the Navy. Never saw him with a girl ever. I'm sure you're right."

"I'm absolutely sure." Skyler could tell that Keith was doing his best not to laugh. Maybe they both should be offended, but he couldn't help but feel the old man with the bad comb-over and thick glasses was cute in his naivete.

Beverly touched her husband's arm with a spotted hand bearing a large, sparkly cocktail ring. "Now stop bothering these nice boys with your questions, Francis. Let them eat their dinner."

"You don't mind all these questions, do you boys?" asked Francis.

Skyler scooped pieces of fish away from the bone with his fork. "Not at all. We're used to answering questions. We're high school teachers. I teach English Literature and Keith teaches biology and he's also head football coach."

"No kidding. Football, eh?"

"Used to play ball in college," said Keith, slicing into his bloody steak. "Almost went pro but hurt my knee."

"What do you know about that? Gay football player. That would have been something. Or—were you gay back then?"

"Francis!" scolded his wife.

"Bev, these boys said they don't mind."

"Well, sir," said Keith, talking like a Boy Scout, "I was always gay. It's not something you turn on or off."

"That's right. Of course," he said, stirring his coffee. "I knew that. In my day, gays were always in the closet."

"Why don't you let them eat their dinner, dear?"

"But this calls for a celebration! They're on their honeymoon. And it's always a honeymoon when I'm with you, Bev." He patted her hand. "So let's have some champagne. On me." He signaled the waiter.

Skyler settled in to eat, but dabbed at his mouth with a napkin before he asked, "How long have you two been married?"

"It will be fifty-three years this November, won't it Bev? My Beverly made an honest man of me and I've never looked back. Here's a piece of advice for you young fellas: Don't go to bed angry. And the wife is always right. Oh. But you can't use that one, can you?"

Skyler kicked Keith under the table when it looked like he might say something. Instead, Keith said, "We'll have to play that one by ear."

When the champagne arrived, they all clinked goblets, ate heartily, and chatted. All the while the ship chugged forth with just the barest of a rocking motion. "What time do we arrive in Catalina?" asked Skyler.

Keith had also ordered a glass of red wine and took a drink. "They said seven-thirty in the morning. We'll have the whole day, and then we sail again at four-thirty."

"Mmm. This ocean air is making me hungry. I was starved."

"You're sure plowing through that. Is it good?"

"Oh, the beurre blanc sauce is heavenly. And this flounder is so delicate. How's your giant piece of cow?"

"Very tender. Would you like a bite?"

"No thanks. Flounder?"

"That's okay."

Beverly and Francis were chatting with some new arrivals, another older couple. "This has been such a relaxing day," said Skyler. "I don't think I've ever had a better vacation."

"And we've only just gotten started."

"That's right. Kayaking tomorrow. I've always wanted to try that, but I've been a little afraid of it."

"Why? You're a good swimmer if you capsize."

"It's that part. Afraid I'll get stuck."

"They'll give you lessons before we head out. And I'll be there."

"To save the day." He toyed with the fish, swishing it in the buttery sauce. "You know," he said quietly so the others couldn't hear. "It isn't that I don't appreciate it, but it kind of hurts a guy's ego to have to be saved all the time."

"Well…I *could* let you drown. But it is my honeymoon. And the room isn't refundable."

"You know what I mean."

Keith's smile faded. "I don't like us to get into a position where I have to 'save' you. Besides, at last count, I think you're ahead in the saving department."

"Am I?"

"Yeah. You saved yourself last time. With those moves you learned in your self-defense class."

"That's right! I threw the perp over my shoulder." He mimed it, still proud of himself. "I — that's funny."

"What?"

"I thought I saw a guy who looked just like Philip."

"There's gotta be a million guys who look like Philip. He's got a 'look', after all."

"Speaking of, uh, by the way, a few days ago, I went back to the University of Redlands bookstore."

Keith set his knife and fork down. His jaw tightened. "What for?"

"Well, you heard what Mike said. The guy who's stalking me had a U of R hoodie. A new one. I used to work in the bookstore so I had a talk with the manager. She came to the wedding. Debbie. Sort of round, middle-aged lady with the Hawaiian print dress?"

"Oh yeah."

"So anyway, she's getting me the list she gave to the cops of all the hoodie purchases since the beginning of the school year."

"Shouldn't we let Sidney handle that?"

"Do you ever get tired of that broken record?"

Keith sighed and snatched up his wine glass. He drank quickly and set it down, caging the goblet in his fingers. "Sorry. We agreed, didn't we?"

"Yes. We did."

"I really didn't want to think about this on our trip." His gazed lingered on the older couples who were fully engaged in conversation, laughing now and again.

"I know. But maybe away from distractions we can think about it, work on it ourselves, you know. And you can call Sidney or Mike for updates."

"Okay. Yeah."

They finished dinner, shook hands with their tablemates, promising to see them again, and decided to go for a stroll along the Lido deck and look at the stars.

In was cold and the wind whirled over them. Skyler hunkered close to Keith, holding his hand tight to his body. "This is just beautiful."

"I'm so happy to be here with you, babe. I can't tell you how much."

They stopped to lean on the rail and watch the water. The moonlight caught on each wave and crest, reflecting the foamy wake of the ship in silver flashes. "This was so unexpected," said Skyler softly. "Not just the cruise — that was an amazing surprise. But…you. Us. Sometimes my head is still reeling…but in a good way."

Keith's arm tightened around Skyler's waist. "It was completely unexpected for me. I know you think that just because you were cute and blond that I was set to fall for you. Everyone says that. But it isn't true. I've hooked up with plenty of cute blonds. But you were something special."

"Was it easier or harder my being at the same school?"

"Much harder. As you might recall, I was trying *not* to like you."

"And doing a darned good job. The names I called you when your back was turned…"

"I can imagine. And you just got cuter and cuter. I was such a goner."

Leaning his arms over the rails, Skyler toyed with the ring on his finger, still a slightly foreign feeling. "But did you ever expect this?"

"No, not really. I hoped I'd meet a guy I could build a life with. Yeah, I was attracted to you, but I wasn't sure you were the One. Well…not right away, anyway."

"I fought it mighty hard."

"I know. I'll still never fully understand that."

"I have a lot of baggage."

"I know. And yet...here we are."

Skyler turned. "Here we are. You know, I think I'd like to go back to our cabin now."

Keith's tender expression flickered with desire. "That's a good idea," he rasped.

They walked together back inside to the elevators. Once they reached their floor they walked down the long hallway and finally to their room.

Inside, Keith turned on a bedside lamp. It offered just enough warm glow for them to see each other, but not too much to blast the room with light.

"Now that I finally have you alone on our honeymoon..." said Keith.

Skyler waggled his brows. "Yeees?"

"I wanted to talk."

Skyler deflated. "Uh...okay."

Keith seemed nervous, which was endearing in one sense but worrying in another. He toyed with the card key before he set it down on the desk. "I just wondered...I mean, we've done a lot of stuff. A *lot* of stuff. Sexual stuff. But I don't think I ever directly asked what it is you liked best."

Eyes widened, Skyler stared. "Are you kidding?"

"Babe, I just want to start out right. Yeah. We've had sex in every which way and you've been a champ about all of that—"

"So have you, but that's not quite true."

"True about what?"

"That we've done everything. We've never done bondage. Or done any dom/sub scenes. Or spanking."

"Oh. D-do you w-want to do that?"

Skyler laughed, mostly at Keith's alarmed expression. "No! I'm not into that. Or threesomes. Or foursomes. Not anymore."

"Not anymore."

"Yeah. Sometimes things get confused. I guess maybe that's part of the charm, not knowing whose cock or whose butt is in your face, but it isn't for me."

"Thank God," he muttered.

"So what is it you mean? Piercings? Do you like pierced nipples? Do you want me to get one?" He stretched toward Keith, shimmying his shoulders. Keith's eyes traveled down to Skyler's chest. "Or tattoos? Would it turn you on if I had a piercing or a tattoo?"

Keith seemed to snap back. "Not particularly."

"Well thank God." Absently he rubbed his chest. "I'm not a fan of sharp things. Especially Prince Alberts." He shuddered. "Not me."

"No piercings for me either. And you don't want me to get a tattoo, do you?"

"And interfere with all that hair? Absolutely not."

Keith chuckled. He shifted closer, closing his hands on Skyler's upper arms. "You do like that, don't you? My chest hair."

"You know I love it. So my preferences. Do I like to be sucked? Why yes, I do. Do I like to suck?" He got in close again, lips inches from Keith's. "Why yes, I do…as long as it's you. Do I like to be penetrated? I most certainly do." He leaned away again, feeling the loss of heat from Keith's presence. "And now you have heard the description of my preferences. Most definitely vanilla and certainly a bottom. But I think you already know that."

Keith smiled sheepishly.

Skyler shook his head. "Sometimes you are so ridiculous. But I'll play your silly game. What's *your* favorite? A little butt play, a little cock frotting?"

His arms slid and took Skyler in an embrace. "I think you know I'm a big fan of fucking you."

"Deep and rough? Because if we're being specific here, that's what I really like."

Keith kissed him, surprisingly gentle for the thread of the conversation. "Okay. And just for the record, I'm pretty turned on right now."

"I should hope so," he said quietly.

Keith said no more, and, steadying his gaze, took off his jacket and pulled at his bow tie.

Skyler scuffed out of his shoes and removed his jacket as well.

They each watched the other undress: shirts, trousers, socks, underwear... Skyler let Keith step out of his but he left his own on, a system of straps where his stiff cock strained against a pouch of black mesh. And when he was sure Keith's eyes were glued there, he slowly turned, showing off how more straps framed his naked butt perfectly. "You like?"

"Damn." Keith reached out and glided his hand over Skyler's exposed ass. "That is fucking hot."

"Well, just for the record, I'm still impressed every time I see that," said Skyler, staring at Keith's considerable erection, standing straight up from his body.

"And I've always been mesmerized by that porcelain skin of yours."

Skyler felt that skin blush a little. "Mr. Fletcher, you say the sweetest things."

"So, are you going to keep on that underwear for a while?" said Keith, already reaching for him.

"Do you want me to?"

Suddenly Skyler was pressed against all that warm skin and furred torso. Their hard cocks — Keith's naked one, Skyler's clothed — slid across the other. *I guess that's my answer.* Skyler lifted his face and planted his mouth to Keith's. They kissed, each heated exchange growing hotter as their lips joined, slid, gnawed. Keith tore away and sucked on his neck. His hand traveled down Skyler's sides until he reached his ass and squeezed both exposed globes.

Keith's nibbling mouth had reached Skyler's chest and found a nipple, licking it to a pink peak. "Don't need these pierced," he growled, teasing them with his teeth. Keith's hand slid down and cupped Skyler's sac over the mesh, rolling his balls gently between his fingers.

Skyler grasped Keith's shoulders to steady himself. "Fuck," he whispered, kissing the top of that dark head.

Keith let him go for a moment and urged him back to the bed, laying Skyler back. Keith covered him, kissing and nipping at his chin, his throat, hands busy, one at the taut nipple, another at Skyler's groin. He released Skyler's cock from the mesh pouch and slowly stroked the rock-hard flesh.

Skyler couldn't reach Keith's dick, which Keith was frotting under Skyler's sac against the soft flesh there, but he did manage to squeeze his fingers into Keith's muscled ass, feeling as the sinews stretched and rolled.

All of a sudden, Keith pulled away and flipped Skyler over.

"Hey! Warn a guy."

"Sorry. I just want to get at your ass." His fingers dug into Skyler's hips and yanked them up so he was bottoms up. He stuffed a pillow under him to keep him that way.

"I guess you do. What are you — ooooh." Keith bit lightly on the fleshy cheeks, pulling at a strap with his teeth before letting it slap back with a delicious sting. He kissed more of his butt, delicately licked, and then pressed his lips tight to the skin and sucked.

"God, I love your ass. It's so round and white and perfect. I just want to bite it." And he did, eliciting a yelp from Skyler.

Keith dug his thumbs into Skyler's cleft and spread him wide before bending forward to kiss his hole. The delicate skin spasmed under Keith's lips, until that tongue flicked and caressed in lazy, sensuous circles.

Skyler's hand reached for his cock, and he stroked languidly.

Keith's relentless tongue licked downward until he nipped at the flesh above his balls over the mesh, tugging on it with his teeth.

Skyler couldn't help but spread his legs and stick out his butt, wanting to get more of Keith's attention. Wide hands squeezed his ass again, pushing the cleft together and then pulling it apart. A tongue speared his hole then flicked away before a wetted finger intruded.

"Where did we put the damn lube?" Keith muttered against his skin.

"You're doing okay for now."

Keith chuckled and nipped again at his butt, taking both sides of the straps and using them like reins, swaying his butt this way and that. "Am I?"

"Yes," said Skyler breathlessly. "Incredibly well."

Keith kissed the place he nipped, nipped again, and then kissed it once more. "I'm getting the lube." The bed rocked when he rose and Skyler watched over his shoulder as a naked Keith, cock jutting away from him and bobbing as he walked, went to the closet in search of the lube.

Skyler waggled his butt impatiently. "Come on. Where is it?"

"Keep doing that and I'll unload before I have a chance at you."

"Then get back here."

The bed dipped and Keith's hands smoothed up his back. One eased down to his butt again, caressing between the straps. "I think I really like this underwear of yours."

Skyler heard the splooge of the tube and then a thumb dipped into his hole. Keith eased it in and Skyler wiggled his ass again. "I am *so* ready for you it's not even funny."

Skyler watched over his shoulder as Keith got up on his knees. "I don't want to hurt you, babe."

"You won't."

Keith lubed himself, and got in close, grasping one side of the underwear straps. Skyler breathed and relaxed as that cock pressed against his hole and pushed inside. Keith took his time, hand rubbing soothing circles at the small of Skyler's back…until Skyler lifted his bottom and drove back at him. He glanced coyly over his shoulder. "You can give it to me, big boy. You know how I like it."

Keith slid his hands under the straps to tighten his grip on Skyler's hips, and slammed in.

Blinking, Skyler inhaled a sharp breath. *Damn*. He was never quite as prepared as he thought he was. "Aaaand if you could give me half a second."

Keith paused. "I told you I didn't want to hurt you."

"And you didn't. Just…a…sec…Okay."

Keith's shallow thrusts were slow, involuntary. "Are you sure now?"

"Very."

Sensation suddenly drove all thought and words from his head as Keith thrust in earnest, and all Skyler's attention focused on that. Keith nipped at Skyler's neck and ran his hands roughly down his sides. He moved with Keith, countering each thrust by backing into it. He massaged his own straining cock and pumped it, running his fingers over the weeping head, until a hand pushed his out of the way.

Keith grunted behind him when Skyler remembered. "Wait! Wait!"

Keith stopped. "What now?" he gasped.

Skyler fell forward and Keith's dick slipped out.

"Skyler, what are you…?"

"Hold on. I brought something for you." He hurried across the room to his suitcase and unzipped an outer pocket. "I slipped this in when I saw the suitcase in the closet. Ta da!" He held it up and Keith, flushed and panting, looked at it with perplexed eyes. A hard, plastic device, curved, with curly-cues springing forth from it, like a three-dimensional wingding. "It's a prostate massager."

"I thought that's what *I* was doing."

"It's not for me. It's for you."

"I'm not putting that in my ass."

"Oh, come on."

"Skyler, I don't do that kind of thing. Didn't we just get done talking about—"

"Live a little. You'll love it. You put that in while you're fucking me. I guarantee you —"

"I really don't want to do that."

Skyler pouted. "Won't you just try it? You might like it. I got it especially for you. It feels real good. And see? It's not like a dildo. It's small."

Keith frowned but, thankfully, his erection didn't flag. He rubbed his hand down his face. "You really want me to try this."

Grinning, Skyler nodded. "I'd like to help you with it," he said, voice low and seductive. "I'll go slow. Promise."

"Okay. Let's give it a go."

"Yes!" Skyler grabbed the lube, gave it a generous squirt, and painted it all over the business end of the massager, wiping his hand off on the sheets. "Now, uh, turn around and show me that plump, gorgeous ass of yours."

Keith did, making a show of arching his back and thrusting out his butt. Skyler swallowed. Damn. He did have a beautiful ass, all round, muscular, and fuzzy. He ran his hands over it, just feeling the muscle twitch under his touch. "I'm gonna start with my finger."

"I'd appreciate that."

"Just breathe." But instead of sticking his finger in, he leaned over and kissed each cheek very tenderly, nibbling with his teeth close to the cleft. He ran his lubed finger down the crease, stopping at the dark, dusky hole and gently rubbed. Keith moaned. "You hate this so much," he whispered.

"Not when you do that. God, babe."

"You know I'll only do what feels good." He rubbed harder, slipping inside, and the strong muscle took him. Gently, he worked the finger, whirling it, loosening. "Okay?"

"Yeah," said Keith breathlessly.

Skyler kept his finger in there, pushing deeper, before readying the massager. "I'm switching. It isn't much thicker than my finger. Am I touching your prostate?"

"Yes."

"Then let's try this." He popped his finger out and eased in the massager. Slowly he pushed it in. Farther, farther…

"Oh fuck!"

"Okay?"

"Yeah. Yeah. Jesus Christ."

"Where's this been all your life, right?"

"Fuck."

"Okay. Now sit back on your haunches."

Keith did and threw back his head. "God damn!"

"Told you. Now. Shall we get back to it or did I just screw myself by giving you a Skyler replacement?"

"Nothing's gonna replace you. But...Skyler *enhancement* maybe."

Scrambling forward, Skyler positioned himself in front of Keith again, ass in the air, pulling his ass cheeks open with one hand. "Got enough lube?"

Keith pumped more in his hand, slathered himself, and plunged in.

"Motherfucker!" he cried.

"He likes it," gasped Skyler, taking all of Keith suddenly. A shower of stars burst behind his eyes.

Keith shoved in deep. *Speaking of prostate massage!* His hand found Skyler's cock again and he milked it like a Wisconsin milkmaid.

"Oh boy," Skyler gasped.

"God, every time I move..."

"Told you."

But Keith wasn't stopping now. His thighs slammed against Skyler's butt, sinking deeply, rippling the pleasure sensations up inside him that pinged off his lower spine and concentrated in his tightened balls.

Each deep thrust in had Skyler slam back to meet it. He clutched the bed clothes to stabilize himself, body jerking as Keith slammed the sensitive nerves, pleasure rising, thrumming in his senses. All the while, Keith's fingers squeezed and rubbed his dick with faster stroking, tipping him quickly toward the edge.

With so much sensation, so much uncontrollable pleasure rushing through him without stopping, he couldn't hold back any longer. He gasped out his release, spurting over Keith's hand and the mattress below him.

But Keith was still pounding behind him. Sparks kept flying behind Skyler's eyes and jolts of pleasure made him twitch as if an electric current were going through him. And just as it might have started to feel uncomfortable, Keith came with a roar. He jutted his hips once, twice, grabbed hard of Skyler's sides, and stilled.

He froze so long, Skyler glanced over his shoulder. "You okay there?"

"Yeah. Yup. I just…can't move. If I move that thing in my ass will…" He moved incrementally and gasped again. "Shit. Too sensitive. How do I stop this?"

Chuckling, Skyler slipped away from Keith and rolled away, getting in behind the man. Momentarily distracted by the feel of Keith's cum trickling down his thigh, he refocused and grasped the curly-cue sticking out of Keith's ass. "Allow me." He pulled it out, tossing it to the bed, and then quickly shed his underwear.

Keith collapsed onto his stomach and flopped down. "Holy shit. You're trying to kill me."

"I assure you, I'm not." He lay down naked beside Keith and ran his hand up the man's smooth, sweaty back. "I told you you needed to trust me."

"I should have known this was your area of expertise."

"Of course it is." He kissed the glistening shoulder. "You like your new toy?"

"Uh huh. And my old one." He turned to the side and scooped Skyler, dragging him up against him. "I like this one a lot."

"I love you, too."

"Definitely, *definitely* love you."

❖

Skyler watched Keith as he slept, but couldn't resist pushing a dark tendril off of his forehead. Blue eyes fluttered open and looked at him.

"Hi," said Skyler softly.

Keith stretched. "What time is it?"

"Late. Or early, depending on your perspective."

"And you're awake."

"I woke and turned over and saw you. And then I couldn't look away."

Keith rolled over and dug his arm under the pillow cradling his head. His gaze traveled over Skyler's face for a moment before a smile broke out. "Yeah, I can see the appeal. Gorgeous man lying beside me. Seems a shame to be asleep."

"Oh stop," said Skyler, grinning. "Tell me more."

Keith reached over, touched Skyler's cheek, dragging his fingers gently down his face to his chin, then up to his lips. "It's a breathtaking sight."

Skyler closed his eyes, letting the words wash over him, just feeling Keith's fingertips. Opening his eyes again, he held his left hand before him, studying his ring in the moonlit room. "I think this married thing is gonna be okay."

"Well, I'm glad you think so, after we spent all that money and everything."

"It's not about the money. It's about you and me."

"Always, babe."

Skyler frowned. "You know, you always use these endearments, like 'babe' and 'sweetheart' and I just don't do that."

"Oh. Does it bother you? I...I don't have to—"

"No!" he said quickly, not liking the frown line forming between Keith's brows. "I didn't mean that. I really like that you say those things. It's just that…I've never done that stuff before with anyone." He got onto his stomach, propped up on his elbows. "I'm just not an endearment sort of guy. But I want you to know that every time I say your name, that's my endearment to you…Keith." He pressed his face close, barely kissing Keith's scratchy chin. "Keith," he breathed, lips just touching.

Drawing back, he measured his husband's face.

Keith's eyes were bright in the near darkness. Emotion rushed through them with startling clarity.

Keith's hand came up again and ran knuckles along Skyler's face. "You're not ready to sleep again, are you?"

Skyler shook his head.

"Good. I'm not ready either." He lifted the blanket and rose, sliding over Skyler and balancing himself over his supine body. He leaned in and kissed his neck. One hand pressed against the bed, while the other explored Skyler's skin. "All I want to do is make love to you all night."

"Sounds good to me."

They kissed. Keith pressed his body to Skyler's and Skyler raised a leg to wrap around Keith's butt, bringing their burgeoning cocks against each other. He raised his hips and mashed them together.

Keith's deep voice rumbled against his skin as his lips left a trail from his neck down to his chest. "You are an amazing man…babe. I can't believe you're mine."

"Believe it…Keith."

Faces close, they gazed into each other's eyes, lips touching, hands exploring. The smell of spent spunk and warm male bodies filled the air like perfume. Skyler's arms encircled the man's brawny torso, and hugged him tight. They could take it slower this time. Stretch it out. But even so, his hole twitched, aching for the feel of Keith's cock.

.

He hoped that they wouldn't move *too* slow.

❖

"Keith," he whispered a few hours later. "Keith! Are you awake?"

"Nope."

"Are you sure?"

"Yes... What's wrong?"

"Nothing. It's just that..." He stage-whispered, "We're married!"

Keith snorted. "Dear God, what have I done?"

Skyler sobered, his smile fading. "I can't stop thinking about today. And everything. I keep waking up, thinking about the wedding, the ship, you and me."

"Skyler, I love you, babe. But we did it three times in a row, and I'm all tuckered out."

"Mind if we snuggle then?"

"Come on." Keith lifted his arm and Skyler scooted in, rubbing his face in Keith's chest hair. God, he loved that! The feel of that scratchy hair, the look of it, his muscled torso like some model or Greek statue. It wasn't long before Skyler started to feel hard again. He caressed his dick gently against Keith's thigh, the delicate skin dragging on the furred leg as he rubbed it back and forth.

"What the...? Jesus, Skyler. Are you on Viagra or something?"

"I'm just a healthy young American male."

"Babe, you know I would if I could. But I'm really —" He yawned. "I'm really sleepy."

There was a pause.

"You know it's really sad."

Grunting, Keith nestled on his back. "What is?"

"A strapping man such as yourself. I would have thought—"

"And then there was the sad end of Skyler Foxe, drowned on his honeymoon. No one found him for days."

Laughing Skyler lay back on his own pillow. "Okay, okay. As soon as you've recovered, let me know."

But the only reply he got was a snore.

Skyler crept into the bathroom in the early morning light and dialed Sidney.

"Skyler? Do you know what time it is?"

"I'm sorry," he whispered. "I just had to call you."

"Is everything okay? Are *you* okay?"

"Everything's fine. Everything is more than fine." He sat on the cold toilet seat and chewed on a nail. "Sidney, I've been such an idiot."

"As I've told you many times."

"But seriously. Why did I fight this so much? God, I love him. He's so perfect."

"That's what you called me about? You are such a sixteen-year-old girl."

"I am not. I just…Okay, maybe I'm a little *enthusiastic* right now. I mean you tried to tell me. Everyone tried to tell me and I just…"

"You can't imagine how happy I am for you, sweetie."

"This is crazy. I'm sorry for calling you so early. It must be lack of sleep."

"Don't be ridiculous. Remember when we used to do this in college? I kind of miss those days."

"Yeah. I used to call at all hours and tell you about my tricks."

"And I used to call you and tell you about my dates. We'd compare notes. And dick sizes. And techniques. The things I've learned from you…"

"That's right. I bet Mike loves that thing—"

"If you ever tell him you taught me that…"

"I won't. I swear."

"So everything's going okay? No…problems?"

"Problems? Like what? Just a sore ass. But in a really good way. He's…he's my husband now, Sid."

"You're in sex shock."

"Sex shock? Is that even a thing?"

"It is for you."

He leaned back, phone pressed to his ear. "I'm just a little overwhelmed, I guess. Thank you for everything, by the way. It was a beautiful wedding. You were a great best man."

"You're welcome. It was a community effort. Now shouldn't you get back to bed to your husband?"

"Yeah, I should. Kiss *your* sexy husband for me."

"Oh. Yeah. I, uh, will."

"Bye, Sidney." He clicked off, holding the phone to his chest.

The bathroom door opened and a naked sleep-ruffled Keith stood in the doorway. "What are you doing, babe?"

"Oh…just calling Sidney."

"Everything okay?"

"Yeah." He rose and walked toward Keith, resting against his warm chest. "Everything's just fine."

Chapter Seventeen

"I FEEL LIKE A HEEL WATCHING THEM," SAID PHILIP. Skyler and Keith were walking in the moonlight and had stopped to lean on the railing and look out over the ocean churning beneath them. Sidney, Rodolfo, and Philip planted themselves some distance away.

"It's very personal," said Rodolfo.

"I know," said Sidney, feeling guilty enough about it, "but we're supposed to be watching *around* them, not *them*."

Philip pushed his glasses up his nose. "So this is really the kind of thing you do, isn't it Sidney? Impose yourselves in other people's lives. Oh I'm not knocking it. It's for a good cause, but I can see how a cop could easily slip to the wrong side of the equation and want to police everything."

"As a cop, you see a lot, I can tell you."

"How do you decompress?"

"We drink." At his appalled expression, she rushed in with, "But not me and Mike. We have each other. We talk. I think if he wasn't on the job, too, it would be hard to talk about it. I wouldn't want to bring it home to a fireman or construction worker."

"Half of the Village People," he muttered.

She knocked her shoulder into his good-naturedly and then scanned the upper decks again. "It's a crazy job, I guess."

"Stressful. You know, I never really thought about it, but I admire you for it, Sid. It's a very tough job, but you manage to keep your integrity."

"Well, either you have it or you don't."

Rodolfo touched her arm. "They're on the move. Where do you think they're going now?"

"I think they're going back to their room. It is their honeymoon."

"Like crazy weasels," said Rodolfo, nodding.

They silently watched them go back inside before following, and stayed far enough back in the lobby to watch the glass elevators go up to the eighth floor and stop.

"See? Okay, guys. Good work. If you want to take a break and do a little dancing or something, go on. I'll be at the security offices."

"Don't stay too late, Sidney," said Rodolfo, "or you'll wear yourself out. What about that list of passengers? Maybe that's something we can do in the meantime."

"I'll email it to you. But you should have a little fun."

Philip looked at Rodolfo. "What do you say, sweetheart? Want to do a little dancing?"

"I think I would like that. For a little bit. Then we can go back to the room. We are here to work, after all."

"Okay. See you later, Sidney. Send the list anyway. Since we can't do anything in the room, we might as well go over the list."

"Will do." She watched them go, wishing that they were all together on this boat just as friends, having a good time. She really loved these men in all their craziness. This life that she had gotten into because of Skyler was pretty amazing. At least his friends were pretty amazing, and loyal as hell.

She made her way to the bridge and to the offices, having been directed from one person to the next with her badge held high. Finally, she made it to the right place and shook hands with Lee Rosten, head of security. She explained what she was looking for, and with a map of the decks in front of her, pointed out the places where she needed to look at the security tapes.

Sitting in front of the monitors, she scrolled through and found the Lido deck hot tub. On fast-forward, she found Skyler and Keith. Scanning around them, she searched for anyone who might have been hanging around longer than they should have. She watched in sped-up time mode, as Skyler and Keith settled in, but then she stopped the tape. At the edge of the action was a woman, just standing there, it seemed. She had a drink in hand, but she didn't move or talk to anyone. And she was watching Skyler. And when they got up to leave, so did she. She seemed to drift close to the elevators, but didn't go up.

Sidney punched in the other tapes, searching for the woman again near Skyler, but in the restaurant and on the desk, she didn't see her again.

It was time to call Mike.

"Hey, Sid. What have you got?"

"I sent you a passenger list. Could you cross reference that with the list of hoodie purchasers I sent earlier?"

"I'll give it my best. How's it looking there?"

"I wish I had more to go on than this. I was thinking it was a woman based on the profiling, and I did see a suspicious chick hanging near Skyler earlier today, but I didn't see her on any of the later tapes."

"You still think it's a woman? I'm not so sure. And our witness, that little girl at the wedding, clammed up. Can't get a thing out of her."

"Damn."

"By the way, I've been checking out the list of Skyler's classmates from the University of Redlands."

"Yeah? Any leads there?"

"One of his former classmates turns up a lot in anti-LGBT stuff online. Has a website. A real redneck religious type. I'm checking him out now. And get this. He still lives in Redlands."

"All right. Keep on that and get back to me soon."

"I know it must be tough. Are the guys giving you a hard time?"

"No, they're actually being helpful." She interrupted herself to yawn.

"Don't work yourself too hard, hon. Get some rest. We had an early start this morning."

"I will. I'll just be at this for a little while longer."

"You should go to bed. I miss you, by the way."

"I miss you, too. I wish you were here and we were having fun."

"So a cruise isn't so bad, then?"

"Not at all. It's just I don't recommend five in a room."

"Do you think that maybe you should tell Skyler?"

"No! You should see him and Keith. He's so unguarded. He's so...relaxed. I've never seen him like that. I don't want to crush it."

"Well...you know best, I guess. But I do think you should knock off for the night. Get some rest. You'll start again fresh in the morning."

"Maybe you're right. I am bushed. Talk to you soon. Love you."

"Love you, too."

She clicked off and stared at her phone. They *had* started out pretty early this morning. And she didn't have it in her to watch one more tape. She thanked the security team, got them to print out the list, and excused herself, telling them she'd be back in the morning.

Trudging back down to their cabin, she stretched and yawned. Opening the door, she noticed Jamie still sitting up reading on his phone, seemingly waiting for her. Dave was apparently asleep. Rodolfo and Philip hadn't yet returned.

"Hey, Sid." Perched up on his bunk bed, Jamie waved.

"Hey. Shouldn't we be quiet?" She gestured toward Dave, gently snoring.

"Oh, God no. Once he's out he sleeps like the dead. It takes a fire alarm to wake him up. Literally. Anything to report?"

"Nothing much. Some woman was checking out Skyler by the hot tub and was generally acting suspicious, but she didn't show up on any other tapes. I'll try to track her down tomorrow. In the meantime, I emailed you the passenger list. Knock yourself out."

Jamie fiddled with his phone and suddenly widened his eyes. "Oh shit. I didn't realize how big this ship is."

"Yeah. I've got Mike working on checking this list against the hoodie buyers."

"What hoodie buyers?"

"Remember? The suspect was wearing a brand new University of Redlands hoodie? I got a list of people who'd purchased one in the last year from the university bookstore. And Mike thinks it might connect to one of Skyler's old classmates who's a big homophobe these days."

"Oh, clever." He scrolled through page after page. "But I think we're overlooking something here."

"Yeah? What's that?"

"What if they aren't a passenger? What if they work here?"

"That would be an incredible coincidence. I mean, how could they be sure they'd get a job on the very ship on the very weekend Skyler would be here?"

"Okay. What if it was a job that didn't need that kind of planning? Something temporary? Or even a stowaway."

"Dammit. That's a possibility too. Maybe I should go back to security—"

"Honey, you are dead tired. Get some rest. We'll get going on that in the morning."

"You think?"

"I do think. Go to bed, Sidney. You're no good to anyone right now. I'll stay up a little and read this list. It would be brilliant to find them on this right away, right?" He sighed and muttered, "Of course I don't know what I'm looking for…"

"Right." She dragged herself to the bathroom to brush her teeth and to change into her sleep shirt.

They'd reached Catalina in the morning and had docked in the isthmus. Sidney headed over to security again.

Lee greeted her and sat down beside her at the monitor. "So now you'd like a list of the crew?"

"Not the crew necessarily. But there must be a list of employees. Temporary employees? People who might be recent hires for a limited time. And also…is it hard to stowaway on the ship?"

"Well, you can't get on without a boarding pass."

"*You* know and *I* know that these things can be forged."

"And they would have to be incredibly clever to do so."

"So just suppose they did get on board. What would be the next clue that they don't have a cabin?"

"The crew are very vigilant. If someone tries to sleep in a restaurant or on the deck, we're always happy to escort them back to their room."

"I see. So it isn't likely. How about posing as crew or an employee in one of the shops?"

"Everyone has IDs with magnetic strips. Very hard to forge."

"How about steal? Say, if you've never met the person."

"They *are* photo IDs."

"But photo IDs can be forged."

"Yes, they can."

"Let me know if anyone has reported any employee that is acting suspiciously. Or they're suspicious of them for any reason."

"Of course, Detective."

She thanked him and returned to the cabin to meet up with the boys. "So what have we got?"

Dave scrolled through his notes on his phone. "Looks like Sky and Keith have kayak reservations on shore. They're scheduled for a two-hour tour."

"Kayak? What is this?" asked Rodolfo.

"It's like a canoe only smaller," said Philip.

"Why would Skyler and Keith do such a thing?"

Jamie called up a picture on his phone and shoved it into Rodolfo's face. "See? It's supposed to be fun, but I can't even." He shuddered.

Dave put a comforting arm around him. "I know you hate that stuff, darlin'."

Sidney tapped her teeth with a fingernail. "Someone has to keep an eye on them. Who's gonna volunteer?"

Rodolfo raised his hand straight up. "I'd like to see these kayaks."

"Fine. Philip, go with him. The rest of us can hang with security and monitor the shipboard cameras."

"Oooo," said Jamie. "I wanna spy!"

She rolled her eyes. At least they were willing to help.

Chapter Eighteen

SKYLER HAD A BLAST KAYAKING, AND THOUGH his nose was getting a little red from the sun, he dubbed the excursion a success. Their personal photographer had taken some shots of them while they were still near shore and then he left them to have their fun.

After Keith carefully and lovingly applied more sunscreen to Skyler's face, they decided to prolong their Catalina stay by walking around Avalon and seeing the sights.

"I was never fond of the beach because of my fair skin," he told Keith as they walked along, watching a slew of people on bicycles whizz past down the middle of the street, "but I'm kind of liking this."

"Not a lot of sunny beaches where I come from, but I did my share of spring breaks."

Skyler stopped. "Wait. This is a side I never knew about. Are you telling me you used to go to spring break and go a little crazy? Are there videos of Keith Gone Wild? Because I would very much like to see those."

Smiling sheepishly, Keith looked away from Skyler, scanning the ocean through his sunglasses. He looked perfectly at home in the sun, what with his tan and the loose shirt hanging open, revealing his toned torso. He was wearing shorts, exposing muscled thighs and calves. Come to think of it, Keith looked at home anywhere an underwear model would be.

"I *hope* there're no videos," he said, a deep dimple creasing his cheek.

"Come on," said Skyler, elbowing him. "Spill it."

"I'm not going to tell you. That was private."

"Oh, come on! *I'd* tell *you*."

"And I don't want to know that either."

"You can't possibly still be jealous. You won!" He raised his hand and waggled his ring finger, showing off the wedding band. "You got me. I'm not going anywhere."

"I still don't want to know details. And I'm not sharing any with you. Now do you want a snow cone or not?"

"You can't distract me with frosty treats—Oh! There's the snow cone guy!"

Momentarily distracted with a snow cone, and spooning out the crunchy, flavorful ice, Skyler sighed, watching swirling clouds hang lazily in the blue California skies. "This is so nice."

"Are you enjoying yourself, babe?"

"You know I am. Thank you so much for this."

"Thank you for all the work you did with our wonderful wedding."

He gave a brief bow. "You know, I—what?" He tore off his sunglasses and squinted into the distance. "I thought I just saw Rodolfo over there." He pointed and Keith looked.

"Maybe it really was Antonio Banderas."

Rodolfo looked remarkably like the Spanish actor, but when Skyler looked again he didn't see him. "That was weird. Why am I hallucinating my friends?"

"You need to get out more."

He smiled and slurped up the snow cone juice. Then he stuck out his tongue at Keith. "Do I have a blue tongue?"

"You do. Is mine red?" He stuck out *his* tongue.

"Yeah, and it looks tasty. Let me try it." He reached up and kissed Keith. When he stood back Keith was looking at him with some surprise, before he casually looked around.

"You're very…*open* these days."

"I don't know what it is. Maybe it's the wedding? I just feel like…fuck everything. If people don't like it they can look the other way."

"Well, all right!" He put his arm around Skyler and continued walking beside him. It was nice to do that, Skyler decided. Even if it still gave him a twinge of anxiety. He ran his self-defense training through his head just in case.

"So what's next on our agenda?" said Skyler.

"Tonight, I thought we'd go to the casino for a while, then hit one of the shows. They're doing *Mama Mia* in the main theater."

"Omigod, yes! You are too good to me! I swear, I'm going to watch tons of football with you when we get back home."

"You don't have to do that."

"Seriously. I will. Because you have been so good."

"I wouldn't mind if you wanted to play bottomless waiter again during those games."

"I thought you wanted to *watch* the games."

"Mostly. But I want you to enjoy them, too."

"Only if you play bottomless patron."

"I think that can be arranged."

"Too good to me," he muttered, shaking his head.

The shops in Avalon were a bit too touristy, and the tour of the Wrigley Mansion would have put them too late to get back to the ship, so they just stopped at a café to people watch and take in the sailboats coming into harbor from the sea.

"Have you ever been on a sailboat, Keith?"

"Yeah, I had a friend in college whose dad had one. We went out a couple of times."

"I can just see you out there with your cutlass and an eyepatch…"

"Are you having pirate fantasies about me now?"

"You'd better believe it. And me, the helpless captive, where you have your way with me. Arrrrr."

"I think all this sea air is getting to you."

"Now hold *on*!" Skyler jumped to his feet. "I could have sworn I just saw *Philip*. What is going on here?"

"Skyler?"

But he was taking off after him, or at least the last place he thought he saw him. He searched the shop but didn't see any sign of him. Keith came up behind Skyler, wearing a scowl. "Babe, maybe it's time to get out of the sun. We should get back to the ship. Take a cool dip in the pool."

"I am *not* seeing things."

"They can't possibly be here."

"I…I guess you're right. Yeah, let's get back to the ship."

Skyler kept glancing behind him, even as they climbed the gangway up to the ship. They got to their cabin to shower and change, which turned into a little lovemaking halfway in and out of the tiny shower stall. Skyler forgot all about his doppelgangers when he sucked on Keith's lips and showered the cum off of each other.

"I like this married life," he said, dressing in his swim trunks and donning a linen shirt.

"Don't get used to it."

"What?"

"I mean, the rest of it; the ship, the vacation. Of course get used to…us."

"That's better. Don't worry. I know we're on track. A little pool time?"

"Yeah. You ready?"

"Let's go."

They took the elevator to the Lido deck and found a place under a cabana. Skyler settled in under the shade while Keith was able to lie in the sun. With his hat low over his face, Skyler got on his phone to check emails. Debbie's list was there, and though he had been successful forgetting for long stretches at a time about the person who was trying to kill him, there were quiet moments when he couldn't get it out of his mind. He knew it was waiting for him when he returned. *No time like the present*, he thought as he opened the file. If he could just figure out who he was looking for. The list was long, and he scanned each name with nothing coming to mind.

Until he hit on it.

M. Carson.

A flash, like a gunshot flaring from the nose of a Glock, startled Skyler, making his heart pound. Their personal photographer was back again, taking another few shots. He seemed taken aback by Skyler's expression and quietly bowed out.

It took Skyler right back to that day. The sound of the gunfire echoing in that room, ringing in his ears, the smell of gunpowder, the shock of pain to his shoulder. That day was burned into Skyler's memory, just as that scar from the bullet was seared into his flesh. Carson had shot him, meant to kill him. And when Keith showed up, and Carson had turned his gun on Keith, Keith hadn't hesitated. He dropped Carson where he stood. At least, Skyler thought he remembered it that way. He had been in the middle of fainting from the pain, after all.

Skyler turned back to his phone. M. Carson. The mere sight of that name sent a chill spearing through him. Coach Scott Carson was the one who had menaced the school and the football team with his outlandish scheme of selling drugs and guns, and forcing his White Power students to do the work for him. The scheme that involved the principal's son changing the grades of his football players. The man who had killed Julia Meyers. The reason Keith had come to the school in the first place as an FBI agent. The man that Keith had gunned down to save Skyler's life.

"K-Keith…"

"Hmm?" Keith was lying face down on a lounger. But Skyler couldn't make his throat speak any louder.

"Keith."

Keith turned. "What's wrong, babe?"

"I think…I think I found the person after me."

Keith scrambled up from the chair and crouched next to Skyler, all in a blink. "What have you found?"

He showed Keith his phone. "M. Carson."

"Fuck. A relative of Scott's?"

"I don't know. A sibling? A son?"

"I'll get this to the agents right away. You call Sidney."

Keith got on his phone and wandered off to talk. With trembling hands, Skyler punched in Sidney's number. Strangely he heard what sounded like an echo of her ringtone nearby.

"Hey, Skyler. What's up?"

"Sidney, I found the guy."

"What?"

"On the hoodie list. M. Carson. I feel it in my bones. It's Scott Carson's relative."

"Okay. We'll check it out."

Just then the ship's horn blared. A half a second later he heard it in his phone. That was odd.

"Gotta go, Skyler." And she hung up.

"Wait…what?" He stared at his phone, trying to make sense of it all through his fear, when Keith was at his side again.

"Did you get through to Sidney?"

"Yeah." He stared at his phone another moment before he put it down. "I…I need to take a walk."

"I'll go with you."

"No, that's okay. I need maybe a few minutes alone."

"Sweetheart…"

He took Keith's hand and squeezed it as he rose. "It's okay. Just a little walk."

Keith's worried face was on his mind as he strode away. It was all getting to him. He thought the wedding and the honeymoon could make him forget but it was only putting off the inevitable. They were safe here, but as soon as they docked back at Long Beach it would all start up again.

M. Carson. Who was it? He obviously wanted revenge. And he hadn't been pulled into the dragnet that had captured the rest of Coach Carson's Neo-Nazi flunkies. A brother, maybe.

He got to the railing and glanced out to the sun-dappled water. Looking down, the sea churned under the wake of the ship in foamy waves. Even as far down as it was it managed to send up salty spray he could taste on his lips.

"Hey, Skyler!" Startled, Skyler turned and was relieved to see Francis and his wife Bev.

"Hi, Francis."

"Where's Keith? You two didn't have a fight, didya?"

"Francis, leave it alone," shushed his wife.

"No, we didn't. I'm just taking in the view."

"It is beautiful," he said. Bev's arm was linked with his and they all stood at the railing. "But it's lonely, too. A vast ocean with nothing between here and there for hundreds of miles."

"That's a cheerful thought, Francis," his wife gently scolded.

"I'm not wrong," he said. "I think it's sort of romantic."

Bev shook her head indulgently. "You always were a romantic, you tomcat, you." They rubbed noses. "We'll leave you to think your deep thoughts, my dear," she said to Skyler. "You look like you're looking for a bit of solitude."

"Maybe he doesn't want to be alone," said Francis, even as Bev dragged him away. She looked back over his shoulder and winked.

He leaned on the rail. It *was* lonely. That big, empty ocean. At least the ship wasn't lonely. Far from it. Lots of people were walking along the deck near him, and there was even a young man who was leaning against the railing along with Skyler. He was blond and slender, like Skyler, and he was looking down over the side of the ship.

"That's a long way down," he said. It took Skyler a moment to realize the man was talking to him. The blond man looked up and sauntered closer and took up his same position on the rail.

Skyler nodded. "Yeah."

"I think I've seen you around. At dinner. By the pool. You're with that tall dark-haired guy."

"Yeah. We're, uh, together. On our honeymoon, as a matter of fact."

The man's face broke into a smile. "No shit. Ah man, congratulations. I'm Jacob." He put out his hand.

Skyler shook it. "Thanks. I'm Skyler."

Jacob laughed. "Then I guess there's no point in trying to hook up."

Now it was Skyler's turn to laugh. "No, not really."

"Damn. Well, good for you. I'm here with my friends. I told them we should have booked the gay cruise."

"Now that does sound like a surer bet."

"No kidding." He smiled as he looked out to sea. "Honeymoon! That's awesome. But...you do seem kind of young."

Skyler shrugged. "When it's right, you know it."

Jacob looked back over his shoulder toward the pool. "Though...dude! Your husband *is* a hunk and a half. Good one."

Skyler preened. "I know."

"I guess I'll tell my friends the both of you are off limits."

"But if we go dancing later, we wouldn't mind hanging."

"That's cool of you."

"I guess I'd better get back to him."

"Before someone hits on him, right?" They laughed.

Skyler waved and turned. Instead of going directly back to Keith, he aimed for the bar, though there was suddenly a crowd of people in his way. He heard a grunt, then a shout, and looked back in time to see Jacob's feet up in the air going over the railing.

Skyler rushed to the side of the ship and saw him splash in the waves. "MAN OVERBOARD!" he cried. "MAN OVERBOARD!" A lifesaver was hanging from the rail, and Skyler grabbed it and tossed it down into the sea. And just as instructed, he kept his eyes glued to him and pointed. Someone else must have given the alarm, because the claxon sounded and soon people were rushing to the rail.

Skyler stayed put, still pointing, still watching the head in the waves grow smaller as the ship surged forward, but even he could feel the ship's engines slowing.

Keith was suddenly beside him. Skyler could tell he longed to grab him but he could see what Skyler was doing. "I thought it was you," he said in a gruff voice, full of emotion.

"No. It was someone else. God, can't they get this boat stopped?"

Suddenly, from aft of the ship, a dingy with an outboard motor was spearing through the water, making a wide turn and popping up over the waves. The ship's wake had settled down considerably. They must have stopped, Skyler decided. And like everyone else, he was leaning far over the railing to see. Two hands clutched at him, making sure *he* didn't go over, and he knew instinctually that they were Keith's.

The dingy bobbed on the ocean and the crewmen were leaning over the side, pulling something up out of the waves. The man was clinging to the lifesaver and they dragged him up and into the boat. Skyler could clearly see that he was alive.

"He's okay," he gasped. Cheers went up from the people lining the rail, even several decks up.

He turned to Keith who looked pretty pale, some feat for that tan of his. "I thought it was you," he said again, softly.

"I'm fine." He allowed Keith to take him in his arms. Until he noticed the purser standing behind him.

"Can we talk to you about this incident, sir?" said the uniformed officer.

Skyler nodded. "Sure. It all happened so fast."

"May I ask your name and cabin number?"

"Skyler Foxe, room 8202."

"What happened?"

"We were just talking, and I turned away, and he was going over."

"Did he say anything that would indicate his wish to jump?"

"Oh, he didn't jump. Someone pushed him."

"Are you sure? It wasn't just that he somehow slipped…"

Skyler shook his head. "No. He was shouting and struggling. He was definitely pushed."

"Did you see who did it?"

"No. There were a lot of people congregating around us. It could have been anyone."

The purser questioned him for almost half an hour, writing down his notes on a clipboard. "Very well, Mr. Foxe. If we have further questions, we'll contact you."

"Okay."

Before Skyler could think, Keith was steering him away toward the elevators. "I figured maybe we should get back to our cabin."

"Yeah, that's probably a good idea."

Turning toward the elevator's windowed wall, Skyler watched the ground fall away as their car rose up the floors. He saw the crowds still there, still milling and talking. What had happened? How had Jacob been pushed? Why? Was it an accident? Of course it was! What else could it be? But as the elevator doors opened and they made their way down the long corridor to 8202, Skyler began to wonder. Jacob looked an awful lot like him. What if it hadn't been an accident? But that would mean…

Keith opened the door.

"I'm going to take another shower," said Skyler. "Feeling a little numb right now."

"Should we skip dinner?"

"No. Let's go to one of the restaurants and have a quiet dinner, just us."

"Okay, babe. You take care of you right now, and I'll be right outside this door."

Thank goodness for Keith. He kissed him and then retreated to the bathroom. He stood in front of the sink for a long time, staring at his reflection.

If it hadn't been an accident, then that would mean the assassin was still after him…and on this ship.

Chapter Nineteen

SKYLER SAT ACROSS FROM KEITH AT DINNER, pushing his food around on his plate with his fork.

"How's your dinner?" asked Keith.

"Huh?"

"Skyler…" Keith put his silverware down. "We don't have to stay."

"What do you mean?"

"You're clearly not eating, so we don't have to sit here. We can leave the restaurant."

"Oh." For a moment, he thought Keith had meant leave the ship. But how was that possible? They were on their way right now to Mexico with no ports between here and there. Just like Francis had said, hundreds of miles in the middle of the ocean. And he was trapped. With a killer.

"You're right. I'm not hungry. Keith, I think…I think — What the *hell*! Now I see Dave. I know I do." He shot up from his seat. The figure ahead of him ducked away. The kitchen doors swung open and someone dove through it. Skyler race-walked through the restaurant after him, skirting around tables and waiters holding trays filled with plated meals.

When Skyler got there, the doors were swinging closed. "What is going on?" With hands at his hips, he looked around the restaurant…and saw someone with flaming red hair ducking down behind the tables. The man crawled along and disappeared for a time, but Skyler was able to follow his progress as various diners jumped and yelped, one after the other, whipping the hems of their tablecloths to look under their tables. Skyler headed him off at the entrance. The man hadn't seen Skyler and popped up from under a table...and obviously hadn't seen the waiter with the tray.

The tray went flying, and the dishes spiraled outward toward parts unknown. The flying tray hit another waiter holding his own tray, and a domino effect had begun. Food flew, silverware clattered as they showered around the screaming guests. Goblets of wine cascaded, men yelled insults, while glasses shattered on contact with the floor. Screams, chairs skidding back, and two trays wobbled to a noisy stop on the floor. Amid the rubble, the scarlet-haired man froze, shoulders covered in salad and beef gravy, with a sprig of parsley poised at the top of his head like a feather.

Skyler winced as the crescendo of noise fell suddenly to silence. "Jamie!"

Jamie turned and glanced sheepishly at Skyler. "Well...hi, Skyler. Fancy you being here."

"Fancy my ass! What the hell are *you* doing here?"

Jamie straightened, glance darting around at all the eyes on him. He brushed lettuce leaves from his shoulders. "Um...what a strange coincidence?"

Keith caught up to Skyler and stared at Jamie incredulously.

Skyler gritted his teeth. "Why are you here? Is Dave here, too? And Philip...and Rodolfo?"

"Don't be silly. Why would *they* be here?"

"The jig is up, Jamie," said Philip. Skyler hadn't even noticed him standing there. He slowly lowered the large, round tray he'd been hiding behind.

"Abort! Abort!" hissed Rodolfo, crouching behind a food cart.

Dave sauntered up from the kitchen, doors swinging shut after him. "Give it up, Rodolfo."

Rodolfo frowned at him before he gradually rose. "Surprise?" he said warily.

Keith pushed past Skyler. "What the fuck is going on?"

"Oh, I think I know," said Skyler, calling Sidney on his phone. Her ringtone sounded at the far end of the restaurant, and he heard an exhaled, "Shit!" ever before she answered.

"Sidney!" he yelled.

Her curly-haired head poked out from behind the bar.

The maître d' rushed over to them, eyes wide. "What is happening? I'm going to ask all of you to leave or I'll have to call security."

Skyler glanced back at the chaos. It looked as if a tornado had blown through the restaurant. Debris was everywhere. Broken glass and plates, trays, waiters desperately trying to clean it up. Patrons, covered in food and wine, glared at him and his companions. There wasn't an eye in the house not looking at them.

"We're leaving," said Skyler to the maître d'. "Follow me," he said to his friends, barely keeping it together.

Clamping his mouth tight, Skyler stalked away out of the restaurant. He didn't look behind him, but everyone damn well better be following him, he decided. He got to the elevator, punched the button, and the doors opened. In he went, pushed the button for the eighth floor, and waited at the back of the elevator with his arms folded tight to his chest. He watched as, one by one, they straggled in, standing silently beside him. Sidney slid in right before Keith. No one spoke as the doors eased shut and the elevator rose.

Once the doors opened on the eighth floor, they parted for Skyler as he proceeded down the length of the corridor, with only the faintest of the thump, thump of marching feet behind him. He swiped his card key in the lock, opened the door, and walked through, standing in front of the bed waiting for everyone.

"Wow," said Jamie, looking around. But any other exclamation he might have made was silenced, when Dave elbowed him and they all faced Skyler. Keith stood behind all of them, as if standing guard.

"Now," said Skyler, clasping his hands behind his back. "Will someone please tell me what the *fuck* is going on?"

Everyone turned to look at Sidney. "Jesus. Okay. I didn't want to ruin your honeymoon, Skyler."

"That ship has *literally* sailed."

She sighed. "Yeah, okay. I'll get to the point then. There was a threatening note left at your wedding reception by your stalker."

"*What?* What did it say?"

"It indicated that he or she knew where you were going. I made the split-second decision of going with you. And then these buffoons wouldn't take no for an answer."

"I object strongly to the characterization of 'buffoon'," said Philip. "Stooge, perhaps, but certainly not buffoon. But may I add before you blow up, that we've been working hard staying out of sight, doing our best to watch over you and Keith."

Now Skyler felt guilty. He slackened his taut posture a little. "Oh. Well…thanks. But…God, you guys." He sank to the edge of the bed and ran his fingers through his hair. "My one and only honeymoon."

"But Skyler," said Jamie, moving to sit beside him. "We didn't want it to be the last thing you ever did, either. This guy was on to you, knew where you were going."

"How is that possible?" said Keith, looking at Philip. "Unless..."

"I swear, my lips were sealed."

"Did you throw out any paperwork about the cruise?" asked Sidney. "Anything they could have dug out of the trash?"

"No, I...I don't think so..." Keith blinked as he thought. "Crap. I could have. That's a rookie mistake. Ah babe, I'm so sorry."

Skyler sighed. "It's not your fault. It's not anyone's fault. It's that stupid stalker's fault." He straightened again, shuddering at the thought. "And he threw that guy overboard. I'm sure he did."

"We all thought it was you," said Rodolfo. "Dave was ready to jump in after you."

"I'm glad he didn't," said Skyler. "He looked like me. I'm sure that's why he was chosen. The stalker made a mistake."

"Did you see anyone, Skyler," asked Keith, "anyone at all near you or that guy?"

"You heard what I told the purser. I saw lots of people."

"Listen, Skyler," said Keith, crouching before him, "you stay here. Sidney and I are going to talk to security."

"I've already been on it," she said huffily.

"Well I haven't," Keith growled. Skyler just knew he was going to whip out his FBI badge. He actually felt better about it.

"Okay," said Skyler as Keith buttoned up his shirt, no doubt trying to look more professional. "I'll stay here and talk to the guys."

Sidney gave him a significant look before she left with Keith. The others found seats on the sofa and desk chair.

"Sky," said Dave, "we're really sorry for barging in on your honeymoon. We didn't want to do it."

"Really, Skyler," said Jamie softly. "We wouldn't have."

He patted Jamie's leg. "I know. And...I really appreciate the sacrifice."

"No kidding," said Philip. "You should see the tiny cabin the five of us are crammed into."

"And I bet this cost you a fortune. I'm sorry."

"Don't apologize to us," he went on. "We're doing it for you. Of course we would. We'd do it for any one of us."

Skyler's emotions overwhelmed and he wiped away a tear. "I love you guys." They all moved together into a group hug.

"We love you, too, *amante*!" Rodolfo wailed.

They all settled back again, and more than one tear was wiped from eyes. "Okay, then," said Skyler. "We've got to work on this like any Scooby Gang caper. What do we know?" He began ticking it off on his fingers. "I found the name of 'M. Carson' on the hoodie list from U of R. 'M. Carson' is a relative of Coach Scott Carson, the guy who held me and Rodolfo captive."

"How could I forget?" said Philip with a shudder.

"He's obviously been stalking me for a while," he said, adding a finger to the count, "knew my movements, knew I was getting married, and somehow found out our honeymoon plans. And now he's on this ship. He could be anyone."

Dave rubbed his chin in thought. "Have you met anyone on the ship? Someone who seems overly friendly to you?"

"Not anyone that seems likely." He thought of the older couple, Francis and Bev. Couldn't possibly be them. He couldn't imagine Francis having the strength to dump anyone over the side. But of course, he could be faking it. He could be less feeble than he made out to be...

Jesus, Skyler, he admonished himself. *You can't be suspicious of everyone.* Though if he was honest with himself, and if he were a cop, he'd have to add them to the list. "Well," he said reluctantly, "there is this older couple."

"How old?" asked Jamie.

"Really old. Married fifty years."

"Oh for heaven's sake!" said Philip. "I think you can rule them out."

"I wanted to make sure everyone is included. So there's Brian and Macy Cherry. We met them in the hot tub."

Philip quirked a brow. "Younger couple?"

"Yes."

"Okay. Who else?"

"Well...the victim. We were both at the rail and started chatting. He's here with his friends. He's gay."

"Do you know that for certain? Did you see his friends?"

"No. But is he going to throw himself overboard at the off chance I'd notice, just to throw suspicion off of him? That seems extreme."

"Skyler's right," said Dave, tucking his hands in his shorts pockets. "We can't include *everyone* on the list. Some things are just too unlikely. Like the older couple."

"I don't know," said Jamie. "There's an old lady at the supermarket I see every time I go there, and she always manages to get behind me and pinch me in the butt."

Dave laughed in spite of the situation. "What? And you let her?"

"I don't *let* her. But she's crafty. Sneaks up behind me even though I have my eye on her every time. She has quite a set of pincers." He made pincer motions with his fingers.

"This is serious," Philip admonished.

"So is my bruised butt."

Skyler head began to throb and he dropped his forehead to his hand. "I don't know what to do."

"Has Sidney given any clue as to who gave that little girl the note?" asked Dave, looking at each in turn.

Philip shook his head. "She hasn't said. But children are unreliable witnesses." Philip pushed his glasses up his nose. "So what exactly does the University of Redlands have to do with it all?"

Everyone stopped and turned toward him.

"What?" said Jamie, perplexed.

"You know. The only lead was this hoodie. How does this connect to Skyler?"

Skyler shook his head. "Gosh, Philip. I don't know."

"Don't complicate things, Philip," said Jamie. "Maybe this relative of Carson's goes there. It's a false flag."

Skyler jumped to his feet and began to pace. "We've got to get some kind of lead. I mean, we are all trapped on this ship and here I am with this tremendous resource."

Jamie elbowed Rodolfo with a smirk. *"We're* the tremendous resource," he said proudly.

"Trapped on the ship…" Skyler perked up. "*He* can't get off either. We've got till tomorrow morning when we dock at Ensenada. We need to find this guy!"

"All right," said Philip. Skyler loved it when he got into logic mode. "You found this name on a list. Which one?"

"The hoodie list, from the bookstore."

"And Jamie scanned the passenger list. There is no 'M. Carson'."

"But I haven't scanned the employee list," said Jamie. "Sidney was supposed to get me that."

"Text her right now," said Skyler. "She and Keith are supposed to be there already, at security. What else?"

Jamie began to text and talk at the same time. "Well, as I pointed out to her, there are also itinerant employees who may not be on the list, who aren't necessarily paid by the cruise line."

Skyler frowned. "Like who?"

"Wait. I'm getting a text back from her." He read silently for a time until Skyler couldn't stand it.

"*Well?*"

"Okay. She said that Mike got a lead on one of your former classmates from U of R."

"Former classmate?"

"Yeah. A very vocal anti-LGBT idiot with a website and everything. Lives in Redlands. He's a kid's photographer, like the kind that goes to schools…"

"Wait. Photographer? Oh shit."

Skyler scrambled, looking under every magazine and sock on their tables and counters.

Dave got out of his way. "What are you looking for, Sky?"

"Business card. Our photographer. His name is Mark. That's 'M'!"

"Oh shit," said Dave.

"Help me look!" Everyone took different directions, spreading around the cabin and even into the bathroom. He turned out his pockets but no business card.

"Can't you remember his name?" asked Rodolfo from under a table.

"No. I wish I did."

"I'm texting Sidney now, seeing if they have a list of the photographers." Jamie's thumbs flew over his phone.

Could it really be the photographer? "How would he know to be on this ship? How could he *get* on this ship?" said Skyler, pacing again.

"He could have stolen an ID," said Jamie, still texting. "Or…" He stopped. "He could have stolen the ID, threw the real photographer overboard or stuffed him in a supply closet on shore, and fixed the ID to show *his* picture!"

Skyler faltered to a stop. "That's horrible!"

"It could have happened."

Philip took two strides and slapped Jamie in the arm.

"Ow! Philip!"

"You don't have to enjoy this so much. Can't you see you're upsetting Skyler?"

"*Amante*," said Rodolfo, putting his arm around him. "It's not your fault."

"But it is. I've ruined Keith's honeymoon."

"You didn't," said Philip.

"But I did. Just by being me. And my stupid, stupid sleuthing. I have no business doing this! And now it's gonna come back and bite me in the ass."

Dave moved closer. "Not if we can help it. We have the advantage over this jerkwad. He doesn't know that *we're* here."

Skyler had been ready to give up. There didn't seem any point to fighting this. Until Dave's words started penetrating his morose thoughts. "That's right," he said slowly. "He *doesn't* know that you're all here. That Sidney's here. He thinks that I'm a sitting duck. Well, I'm not!"

"That's the old Skyler spirit!" said Philip.

"Yeah. And you know what? We're going to go look for him. All of us. Except...you guys are going to hang back. Let me be the bait."

"Is that such a good idea, *amante*?"

"I'll stay away from the ship's rails, but...yeah. I'm not just going to sit around waiting for Keith and Sidney to look through some files."

"I don't know, Skyler." Jamie worried at his fingernail.

"I'm going. This only works if you guys are with me."

Dave exchanged glances with everyone. "Sky's right. And this isn't his first rodeo. I'm in. It's one for all, and all for the SFC, right guys?"

Jamie relented. "For the SFC!" He put his hand in the middle of their circle. Dave rested his hand on top, and gestured for Rodolfo.

"For the SFC!" he said, putting his hand on top of Dave's. "Come on, Philip."

"You'll do it anyway, won't you. Oh, all *right*. For the SFC!" And his hand went on top of Rodolfo's. Skyler smacked his hand on top of all of them.

"For the SFC! Let's go!"

Skyler strolled the decks, trying to look nonchalant. All the while the SFC stayed well back, some in front, some behind him. Far enough away that they didn't look as if they were with him. It was tempting to loiter near the railing but he stayed away as promised, taking his time to be where other people were not.

Where was that photographer? He was always around when you didn't want him. Now that Skyler wanted to find him, he did a disappearing act.

He made sure his friends could see him go to the elevator. He signaled with his fingers casually against his thigh what floor number he was heading for.

Rodolfo and Philip got into one elevator, Dave and Jamie in another, and Skyler in yet another. Just as the doors closed, someone slipped through at the last second.

"I almost missed you," said Mark.

Chapter Twenty

SKYLER BACKED UP TO THE GLASS WALL AS THE elevator doors slid closed and the car rose.

"I was hoping to catch you alone."

"W-what makes you think I'm alone?" squeaked Skyler.

Mark slid his gaze around the empty elevator car. "Uh…unless your husband is invisible, you look alone to me."

There was no use looking around. He was effectively trapped until the doors opened. And Mark was standing in front of them. "Why?" he asked, trying to keep the tremble out of his voice. "Why are you doing this?"

Mark reached back and hit the stop button. The alarm rang for a moment and then stilled. "Don't you know? Some private shots are called for, I think."

Mark brought up his camera and took a few pictures. "Why don't you look out the window? Yeah, that's the expression. Pensive."

Terrified, he mentally corrected. "Why?" said Skyler, chin trembling. He thought they'd planned it so well. But all he could think of was Keith. What would he do…afterward? How would he take it when Skyler was found dead?

Mark hit the button for the car to resume. Skyler flashed a surprised look at him.

"An arty shot. Everyone likes them. Let's see what we can accomplish on the deck. It's almost deserted out there. Let's just take care of this now."

The elevator doors opened, and Mark stepped aside, gesturing. "After you."

"We don't have to do this," pleaded Skyler.

"We don't?" Mark looked more puzzled than angry when he stepped out after Skyler. "But we're already here. Just step back. This won't hurt a bit."

"Did I offend you in some way? I'm sorry, but I don't even remember you."

"Uh…I'm your photographer."

"No. From college. I'm sorry, but I don't remember you. And I was a little crazy back then. Just coming out, so maybe I offended you…"

"From college—"

Streaks of color whizzed by Skyler's sight. It happened so fast. Dave and Rodolfo each darted forward from different directions and tackled Mark to the ground. It wasn't pretty. They all tumbled together, legs and arms flailing. Mark certainly wasn't prepared, and his camera flew heavenward before hitting the deck with a loud crack, pieces flying everywhere. Then there was a pile-on as Jamie and Philip joined their companions and clustered on top of the photographer/stalker.

"Got you, you son of a bitch," grunted Dave.

"Get off of me! I think you broke my collarbone."

"I'm going to break more than that," cried Philip.

The guy still struggled and the four friends smacked and punched him.

Skyler backed away out of the line of fire. He bumped up against a pillar and rested there, breathing hard. It was over.

"Oh my God!" said a female voice beside him. He turned and saw Macy Cherry, the lady from the hot tub. "What is going on, Skyler?"

He grabbed her arm and ushered her away. They got to the deck where the hanging lights were beginning to come on as night fell and a cold breeze swept up from the sea. "It's nothing. I've been having a little trouble with a stalker."

"What? That's terrible. Where's Keith?"

"He's talking to security. That guy's been stalking me for a while. I thought I lost him back at home, but he found out where we were taking our honeymoon."

She shook her head. "I can't believe that. Are you all right? We should call Keith."

"In a minute. Hoo! I'm just catching my breath." He put a hand to his chest and inhaled deeply.

"Well that was a lucky thing those guys coming to the rescue."

"I know. They're my friends."

"I never heard of a group honeymoon before."

"Well…it isn't exactly —"

"But maybe that's what faggots do."

"It's — what?"

"I mean…" She reached into her purse and drew out a large steak knife she'd obviously stolen from a ship's restaurant. "It's like my brother always told me. You can't trust a fag."

Suddenly her hand darted out and closed painfully on Skyler's wrist. She held the knife to his throat, the serrated edge digging into his flesh. He found he couldn't scream. Not with his throat closing up with fear. Not with that sharp edge so close to a vein. "Meanwhile, your stupid faggot friends are beating up the wrong guy," she went on. "Oh well. Let's go back here where we can be alone."

*"You're…'*M. Carson,'" he managed to gasp.

"My maiden name. I tell you. You are a hard man to kill."

"Why are you doing this? You don't want to come to the same bad end—"

"Shut up. It's your fault my brother's dead."

Skyler let her pull him along but he dragged his feet, trying to stall. "So you agree with what he was doing? Recruiting innocent kids to sell drugs for guns?"

"He wasn't doing any such thing!"

"But he was! There are tons of witnesses. The trial of his coaches…"

"Scott never had a chance. It was those guys that made him do it."

Could he reason with her? Appeal to her better nature? "Where's Brian? What about your own kids?"

"Brian…will understand."

"But your kids? Isn't it bad enough about their uncle being involved in these crimes? But their mother? You could walk away now. When the boat docks at Ensenada. Run away and don't come back."

"You'd like that, wouldn't you? But I'm here to get the job done."

"Your kids, Macy. Think of them."

She slammed Skyler up against the changing rooms, away from the people still at the bar by the pool. It was sparsely populated as cold as it was.

"You don't get to talk about my kids."

"They'll be forever tainted. They'll be bullied and ridiculed at school."

"I said…" She grabbed him by the shirt and slammed him into the wall again. "Shut up about my kids."

Where were his friends? *Stall, Skyler!* "What about Sunday school? What about Brian? What about that innocent guy you almost drowned?"

"And he's fine."

"But he might not have been. You can stop this now, Macy. Right now. You got your point across. Boy, did you. I'm really sorry things ended the way they did. But Scott Carson tried to kill me. And he was responsible for the death of another teacher."

She pressed her lips tightly together. With a determined look in her eye, she grabbed Skyler by the back of the neck, pinching hard, and shoved him forward toward the railing. *No!* he screamed in his head.

"I won't let you do this, Macy."

"You can go over *with* or *without* a slit throat. I don't care which, really."

"You don't want to do this."

"I do. I really do. Then your so-called husband gets it. He's the one who actually shot Scott."

"You leave him alone!"

"Isn't that cute. Oh man. You don't know how disgusted I was sitting in a Jacuzzi with you guys. Took me the hottest shower of my life just to decontaminate." They were standing at the rail. She looked one way down the deck, and then the other. No one in sight.

Skyler measured the situation. There was no way in hell he was allowing her to dump him over the rail. He wasn't going to let her cut him, either. He searched around for anything he could use as a weapon.

And then he remembered.

Without overthinking it, he stepped back, grabbed her arm, bent, and hurled her over his shoulder. She hit the rail, but Skyler flung his hand forward and grabbed her wrist. She dangled over the side, screaming.

He pulled with all his might, but he was in an awkward position, and all the weight was on her side, dragging her further down.

He didn't know how much longer he could hold her. He braced a foot at the bottom of the rail and tugged, but her wrist was slipping from his sweaty hand.

"Don't drop me!" she screamed.

"I'm trying!"

A large figure appeared beside him, reached down, and clasped her arm, pulling her up. He dumped her on the deck.

Keith kicked the knife out of her hand and slammed her down, holding her arms behind her back.

"Couldn't you even text me?" he growled, looking up at Skyler with narrowed eyes.

"I was with the guys. We…we had this one…"

"Yeah, I can see that." Keith mashed her face down even as she squealed. Ostensibly he seemed to be waiting for someone with handcuffs to show up. But Skyler could tell it was payback.

"Are you the bitch that's been after my husband?" he snarled.

"'Husband'?" she snorted, quite a feat with her mouth mashed against the deck. "I'd spit, if I could. You were next, by the way. I wanted maximum pain."

Keith's elbow found its way to the middle of her back and she gasped as he pressed down hard.

"Oh…sorry," he said unapologetically. "Are you working alone? Are you with someone?"

"I'm alone. Not even my husband suspected. You…you can leave him out of it."

"Not a chance." He glanced once at Skyler. "In light of this, I think you'd better go rescue the other guy."

"Mark! Oh shit!" Skyler spun and ran, skidding around the corner and wincing at the sight of all his friends burying the hapless Mark with their bodies.

"Um...guys?"

"We got 'em, Sky!" said Dave proudly. He had a bruised eye. Come to think of it, they all looked beaten up and rumpled. Philip's normally perfect hair was all mashed to one side and sticking up in a flip. Jamie looked like he was nursing a hurt wrist.

"Yeah, heh. I see you got him. But, uh, maybe you should let him up."

"Nothing doing," said Philip. He looked a bit proud of himself, too. "He's going to pay for what he did to you."

"Well, that's the thing. You see, he didn't do it."

"What?"

Jamie snapped his head up. "Skyler, what are you saying?"

"I'm saying that...we made a mistake?"

"We?" said Rodolfo. He had his arms wrapped around Mark's leg, and by the look of the rucked-up pant leg, he'd been biting it.

"Uh...me, then. Could you...could you all just let him up?"

Philip managed to put a hand to his hip while holding Mark down with the other. "Are you absolutely sure?"

"Yeah. Dead sure. Because while you were wrangling him, the real stalker had me at knifepoint at the railing."

That was enough for Rodolfo. He released Mark's leg and the man was able to wriggle them.

"Sky," said Dave, wilting a bit. "Say it ain't so."

"It is." He bent down and looked Mark in the face. "I'm really sorry about this. I'll replace your broken camera."

"You'll do more than that."

Skyler winced again. "Let him up, Dave."

Dave and Philip released him at the same time. Skyler tried to help him to his feet but he shook him off. "What the *hell* was all that about?" He pressed a hand to his shoulder and whine, "I think it's dislocated."

"I'm so sorry," said Skyler. "You can let Dave look at it. He's a fireman."

Mark didn't look as if he would warm to that idea.

"You see," said Skyler in his most apologetic voice, "there has been this person stalking me, trying to kill me. I thought it was you."

"It isn't! I don't even know you."

"I know that now. Keith's got the perp back there. She…she held a knife to me." Skyler put a hand to his neck. He was surprised to look at his hand and see a smattering of blood.

"Well good for you."

The sound of feet running toward them thundered on the deck. Security. Some of the uniformed men passed them and headed for Keith, while three slowed and stopped around Skyler and his friends. Sidney came running up from behind them. "Skyler, what's going on?"

He looked back over his shoulder and sighed. "A little of this, a little of that."

EPILOGUE

THEY'D SPENT HOURS IN SECURITY. THE CRUISE line had papers for them to sign, and Philip, drawing on his earlier lawyer training, looked then over meticulously. A lot of release of liability forms, security reports, and police reports. They had reached port by this time in the early morning, and the Ensenada police had been asked to board. They took temporary custody of Macy, escorted by Sidney, until she could fly with her back to the United States.

Mark the photographer was convinced not to press assault charges, especially since the cruise line representatives told him that if he did he would never work their cruises again. But Skyler promised again to buy him a spanking new camera and even purchase all the photos he'd taken of him and Keith.

Mollified, the man was released and the ship's doctor declared him fit, if somewhat bruised and sprained.

With the sunrise, the ship had gotten back into the swing as if nothing had happened. They certainly hadn't told the rest of the ship's compliment what had transpired. Oblivious passengers were lining up to disembark to Mexico, with hats and bags. The aroma of sunscreen hung heavily in the air.

The SFC had packed their bags and were waiting to leave as well.

"You guys, you don't have to leave," pleaded Skyler. "You're already here."

Philip waved him off. "We accomplished what we came here to do. And this is *your* honeymoon. We have no business sticking around."

Skyler dithered. "Well, it's not exactly the dream honeymoon anymore…"

"Nonsense," Philip reassured. "Keith is here. You're unhurt. It's still a romantic cruise, or can be again." He leaned in. "I think, if you—ahem—put your mind to it, you can get yourselves back in the mood. But not if we're around."

"Do you all feel that way?"

"God, Skyler," said Jamie. "We felt bad enough being here spying on you. It's time for us to go. We'll catch a flight back to Long Beach."

"We never wanted to be here in the first place, Sky," said Dave. "We just didn't want anything bad to happen to you." He put his hand on Skyler's shoulder. "We care about you, dude. And we care enough now to leave you two alone."

"They are right, *amante*," said Rodolfo. "We will all travel together on a cruise another time. But a honeymoon comes only once." He grabbed Skyler and kissed him once on each cheek. "Bless you and your Keith." He raised his face to Keith. "We leave our friend Skyler in your hands."

"I'm so glad it's over," said Jamie. "But I still don't get the U of R hoodie thing."

"It was her husband," said Skyler absently.

Philip shook his head. "But the police were saying he had nothing to do with it."

"She said as much. Said he was into all kinds of football. Even local college ball. Bought the shirts. I'm sure she bought the hoodie for him. It was a red herring."

Everyone fell silent as they seemed to consider this.

Skyler sighed heavily. "I don't know if we should continue on this cruise. Maybe the bloom is off the rose."

Keith wore a serious expression. It wasn't Skyler's favorite. "If you want to leave, babe, we will."

"Do *you* want to leave?"

"I'll do anything you want."

"But what do *you* want to do?"

"Anything you want."

"Oh, for God's sake!" cried Philip. "You obviously both want to stay. Stay! Enjoy the rest of your trip. The crisis is over. The marriage has begun. Make the most of it."

Skyler locked eyes with Keith. "What do you think? Should we continue?"

"I'm willing if you're willing."

"Awww," said Jamie. If he was a cartoon there would be hearts in his eyes. "You two, kiss and seal the deal."

Smiling, Skyler reached for Keith. "I can go for that." And they did.

Skyler had thought that the dynamic of the trip would be darker after all that had happened, but instead, his mood had lightened considerably, knowing that it was all over. There was no worrying when they got back that it would all start up again. It was done. The guilty party had been dragged off to jail, her hapless and clueless husband trailing after her, and his friends had left the ship. He loved them, would have accepted it if they had stayed, but he was equally glad that they'd decided to go, because now he and Keith could be alone again.

Keith, too, seemed to have sloughed off his bad mood. Skyler supposed it was his FBI training that allowed him to separate crimefighting from his personal life. He seemed relieved that Skyler had wanted to stay, and it made Skyler feel one hundred percent that he had chosen the right course.

They had staked out a place by the pool, Skyler in the shade, Keith out in the sun, his furred chest glistening from sunscreen and sweat.

Skyler had eschewed Ensenada. He didn't want to take any chances on anything else unexpected happening. He was satisfied looking out to the harbor and enjoying the rest of the cruise from the ship.

But even as he relaxed with the latest book on his phone, he kept thinking of Macy and the possibility of others like her. Her hatred had gone so deep that she had taken the time, without her husband ever being the wiser, to plot and plan. Were there others out there, waiting to do as she had done?

"No, Skyler," said Keith softly beside him. "I can see it on your face. You can't worry about this. This was a one-off, a million to one chance."

"But I ruined our honeymoon."

Keith sat up and turned, throwing his legs over the side of the lounger, and bending toward Skyler. "You did *not* ruin our honeymoon."

"But I did. We were having a perfectly good time and then this happened. And it's all my fault. I never should have gotten into sleuthing."

"Except that you have a gift for it."

"I—what?"

"Sweetheart, why do you think some people go into law enforcement? Yes, some are gung-ho to right wrongs, but others are good at the puzzles. They have a gift. And so do you."

Taken aback, Skyler considered Keith's words, flattered by their very nature. "You think I have a gift?"

"You've proven it. True, at first I just felt as if you were meddling, getting in the way of *my* investigation. But you kept coming up with pertinent information, thinking outside the box of us veterans, finding out more in-depth clues. You cracked case after case. I actually realized it when we first went over the possible stalkers, and I really did marvel at all the crimes you solved in so short a time. It was staring me in the face. You have a gift, babe, and I told you back at the White Party—maybe reluctantly— that I would no longer stand in your way, but I'm proud to be able to help you. I really am."

"Wow. You really think I have a gift?"

Keith laughed. "Did you think you didn't?"

"I don't know. It just seemed to keep bugging me until I did something about it."

"Well, it's obvious to me."

"But I did screw up this last one. I thought it was the photographer."

"An honest mistake. I would have gone for him, too."

"Really? You're not just saying that?"

"You're the most insecure confident person I've ever met."

"I have confidence in some things, and not others."

Keith edged closer and said quietly, "You can have complete confidence about the spell you've cast over me. Because I love you so much."

"Enough to keep sleuthing with me?"

Keith got up and sat beside him. With his arm around Skyler, he pulled him close. "Just ask, Skyler. We're a team, you and me. Watson to your Sherlock Homo, as Jamie would say."

Skyler smiled. "Mr. Fletcher, you say the nicest things."

AUTHOR'S AFTERWORD

I'm a big fan of Lord Peter Wimsey, that dapper sleuth from the 20s and 30s written by Dorothy L. Sayers. In fact, I preferred him over Hercule Poirot or Miss Marple simply because he was a fully realized character with an interesting backstory, and Ms. Sayers wasn't afraid to let him change and grow over the series, a truly modern innovation in mystery writing at the time. Poirot never changed. That's what makes him a little boring for me. Now, in the Lord Peter Wimsey series—SPOILER ALERT—he finds true love later in the books and in the last full novel, gets married and goes off on a honeymoon. In fact, the book is called BUSMAN'S HONEYMOON, a play on the saying "Busman's holiday," meaning, the bus driver, even on vacation, has to drive his family around. And so Lord Peter, peer and amateur sleuth, solves a murder even when on his honeymoon. It has been called a perfectly good love story interrupted by a mystery. That was definitely the inspiration for STONE COLD FOXE, except the murder Skyler must solve is his own impending one.

I do enjoy moving the character story arc of Skyler and Keith along. It's sometimes hard to remember—even for me—that their timeline has only moved on a year, rather than the six plus years since the first book's release.

So, Skyler and Keith are married. What a whirlwind courtship that was! I've been asked whether the series will be coming to an end soon, or will I be writing them forever. I'll confess right now that I *won't* be writing them forever. And, in fact, I am sad to say that I have decided that this is the point that we'll have to leave the Skyboy and his friends to live their lives without us peeking through the curtains like a bunch of pervs. I mean, this is actually a great place to stop. It sort of revisited all of Skyler's cases and bookended the first novel. I've loved telling Skyler's story but everything in its season. I might write another in the future. You never know. But now seems like a good time to put this series to bed.

With grateful thanks to all my readers and fans. You have sustained me and encouraged me on this long journey. Thank you all for coming with me. I hope you had a pleasant time.

Remember, if you want to talk to me or ask a question, you can reach me on Facebook at facebook.com/skylerfoxe.mysteries, and on my website at SkylerFoxeMysteries.com.

I love you all.

Made in the USA
Middletown, DE
29 October 2020